KT-529-681

LUCY COURTENAY

THE KISS

Hodder
Children's
Books

A division of Hachette Children's Group

A Catalogue record for this book is available from the British Library

ISBN: 978 1 444 92286 8

Typeset in Berkeley Oldstyle by Avon DataSet Ltd, Bidford-on-Avon, Warwickshire

Printed and bound in Great Britain by Clays Ltd, St Ives plc

The paper and board used in this book are made from wood
from responsible sources.

An imprint of Hachette Children's Group
Part of Hodder & Stoughton
Carmelite House
50 Victoria Embankment
London EC4Y 0DZ

An Hachette UK company
www.hachette.co.uk

THE KISS

For Stephanie Thwaites my agent who, for all her hard work, has never had a printed word of thanks from me. So . . . Thank you!

The moon is insanely full on the beach at Argole-sur-Mer. It hangs there like one of those massive concertina lampshades that fill your bedroom and make you wish you'd chosen something a bit smaller. It's also indecently close to the sea, making the midnight Mediterranean glitter with promise.

I look with excitement at the smooth brown hand holding mine as we walk along the soft, cold sand. Rubbing my thumb with his, Laurent tosses his head towards the still-thumping nightclub behind us on the beach front.

'You dance very well. Like a mermaid.'

The correct term for my dancing is 'unhinged'.

'Thanks,' I gulp. 'So do you.'

Witty backchat is impossible. Not in the moonlight, on a French beach, with the Mediterranean swishing away in the background like a big wet theatre curtain. Right now, it's all I can do to keep one foot moving in front of the other.

Laurent picks up one of my long blond curls and twirls it around his fingers. 'What is your name, mermaid?'

'Delilah,' I say, bracing myself for The Song.

Vinyl smells awful when it catches fire. I know this because Dad burned all Mum's records when she left. The inferno wasn't as dramatic as he would have liked, but that's gas fires for you. The house reeked for weeks. When I put Dad's record collection in the flames, which I plan to do the next time someone sings The Song at me, I will do it in the back garden.

Laurent doesn't react. He's too busy circling the back of my hand with his thumb. Round and round and round. Clearly, Tom Jones is no biggie on the Med.

I love France.

We stop by a big sand dune and he moves a little closer. I am giddy. I've heard French boys are excellent in the lip department.

'It is a beautiful moon, *non*?' he murmurs, his mouth grazing my ear.

'*Pas mal*,' I manage.

I feel a flicker of concern in case I've just said 'My dad's sick' by mistake. Laurent's mouth on my ear is scrambling my head. I half expect an accordion to warble into action behind the sand dune. This is all just so – *French*.

I'd spotted him at the bar half an hour earlier. Fatima had already pulled and was kissing her prey in one of the darker corners of the club when he walked across the pulsing dancefloor with its flashing lights and silently started dancing with me. Unsmiling. Utterly lush. It pushed my whole unhinged-dancing thing to new heights. He's tall, and blond, and there's a smudge of sand still sitting on his collarbone under the soft cotton collar of his shirt.

'It is the moon of Aphrodite,' Laurent informs me now. 'The moon of love. You know about Aphrodite, *non*?'

'There's a Greek bar back home called Aphrodite's Moon,' I say like an idiot. 'They do excellent mezze.'

Laurent's voice gets lower. 'Aphrodite kissed a mortal once by the light of this moon, many thousands of years ago. It drove him crazy. The next person that he kissed – *boum*. The craziness travelled like this . . .'

His lips start making their way along my jawline. I think I say 'meh,' like a goat.

'It travelled from person to person. It travelled through time. Everywhere – *boum*! Like a bomb. *Tu comprends?*'

'Where did it end up?' I whisper. His lips are on my cheek now.

'It ended with me. And now I am going to pass it to you. You will like that, mermaid?'

I'm not proud. I make the first move and grab his chin. It's the moon, OK? That crazy lampshade moon.

As he kisses me, a ball of white heat travels from my lips all the way down my legs. My knees turn to rubber as it ripples on, right to the tips of my toes. I seriously think my toenails are going to blow right off as Laurent tightens his arms around my back and gets stuck in. This is it! THIS is what all the fuss is about! Lips, doing precisely THIS THING! Never in the field of human conquest has Delilah Jones been kissed as well as this. It's like the moon itself is inside me, filling me with light.

I don't know how long we kiss for. It's delirious. Glorious. Wondrous with great big dangly bells on. And when it's over, I want to fly up to that big fat moon and thank it from the bottom of my poor old broken heart.

Home is already wetter than a fish in a bikini, and it's only early September. I look crossly out of the window, and think of moonlight, and beaches.

'*Delilah!* I'm telling you the most important thing that has EVER happened to me and you're looking out of the window!'

I pull my eyes back into the room.

'Look!' Tabby thrusts her phone under my nose again. 'This is him. Isn't he gorgeous?'

I stare at the picture of the smiling boy. Tabs has told me his name is Sam. I get as far as registering that his hair is sandy, but then the thought of sand catapults my brain back to Argole-sur-Mer. The evil rain slaps against the darkening windows. Why aren't I still in France?

'He looks like an onion,' I say.

'How can a person look like an onion?' Tabby demands,

5

tenderly closing Sam's picture down.

'Round head. Brown skin. Tufty bit on the top. Onion.'

I'm right.

'You are so completely wrong I can't even *talk* about how wrong you are,' Tabby says hotly. 'You haven't even met him and already you're comparing him to a root vegetable.'

'Onions aren't root vegetables.'

'Not helpful, Delilah! Are you jet-lagged or what?'

I make a massive effort. Tabby is my best friend after all, and I am giving her about as much attention as I give Wellington, her dog, after he's been kayaking through the puddles in the local park.

'I'm sorry, Tabs,' I say, impatient with myself. 'France scrambled my brain like eggs. I've been looking forward to this conversation for AGES. Losing my phone was the worst thing that's ever happened to me.'

Shortly after the best thing that's ever happened to me. The two events aren't entirely unconnected, if you must know.

'I feel as if I've been in solitary confinement for some heinous crime I never committed,' I go on. 'I keep picturing my phone, beeping sadly on a French sand dune while being eaten by a crab. So tell me everything again and I promise I'll focus.'

Tabs is happy to go right back to the beginning. I settle into my beanbag and listen properly.

My best friend has been going out with Sam for three

weeks and four days. He is her first proper we-go-on-dates boyfriend, so the days thing is important.

'And you won't believe how we met. It was SO romantic. He was at the water fountain during the break in our choir workshop and I was at the water fountain too and we both bent down to drink the water at the same time!'

'Cute,' I say.

Tabby rolls on to her back with a sigh. 'And then we had sectionals.'

That gets my attention. 'You what?'

'Sectionals. It's where the choir gets divided into small groups that rehearse separately,' Tabby explains. 'Sam was in my group. He sat next to me. He had water from the water fountain all down his shirt.' She lowers her voice. 'You could see bits of his chest through the material.'

'Describe,' I say with interest.

'Muscly,' says Tabby happily. 'Like a big ripply walnut.'

'A *walnut*? First an onion, now a walnut? What are we making here, a salad?'

We howl about this for a bit.

'So after the sectionals—' Tabby's eyes widen. 'That actually sounds really rude, doesn't it?'

We both fall to the carpet. Neither of us can speak for a full minute and a half. I love Tabs. She's so adorable, with her spiky brown hair and glasses and habit of getting jokes several hours after everyone else.

'So,' says Tabby when we've got our breath back, 'at the end of the first day he walked me to the bus stop and took

7

my number. And then he called and picked me up from the bus stop the second day. And then at the *end* of the second day, he walked me to the bus stop again—'

I hold up my hand. 'Enough with the travel information. Tell me about the kissing.'

Tabby blushes. 'He kissed me on the last day.'

'Where?'

'On the lips,' says Tab, surprised at my question. 'Oh, *where*! In the wings of the hall, just as we were about to go out for the performance we'd been working on all week. He took my hand and squeezed it.' She grabs my hand and gives it a scrunch to demonstrate. 'And I turned round to say good luck, and then his nose was, like, there.'

Tabby is really getting into her story now. She looks particularly adorable as she talks, eyes all shiny behind her glasses and cheeks as pink as candyfloss.

'I thought I was going to stop breathing! I'd been totally desperate for him to kiss me all week and now here we were with just seconds to go before we were supposed to be singing in German. And he kissed me on the spot!'

'In German?'

'In French, actually,' Tabby says. 'You know. Tongues.'

I smile mysteriously. 'Believe me, I know all about kissing in French.'

Something in my tone of voice catches Tabs' attention. 'You got with someone in France!' she gasps. 'Didn't you? That's why you've been on the moon all evening. You got with someone and you haven't TOLD me!'

'Your kiss is way more important,' I inform her piously. 'Because yours led to a boyfriend while mine was just . . . THE LUSHEST KISS EVER IN THE ENTIRE UNIVERSE FOR ONE NIGHT ONLY.'

We both squeal extremely loudly.

'Oh my God!' shouts Tabby. 'I can't believe I've been going on about Sam when you've got juice too!'

'I can't tell you how incredible it was,' I say in a dreamy voice. 'My head literally caught fire. There was smoke coming out of my nostrils and everything.'

Tabby beams at me. 'The first guy you've kissed since Dave! That's *massive!*'

I can't help flinching at the D-word.

'How "incredible" are we talking?' Tabby says eagerly.

I focus on remembering Laurent's kiss instead of the other thing. How am I supposed to find the words? The memory alone is making my tummy melt like ice-cream: warm fudge sauce, sprinkles, *the works*.

'It was magnificent,' I say at last. 'He had this whole Aphrodite line going about this godlike kiss that's been breaking hearts since the world began, and then he demonstrated its godlikeness. There were bits of me scattered all over the sand dune by the end. I tell you, no-strings-attached lust is totally my new favourite thing. That first kiss . . .' I swallow. There really are no words to do it justice. 'You know the feeling when . . . *mmmm?*'

'When mmmm what?'

I dig Tabby gently in the arm. 'I think we can agree that

most of the guys we got with from Year Nine onwards were terrible, with the exception of Ali who did something oddly twisty with his tongue—'

'I never got with Ali,' says Tabby.

'Didn't you?' I say, momentarily diverted. 'I thought everyone did. But that aside, now you're properly loved up – well. *You* know.'

Tabby looks worried. 'Do I?'

'Don't you?'

There is a strange silence. Oh. *Whoa*. Hold the ketchup, this is serious.

'Don't tell me the Onion can't kiss?' I say in dismay.

'He kisses really well!' Tabby protests. 'And he's not an onion!'

Snatching her phone, I study Sam's picture again. There is a stab of doom in my guts. He just looks so – *ordinary*. No way can he kiss a girl until her head blows off.

'Tell me honestly, Tabs,' I say, pressing the phone back into my best friend's hands. 'Does he kiss like a water fountain? Wet, gushy, dribbling?'

Tabby's big green eyes shimmer at me. 'No!'

'But does he get you *here*?' I press my hand into her belly.

Tabby pushes my hand off. 'Kissing isn't food, Delilah. That's my stomach you're prodding. He gets me here.' And she touches her heart.

I owe it to my best friend to tell her the truth. To tell her what's really out there. She's so young and inexperienced.

'You have to listen to me, babe,' I say. 'Do you

fancy him, or is he just . . . nice?'

'I'm mad about him,' Tabby says defiantly. 'And he's mad about me too. He texts me a hundred times a day and he phones me every evening and I think he kisses just fine.'

Fine? This is worse than I thought.

'Oh Tabs.' I shake my head. 'You have no idea. Now you have a boyfriend, you're going to be kissing this guy a *lot*. His kiss should make your entire body explode. Turn your hair into fuse wire and your guts into dynamite. You should want that kiss over and over and over again because otherwise, frankly, what's the point?'

'You should be an agony aunt,' Tabby grumbles. 'So tactful and understanding.'

'What did the Onion's last text say?'

'*Delilah . . .*'

'Sam, the Onion, whatever.'

Tabby slowly flips open her phone again.

Just wormed the cat. Was tough. See u at bandstand in 10. I'll be the 1 covered in Elastoplast.

She tries to hold my horrified gaze.

'It's funny,' she points out a little sadly. 'The Elastoplast bit.'

'You can't go out with a guy who worms a *cat* before meeting you,' I say. 'Did he even wash his hands? Did you actually touch palms?' I gaze at Tabby's fingers. 'Tabs! You could have CAT WORMS!'

Tabby is laughing now, although it sounds a little reluctant.

11

'That is so unbelievably gross,' I say, grinning. 'If you love me at all, don't go all exclusive with the Onion. We're young and free. Don't you want to stay like that for a bit longer? Not answering to anyone and doing what you want when you want and not so it fits in with football-practice nights?'

Tabby looks at the floor. 'But I really like him.'

'And we all know where really liking someone gets you,' I say sharply.

This whole heartbreak thing, right? The way you see it on TV, it's awful for about five minutes and then there's an ad break for some super-strength mascara that gives you eyes like a demented panda and then you're out dancing with your friends and fancying someone else. No one gave me that script. Crying yourself to sleep for months until your pillow grows mushrooms? Reliving conversations until they're as worn and tattered as that piece of tissue in your coat pocket from the last time you had a cold? Imagining how things Should Have Been? Burning with shame every time you remember the completely-not-cool texts you sent when you were 'believe me, totally caned' i.e. stone-cold sober, lonely and desperate? That's the reality.

'There's a college party tomorrow night at the Gaslight Theatre, welcoming the freshers,' I say firmly. 'You and I are going, and we're going to get you a *proper* kiss so you know what you're missing before you go and settle down with an Onion. End of.'

The Gaslight Theatre is right in the middle of town, near the river. It's a classic concrete monster from the seventies, rows of tall thin windows on it like the open mouth of a basking shark feeding on plankton. Mum and Dad took me to a pantomime there when I was six, and for months afterwards I thought it was a place where magic came through the plugs instead of electricity. I gazed on it in rapture every Saturday morning when we went shopping, remembering King Rat creeping through the auditorium with his long tail dragging behind him. Most of the other kids screamed with terror, but not me. King Rat was the bad guy, and bad guys never got away with it. You just had to wait for the end. What was there to be scared of? Then Mum left. I understood better about King Rat then.

Tonight the Gaslight has green lighting all up the front: strips of Kryptonite beckoning Superman into the bad guy's lair. Tabby and I stand on the steps, shivering in the evening air, listening to the roar of people inside and working up the courage to go in. We're already a couple of drinks to the good, but a couple more are needed.

'How do I look?' Tabby asks.

'Sensational,' I say.

The petrol-green fabric on Tabby's dress really suits her colouring. I have persuaded her to ditch the glasses in favour of contacts tonight, even though she hates wearing them, and we've spent ages on her eye make-up. She resembles a beautiful dragonfly, all legs and shimmer.

'You look hot too,' Tabby says, checking me over.

I sort out the gussety bit of my cherry-red playsuit and fluff my hair a bit. 'Sure I'm not too curly?' I check.

'I'd kill for your curls.'

That's what everyone without curls says. They have no idea.

'Guess what?' I say. 'I'm saving up for—'

'Don't say straighteners,' Tabby interrupts, looking worried.

Give a girl a chance. 'I was *going* to say, for a haircut. I thought I might go really short, like you. A whole new look. Leave the past behind.'

I have pictured it many times in the past months. Goodbye, dumb curly walk-all-over-me kid. Hello super sophisticated French-boy-kisser-among-dunes vamp. The hair's as good a place to start as any.

Tabby looks horrified. She grabs a fistful of my hair

and shakes it at me like an angry, very curly horse's tail. 'Cut this? Don't you know how lucky you are? Mine only grows to my neck, and then it just hangs there, splitting at the ends and getting snarled in the zips of my cardies.'

Tab has a definite way with words. She almost makes me change my mind. I decide to leave the decision another week.

'Does Sam know you're out with me tonight?' I ask.

'He wanted to go out, but I told him we were having a girls' night,' Tabby confesses. 'How I hadn't seen you in ages and how he'd feel left out of all our conversation and how it was better if we saw each other tomorrow instead. I feel bad about it, to be honest.'

'You *haven't* seen me for ages, apart from yesterday, and we are girls out for the night, which makes it a "girls' night",' I point out. 'Don't lose the buzz.'

I take twenty quid from the cash machine at the foot of the Gaslight steps, then grab her hand to drag her in with me. As I haul her towards the doors, Tab suddenly gives me a nudge.

'Check out those two,' she whispers.

Two guys are standing in a street-lit patch not far from us. One is tall and well-built, with a fitted black T-shirt and a mess of dark hair. The other is whippet-thin, his white trainers gleaming brightly in the green light flooding through the glass doors of the theatre.

'Let's go in,' I say abruptly. And I shove Tabby hard

between the shoulders, into the thumping warmth of the theatre bar.

I happily admit to being a party girl. I've danced on tables before, and once puked in a flowerbed. But I suddenly find that I'm as shy as a new-born lamb. I don't recognize a single face. I am frozen to the doormat and more than a little freaked out.

'Sure this is the right party?' Tab whispers in my ear.

I spot a group of familiar faces huddled by the loos, all looking as shell-shocked as I feel. I unglue my mouth. 'It is,' I manage. 'We're college girls now. This is where we belong.'

Tabs looks happier. Excited, even. I wish the same could be said of me, but seeing Studs outside has thrown me like a discus at the Olympics. I have to pull myself together.

We gaze around the room in bemusement, standing close together for courage. Brightly coloured *Welcome* banners are slung up over the bar. The girls are all wearing practically nothing and the guys look like they've found the mother lode. Half the room is already wrecked.

This seems like a very, very good idea.

I consider fighting my way to the bar, but a sea of drunk people are in the way. I put some money in the vending machine by the door instead. Two cans of soda roll out with a familiar clank. Open, drink a third, top up with a mini-bottle of vodka nicked from Dad's drinks cupboard which has, in turn, been nicked from a hotel mini-bar.

'Get this down you,' I advise, handing Tabby her

doctored soda and taking a slug of my own.

Tabby knocks back her drink in one, producing a burp somewhere on the Richter scale of burpiness. 'Wow, sorry,' she says, wiping her mouth. 'Do you think anyone heard? Let's dance.'

Guys are checking her out already. I feel a brief flash of conscience about the Onion. Then again, we're sixteen. No one's faithful at sixteen, apart from me, and *that* is a mistake I'll never make again.

'Did you know those guys on the steps?' Tabby shouts through the music as we throw ourselves around the dancefloor. I am still feeling weird, but the evening is improving with every thud from the speakers. 'You acted like you maybe did. The tall one was cute. Did you see his shoulders?'

I don't answer her question. Jonny Osgood has just loomed on the dancing horizon like an overweight lighthouse in a stormy sea. He's even wearing stripes to complete the illusion. I'm ridiculously pleased to see him.

'OZ!' I roar, waving like a madwoman.

Oz forces his way through the crowd to join us, holding a beer bottle aloft. His button-black eyes are gleaming with good humour, his hair gelled into a kind of pyramid. He already seems to know half the people in the room, to judge from the head-nods and high-fives going on. As he gets closer, he waggles his tongue at us like a thirsty dog.

'Fancy a kiss, ladies?'

'You're such a lech,' I say, cheerfully shoving him in

the chest. 'Keep your tongue to yourself and get us more drinks.'

'Eighteen already and college hasn't even started,' Oz says happily. 'It was worth redoing last year for this very pleasure.'

'You quoting your dad now?' I inquire. 'I'm guessing not.'

'A blip,' he says, waving all mention of flunked GCSEs to one side. 'Nothing more. Whoops, none left,' he adds, frowning at his bottle. 'Another, I think. What are you two drinking?'

'You could do worse than get with Oz tonight, Tab,' I observe as Oz heads to the bar. 'He may need to lose a little weight, but he's been into you since last summer and has the attention span of a gnat. He wouldn't give you any trouble.'

Tab looks appalled. 'Oz? No way. That would be like getting with my *dog*.'

The music goes up a notch. Ultraviolet lights come on, and everyone wearing white starts to glow in bright, uneven patches. Tabby's eyes skim off the top of the dancing crowd and come to rest on a dark head standing some way above everyone else.

'Hey!' she says with excitement. 'The big-shouldered one from outside is behind the bar!'

'If his friends are anything to go by, he's probably robbing it,' I mutter.

Tabby jabs me a little unsteadily in the chest. 'You *do* know him! Who is he? Can I meet him?'

I glance around the room at floor level. Studs' white trainers will be glowing like lightbulbs in here. I think I glimpse him on the far side of the dancefloor. 'Far side' is good, though 'Australia' would be better.

'I don't know him, but I know his friend,' I say. 'Avoid.'

'You can't bring me out and tell me I'm going to kiss someone but I don't get to choose who,' says Tabby with a grumpy hiccup. 'I'm going to give Oz a hand with the drinks and check out Shoulders for myself.'

I sit for a while, waiting for Tabs and Oz and watching the crowd, smiling flirtatiously at any half-decent guys looking my way and feeling more like myself. This isn't so strange. It's just bigger. As a kicking tune crashes in, I leap to my feet and dance on a wave of affection for all the faces that I know and several that I don't. It's good to be back.

'Well now, Delilah.'

My good mood evaporates like steam off a cowpat.

'What are you doing here?' I say warily.

'Business, babe. It's a well known fact that college kids like to partay.' Studs pushes his cap back on his head and looks me over. I feel his eyes, hot and wet, like a pair of little tongues licking my skin. The diamond studs in his nose wink in the flashing lights, on and off, on and off. He whistles. 'You're looking hot tonight. Dave's a fool.'

I lick my lips, which are suddenly dry. 'Dave who?'

'I always liked you, Delilah.'

'It's not mutual,' I snap.

As he melts away into the crowd, I half expect a flash of

sulphur-smelling smoke. This is the Gaslight after all, home of magic and illusion.

'Wanna dance?'

The smiling guy who's approached me is OK-looking, but all my energy has drained away like dishwater. Flirting is suddenly beyond me.

'Sorry,' I mutter. 'No thanks.'

I grab my bag off the table and walk as quickly as I can across the pulsing dancefloor. I have to find Tabby. We have to leave. Right now.

I stop in dismay.

My best friend is lolling over the bar, her fist wrapped firmly in the neck of the big-shouldered barman's T-shirt as she kisses him across the beermats among cheering onlookers. Standing beside her, Oz is holding three bottles of cider and looking fed up.

But not nearly as fed up as the guy in the Gaslight's double doors, frozen and gaping and as unlike an onion as it's possible for a human to be.

Talk to me babe. I miss u xx

'*Send*, will you?' I snarl, pressing buttons. The message sits there, looking at me like a particularly stupid dog that's been instructed to fetch a stick but would rather stay where it is and lick its butt. I whack the send button hard one more time and it disappears. It's a pig, being back on my old phone. Everything is clunky and dates from a hundred years ago. There's an app for sending smoke signals somewhere on it, I swear.

My whole life is a pig just now, to tell the truth. I haven't seen Tabby all week, despite calling at her place four times, both before and after college. She's avoiding me. I can't blame her. Sam dumped her in spectacular fashion, and her devastation is all my fault.

College isn't supposed to start this way. I've been so preoccupied with the Tabby thing that my first few days have passed in a blur of grovelling voice messages and texts which – when my phone bothers to send them – haven't had any response at all. I have to get a grip. This year is *important*. I can't afford to lose the plot in Week One.

Tabs does all different subjects to me – Classics, English, Ancient History and Music. College is huge, and my bit is miles away from the Arts Department. I have been lurking as much as I can in the canteen, but even at lunch the two sides never seem to meet, as if they function in parallel universes. At this rate, I'll never see my best friend again.

'Hi Delilah. I'm thinking of running away to the circus. I reckon I'd be good on the trapeze.'

Oz is in front of me with his canteen tray.

'It was our first Economics class,' I sigh, dropping my phone on the table with irritation. 'Only Einstein would have understood it.'

'Einstein . . .' Oz sets his tray down and then clicks his fingers. 'The dog from *Back to the Future*. Classic! Am I right or am I right? Thanks for the text. I'm here and I've missed you too. Let's talk.'

'What?'

'Your message.' Oz looks expectant. 'You just sent it. About five seconds ago.'

I groan and slap myself round the head. 'I was trying to send that to Tabby. Stupid, *stupid* phone.'

Oz unwraps a sandwich the size of my head and takes a bite. 'What are you missing Tabby for? You guys are joined at the hip.'

'We had radical separation surgery,' I say.

'Is this about the party at the Gaslight?' he asks in a surprising flash of intuition. 'That whole ugly scene on the steps when Tab got canned? It was nasty. But may I remind you that you're not the one who got with the barman?'

I rest my forehead in my hands. 'I may not have done it, but I talked her into it. Well, not the bar guy – I suggested you, actually – but if I hadn't practically ordered her to slum it she'd still be with Sam and taking my calls.'

Oz brightens. 'You suggested me? What did she say?'

'That's not the point. The point is that I made my best friend lie to a guy who made her happy and is now making her extremely unhappy. What kind of friend am I?'

'A bad one.'

'Tell it to me straight, why don't you.'

'You asked,' he points out.

'Oz, what actually *happened* that night?' I ask in some desperation. 'I only saw the end. Give me details. I need facts to get myself out of this mess.'

Oz obliges. 'I was getting in the drinks when Tabby swung up. She was quite pissed and started chatting to the bar guy.'

It never takes much to get Tab drunk. She once slid down some banisters after one glass of punch, catching her dress on a splinter halfway down and ending up at the bottom like a blown-out umbrella. Come to think of it, it was the same party where I puked in the flowerbed. Maybe there was more than cider in the punch.

'We were flirting and it was going well,' Oz continues. 'Then I realized her efforts were all aimed at the bar guy, not me. The kissing part happened when I wanted to get some crisps. Tabby ups her game with the bar guy about getting some for free. He makes some idiot comment about them costing her a kiss, so she grabs him. You know the rest.' He frowns. 'We never even got the crisps.'

I'm not surprised the bar guy lies at the heart of this. He's mates with Studs, isn't he?

My phone rings. I leap on it like a kid on a lilo.

'Tab!' I cry, almost sobbing with relief. 'Oh Tabby, I'm so, so sorry about Sunday night! Are you OK?'

Tabby sounds cool. 'Not really.'

I'm gabbling but I can't help it. 'I'm with Oz. He told me what happened. It's not your fault, hon. The bar guy started it.'

'We shouldn't have gone to the party without Sam.'

'I know. It's totally my fault,' I say humbly. 'All of it. I swear to you that if I could change Sunday night, I would.'

Tabby's voice softens. 'I've got a brain, and I make my own choices. I *was* angry with you, but I have to face facts. You weren't the one doing the kissing.'

'That's what I said,' Oz puts in, listening shamelessly.

'Shut up, Oz,' Tabby and I say together.

Oz stands up. 'My work here is done.'

'What can I do to put things right?' I beg down

the phone when he's gone. 'I'll do anything to make you feel better.'

Tabby starts to cry. 'I don't know. It's so awful. When he saw me . . . I'll never forget his face as long as I live. He won't speak to me. We sit in the same classes and he looks through me like I'm not there.'

I'm on the verge of crying myself. 'That means he still likes you.'

'How do you figure that?'

'If he wasn't that bothered, he'd be talking to you by now.'

Tabby is silent on the other end. I can feel her hope snaking down the phone into my ear.

'I'm going to sort this out,' I promise. 'Do you want me to call him?'

'He won't believe you. You're my friend, which doesn't exactly make you objective.'

I am determined not to let this opportunity to make amends pass me by. I've done plenty of things in my life that make me break into a sweat of misery. Tabby is not going to be one of them. She's not getting away.

'Well, how's this?' I say. 'I'll go to the Gaslight this weekend to talk to the bar guy myself. I'll give him Sam's number and persuade him to call and explain what happened. You were *drunk*. Are you telling me Sam's never got drunk?'

'He doesn't drink,' says Tabby.

'Well he should,' I say crossly. 'Then maybe he wouldn't

be so quick to judge others. Are you free after college? I want to take you out and buy you something nice to say sorry. I saved up some money from the lido to get me through college this term and the least I can do is spend some of it on you. Can we do that?'

'That would be nice,' says Tabby gratefully. 'I love you, Lilah. Let's not fight ever again.'

I can tell you now, sobbing in the college canteen is up there on my list of Uncool Things I Have Done. But it's worth it.

'OK,' I say, disentangling myself from Tabby's arms in the college car park, where we've been hugging for approximately five years. 'Let's do this shopping thing. There's a fabby vintage shop by the Gaslight. I'll take you there.'

'Actually,' says Tabby, 'can we go to M&S?'

'M&S?' I reply in shock. 'What are you, seventy-five?'

'Is this my treat or what?' Tabby reminds me. 'I would quite like some new undies, actually. Mum says M&S do the best knickers in the business.'

'You are so uncool,' I grumble. 'You'll be telling me about their three-for-two deals on socks next.'

Marks and Spencer's is only a couple of doors away from college. I don't think I've been inside since Mum left. Dad's not much of an undies shopper. Tesco's with the odd market pair thrown in is more our style. Still grumbling, I usher Tabby through the big glass doors.

Pants are on the first floor.

'Exactly how many bums are there in this town?' I say, reeling from the banks of underwear stretching away from us in every shade from white to shocking pink.

It's so nice to hear Tabby giggling again. She chooses a set of pants and a bra in blue and white polka dots and thrusts them at me.

'Are you sure about this?' she says suddenly, pulling them back again as I reach for them. 'They're twenty quid.'

'I saved four hundred pounds this summer, even after France,' I say with pride. 'Twenty quid is a drop in my vast cash ocean, and it's worth every penny to see you smiling. Hand them over.'

The till lady rings them through. I take out my card and flourish it at her, proud that at last I have a bank account. The card is still quite shiny and new, and I've personalized it with a picture of myself looking about as straight-haired as I ever get.

'Sorry love,' says the till lady, handing it back. 'It's not going through the machine. Have you got anything else?'

With only two pounds in cash on me, the undies are returned. We head for the food department instead.

'That was embarrassing,' I say as we leave with our purchase. 'I'm really sorry. I've probably set something up wrong with the bank. I'll talk to them about it tomorrow.'

'Don't worry,' says Tab. 'I love Percy Pigs.'

'Stick with me and I'll treat you to pig-shaped chews forever, babe,' I sigh. 'I know how to impress a lady.'

27

The Percy Pigs are gone before we've made it halfway down the High Street. The Gaslight glimmers at us, a hundred metres further on. It's cloaked in pink lights today, and is already shining in the grey September afternoon.

'We're going in there,' I say, high on Percy Pigs and sudden resolve. 'We're going to sort this out with the bar guy right now.'

Tabby looks pale. She stares at the Gaslight. 'I don't think I can face him,' she says in a small voice. 'And I've got an essay due on *The Odyssey*. I think I'm going to – you know. Head home.'

I pat her on the arm. 'I'll deal with it by myself. Give me Sam's number so I can hand it over.'

Tabby messages me the number. Her eyes look a bit watery at Sam's smiling photo on her phone.

'Shoulders may not work there at five-thirty on a Thursday afternoon!' she shouts after me as I stride towards the theatre.

'We've got to start somewhere!' I shout back. 'I'll call you later!'

And I walk up the theatre steps into something completely unexpected.

The Gaslight is quiet and the familiar smell of stale beer hangs in the air. Someone is hoovering, somewhere. The pinboard by the double doors is covered in flyers about shows, art exhibitions and animal sanctuaries, as well as singing lessons and job vacancies at the theatre. A big poster for the Christmas pantomime – *Cinderella* – beams down at me, looking about as funny as a dead clown. The brown zigzag carpet, invisible beneath a thousand partygoers at the Start of Term party, is the same one I remember from when I was six. It crunches under my feet as I go past the box office with its cheery displays of old Gaslight productions.

A woman comes out of a door beside the bar, carrying boxes of crisps stacked up to her nose. A pair of heavily mascaraed eyes regard me, sandwiched between bleach-blond fringe and brown cardboard. I think I remember her from the party night.

'Bar opens at six, love.'

I clear my throat. 'I'm looking for a guy.'

'Aren't we all?' Smoky laughter makes the cardboard tower of crisps shake as she sets it down on the end of the bar. She wipes her hands down the legs of her tight-fitting jeans. 'You want to get specific?'

This is suddenly feeling like one of those things you talk about but never actually do, like, *Hey, let's leap in the river to see how deep it is!* or, *I'm going to dye my hair green and get an undercut!* I cast my mind back to Sunday night. I don't know the bar guy's name. What does he even look like? I hardly saw him, except on the dark theatre steps with Studs and then with half his face attached to my friend. 'He's, er, tall? Dark hair? Works here?'

The woman tilts her head towards the bar door. 'JEM! Get out here!' She rests her arms on the bar and assesses me. 'Friends, are you?'

'I've never met him,' I say.

'Internet date, is it?'

'I'm here on behalf of a friend.'

She gives me a look. I get the sense that she has lots of girls coming here 'on behalf of a friend'. All my resolve about making it up to Tabby teeters like the pile of crisp boxes on the bar. I'd like to go home now because I know this is going to be *very* embarrassing.

Jem comes out of the door with both hands full of beer glasses still shimmering hot from the dishwasher. He *is* tall, even by my five-foot-three standards. His shoulders are exactly as wide as I remember, and encased in a close-fitting grey T-shirt that brings out the ashy flecks in his blue eyes. A red and white teatowel is wrapped inexplicably around his head.

I stare. He stares back. Even with the teatowel, he is divine. No wonder Tab went primal. He sets the glasses down on the bar and pulls the teatowel off, revealing black hair spiked up and a little sideways.

'What's with the teatowel?'

My appropriate-first-question filter is apparently in the 'off' position.

He regards the teatowel in his hands. 'It's a teatowel,' he says.

The blond woman has vanished so it's just me, him and the distant hoover. He slings the teatowel over his shoulder. I try not to think about the *actual* shoulder under the T-shirt under the teatowel, which means my imagination paints it in total clarity. He leans his extremely fit arms along the bar and grins at me.

'What do you want to talk about?' he asks.

'My friend. You, er . . .'

I fumble around for the words, and know I'm looking increasingly stupid. This is hideous. I would swap Tab's stair incident for this any day.

'Slept with her?' he suggests helpfully.

I am stunned into action. 'No!' I say in outrage. 'Kissed her, I was *going* to say. And now there's this nightmare going on in her life that you have to help me with, because you caused the problem in the first place.'

It's his move now. I look at him in an expectant way. Then I realize that he might think I'm looking at him in the *other* sort of expectant way – which I'm totally not – and I stare at the bar instead.

'What's your friend's name?'

I make myself look up again. He's even better looking second time round. 'Tab,' I say. 'Tabitha. Tabby.'

'What, I got with all three?'

He's laughing at me, I realize.

'Tabby,' I say, holding on tightly to my dignity. 'On Sunday, at the college party. Across the bar?'

His flecky blue-grey eyes clear. 'Spiky brown hair? Big . . .' He makes the gesture that translates in boy language as 'boobs'.

'Yes!' I point at him in emphasis, then put my finger down because it looks a bit pervy, agreeing with the boob thing he's just mimed. 'Spiky brown hair. Angry boyfriend.'

'Oh yeah, the angry boyfriend.' Jem scratches his head, close to his hairline. 'He should get over himself. It was a party. Everyone does dumb things at parties. Anyway, she was cute and asking for it.'

I colour angrily on Tab's behalf. 'She's not a slut!'

'I wouldn't know. We didn't get that far.'

His fingertips are pinkish-white. I notice the same pink-white colour all around his hairline. The teatowel thing suddenly becomes clear.

'Have you been doing a *facepack*?' I say in astonishment.

'Face*paint*,' he corrects, colouring slightly.

'Facepaint?' I have him like a spider under a glass, scuttling helplessly beneath my scorn. 'What are you, Krusty the Clown?'

He's gazing into my eyes. I'm not sure he's listening. 'Why are you staring at me?' I demand when he fails to respond to my clown remark.

'Your eyes are different colours. One's like chocolate. The other's more like poo.'

I lose my thread. Understandably, I feel.

'I— it's my contact lens, I just wear one because the other eye doesn't need anything so it makes my eyes different— I'm sorry, did you say poo?'

Stretching up from the bar, he links his hands and cricks them above his head. His chest does this expanding thing that always happens when guys do that. At that moment he seems as big as a tree, if you can get ripped trees.

'What's your name?' he asks, lowering his arms again.

Visions of burning vinyl rise once more in my mind's eye. 'That's actually irrelevant, but since you ask, *Krusty*, it's Delilah.'

'Nice.'

'I could say the same of you,' I shoot back, stung. I am still battling with the poo thing.

'I mean it. I always mean what I say.'

'So you're saying my eyes actually look like poo?'

33

'Only *one* of them,' he says agreeably. 'I could go with mud, at a stretch.'

I take a deep breath. Where and how has this conversation gone so wrong? 'I came in to tell you that my friend needs your help to get her boyfriend back. That's it, basically. That's what I came in here to say.'

'I'm not convinced this is any of your business,' he says, 'but you're here and not her because . . .?'

'Because it's my fault,' I reply after a pause. 'And I promised I'd fix it.'

He looks genuinely curious. 'Why is it your fault?'

Time out, people. Stuff here needs to be explained.

You only have to scrape the surface of Delabby/Tabilah in order for things to become clear. We are *as one*. As luck or puberty or whatever would have it, I've always been one step ahead of Tab on boobs, periods, cigarettes, alcohol and boys. We have grown together in this way, like this amazing photo I once saw of a bicycle inside a tree. Tabby is the bicycle – in a genuine steel-and-rubber way, not a slaggy one – and I am the tree that has grown *through* the bicycle and *around* the bicycle, raising the bicycle from the ground as *part of the tree*. The bicycle wheels spin in the wind, but the tree calls the shots. All of which makes me responsible for stuff like this, whether Teatowel likes it or not.

I don't say any of this out loud. It would sound insane.

'You don't need to know that,' I say briskly. 'I just want to give you Tab's boyfriend's number and ask, very nicely, if you could call him and explain what happened and how it wasn't Tabby's fault.'

He disappears into the kitchen, which isn't supposed to happen when you're in the middle of a conversation. I hear the clank of a metal locker being opened. 'How do you square that?' he says, re-emerging in a dark grey jacket. 'She jumped on *me*, not the other way round.'

This is like wading through treacle in a big Victorian frock with my feet tied together. On a very cold day so the treacle has set like toffee. I am close to breaking point.

'She'd never have done it if you hadn't given it all that with the free crisps thing!' I say through my teeth. 'Can I *please* message you his number?'

He flips up a hinged part of the bar and comes out to join me, adjusting his collar. 'Let's walk and talk,' he suggests, and heads for the double doors.

The afternoon is gloomier than ever. I hurry after him, the double doors swinging shut behind me. 'What's to talk about? Will you do it or not?'

'You expect me to call up the angry boyfriend when I don't have the full facts?' he asks, jogging gently across the car park. 'I think not.'

'You want more facts? Fine.' I break into a run, trying to keep up with his long legs. 'I told her to do it.'

'Did you know she had a boyfriend?'

'Yes, but—'

'So why did you tell her to kiss me?'

This isn't painting me in a good light.

35

'I messed up, OK?' I say in frustration. 'And for the record, I didn't tell her to kiss *you* specifically.'

He swings round so I practically collide with his chest. He smells warm.

'Are you busy?' he asks, looking down at me.

'Yes!' I practically shout. 'I'm busy trying to unscrew my screw-up! Will you help me or not?'

'I'm thinking about it. Keep walking or we'll be late.'

We make an odd pair, him striding easily along and me scurrying beside him like a pet mouse on a string.

'Late for what?' I pant as we pause at a set of traffic lights.

He shoots me a sideways look. 'My Krusty the Clown convention.'

I am too breathless, too curious, too annoyed to ask anything more about where we are going. We rush along, up narrow streets and through little alleyways, heading into the yellow lights of the Watts Estate – a cluster of uneven concrete high-rises that crown the town like rotten teeth. The views across the Downs are breathtaking up here, even in the gloom of six pm.

Jem switches left and right, with me still grimly on his tail. I lose my bearings and find a whole bunch of misgivings to replace them. Why am I following a total stranger into this ever-darkening place? Have horror movies taught me nothing? I stroke my house keys in my pocket, and tuck the sharp end of the latch key between my fingers. If he tries anything, I'll be ready.

He is the answer to Tabby's problem, I remind myself. I can't let him out of my sight until he agrees to help. If he thinks he'll lose me in this badly-lit maze of twists and turns, he can forget it.

'I have other stuff to do tonight!' I complain as he makes what feels like the fiftieth left turn, past a collapsing fence and a couple of mildewed greenhouses.

'No you don't.'

'You're not the one who has to explain Keynesian theory in class tomorrow afternoon!'

I don't actually have to do that for another fortnight – fortunately, as I'm having trouble even spelling Keynes, let alone getting my head around his ideas on macro-economics – but I have to fight back with *something*.

'What's Keynesian theory?'

'I don't know!'

I never plan on making him laugh, but I seem to do it with tragic ease.

We've reached a tower block at the top of the estate. He goes through a set of doors and down a bleach-smelling corridor towards a lift. I follow, practically snorting with determination. No way am I letting go now. I am double-sided Sellotape. I am No More Nails.

The lift is steel and way too small. He fills most of it. I plaster myself into the smallish corner that remains, and hope we aren't going to break down halfway. Being stuck in a tiny space with the hottest guy I've ever met would be a *nightmare*.

'You remind me of an angry squirrel,' he says as we crank upwards. 'You're actually chittering.'

'I bet you say that to all the girls,' I snarl.

'Not all of them,' he says, looking at me consideringly. 'Just the cute ones.'

Cute?

Oh my God. Right here and now, perhaps even before the lift has reached its destination, I have an opportunity to dust off my newly minted no-strings-attached approach, as perfected with Laurent in the summer sand dunes, and kiss this teatowel-wearing god.

Yay! woofs the Lust Labrador.

Don't even, hisses the Cat of Mistrust.

I have always found that the big questions in life boil down to the Lust Labrador and the Cat of Mistrust. It's a useful distinction. The Lust Labrador acts without thinking while the Cat of Mistrust does it the other way round. The Cat of Mistrust is a big thing with me and getting bigger all the time. I think Laurent was a weird one-off.

Beyond the lift, a corridor takes us to another door, a battered red one this time, and into an open-plan space stretching the width of the block and filled with the sweet smell of hash. The walls are painted a riot of different colours and long windows face the setting sun, which hangs low in a sky striped with oranges and reds and greys. Music is playing quietly somewhere; there are mirrors, and curtained-off areas, and a studio set-up with lights and a white backdrop and a camera on a tripod.

The place is full of people of different colours. Greens, golds, reds, blues and pinks, all swirled up together, some abstract and some not. There's a girl with eyes like peacock feathers; a guy with a red snake around one thin arm; silver-skinned boys with rivets studding their chests. A red-haired girl in a black dress is poised over a boy's bare back, painting a delicate set of angel wings on to his shoulder blades.

Jem goes to high-five a full-on jungle vine heading for the camera and the white backdrop.

'If you smudge Sukhdev, I'll murder you, Jem,' says the red-haired girl, barely looking up. 'He took me three hours.'

Jem lowers his hand, leaving the jungle vine hanging. 'Anywhere free?'

'There's a space by the window. Light's terrible so no one else wants it. 'Scuse me for not chatting but if I don't keep my eyes down, these babies are going to turn into chicken wings. Kev! How's the lighting?'

A big guy with a bullet hole painted through his cheek lowers his light-meter. 'When are we getting blinds in here? Sunset keeps changing the readings.'

'Take Sukh's pictures as quick as you can then.'

'Guys, this is Delilah,' says Jem.

I lift my hand to say hello, forgetting that I am still holding my house keys. They fall with a clatter to the paint-stained floor. The red-haired girl's hand jumps, sending a feather shooting off at a strange angle across the ribcage of her canvas.

'All that's missing is the tambourine,' she growls, dabbing at the splodge she has made.

I flush and scoop my keys up. 'Sorry.'

'Ignore Ella,' Jem tells me, steering me on to a stool beside a tall mirror reflecting the swiftly changing sky. 'She's brilliant and she lives here, so it pays to tolerate her moods.'

My curiosity wins over my embarrassment as I gaze around at all the activity. 'What is this place?'

'A body art collective. We paint each other most Thursdays.' He points at his hairline. 'The remains of this afternoon's skull. I practise whenever I get the chance.'

That explains the teatowel, I realize.

He rubs his ear. 'How did our first conversation go again?'

'"What's with the teatowel?" "It's a teatowel."' A smirk is snaking across my face. I can feel it, wiggling in there.

'That's bad,' he says.

'It wasn't *Romeo and Juliet*,' I agree.

I could bite my tongue off. Why didn't I choose *Hamlet* or *Macbeth*? Or even *Eastenders*? He gives me the same searching stare he gave me in the lift, like I'm a layer of paint or a sheet of old wallpaper ripe for stripping.

'You're lovely,' he says.

Whoa, whoa, whoa. Not going there.

'Now that I've got you standing still,' I say, whipping out my phone, 'can I message you this number or what?'

He takes the phone from me and places it beside the long mirror. 'Later. I was going to do my skull, but I've changed my mind. I'm going to paint you instead.'

The jungle vine posing for photos is wearing pants and paint and nothing else.

'No way,' I say, horrorstruck.

'I'm not asking you to take your clothes off,' he assures me, pulling small pots of paint and different brushes from the pockets on his jacket. He pauses for a beat. 'Not yet, anyway.'

I want to flirt back but the Cat of Mistrust holds me in its amber gaze. I glance around the room to regain my composure. I feel him grinning over his paints, opening lids and checking colours.

'Does it wash off?' I ask at last.

He circles his face with his finger, reminding me that he was a skull less than an hour ago. It has the distracting effect of centring my gaze on his features: long-lashed eyes the colour of the sea at Brighton, a strong straight nose, a small scar on his upper lip.

What choice do I have?

'You can paint my hand,' I say reluctantly. 'But you have to promise you'll call Tab's boyfriend.'

'Deal.'

'You mean it?'

He takes a packet of make-up wipes from his pocket and cleans the back of my hand. 'Not everyone in this business uses wipes, but I prefer it,' he says, blowing to dry the surface of the skin. 'Paint is useless over moisturizer, and these make sure the skin is clean and dry. And I already told you that I always mean what I say. Keep still now.'

This is the point at which I should relax. Job done, promise made. But I can't. Him blowing on my hand has just sent me into orbit.

He paints on a base layer and blows again, waggling my hand in the air like it's a straw-filled rubber glove on a scarecrow's arm. When the base is dry, he dips the point of a smaller brush into a pot of red paint and puts the tip of the brush on my skin. I bite my lip. It tickles, and is cold. It is also the sexiest thing anyone has ever done to me. Seriously. If hands could dribble, mine would be dribbling. Mesmerized, I watch him stroke the little brush between the veins leading from my fingers to my wrists.

I do my best to sound cool. 'What are you painting?'

'Blood, bones, veins and arteries. The things that make us real.'

I think about this, mainly because it stops me thinking about other more dangerous things. 'You paint what's real in the same way that you mean everything you say?'

He pauses, as though surprised by what I thought was obvious. 'Truth is a big thing with me,' he says at last.

'Get you, Gandhi.'

I shut my eyes at the warmth of his breath on my fingers as he leans in closer. The brush sweeps up and down my skin. I have to say something else or risk bursting into flames.

'Is this a hobby or a life plan?'

'I'm not working in bars all my life. All those sci-fi lizard men and undead zombies you see at the multiplex? Some day they'll be down to me.'

'So much for keeping it real.'

He laughs. 'You may have a point.'

As he blows on my skin again, my hand zings urgent messages all over my body. The Lust Labrador starts to drag me down dark and sultry paths.

'Do your friends let you practise on them?' I squeak.

Blue paint next, following the tracery of my veins. 'They're generally too busy stealing cars.'

I laugh in a mildly hysterical way. He raises his eyebrows.

'You're serious?' I say, realizing.

'You're learning, grasshopper.'

He keeps painting me as the rest of the artists and models take turns before Kev the bullet man's camera lens. The smell of hash grows stronger; the music grows louder. I remain on my chair, lulled into a state of highly charged semi-sleep.

'Photo time,' says Jem.

I peel my eyes open at the cold blast of a spray sealant on my skin. The internal workings of my hand lie before me in gory detail. Bone, blood and tissue glisten. Veins bulge. It's grotesque and amazing at the same time.

'I should be in A and E,' I say incredulously. 'How do you get the detail so perfect?'

'Reading lots of anatomy books.' Jem checks his watch. 'Whoa, that's the time? I have to be back at the Gaslight by nine. Val'll dock my wages if I'm late.'

When in doubt, feel guilty. It's the English way. 'Coming here was your idea, not mine,' I say quickly.

'I know.'

He plants a hand on the wall either side of me so I am trapped on the stool. His eyes are more blue than grey this close up.

'So,' he says. 'Can I kiss you now?'

He says it like it's the most normal thing in the world. Like he's offering me a cup of tea or something. He's so blinking *close*.

'What?' I stammer.

'You don't have to sound so shocked,' he says reasonably. 'Your pupils are enormous, which means you like the idea as much as I do.'

'I—' No one has ever read my eyes like that before. 'It's the pot, OK?'

'That makes your pupils smaller.'

I fight back feebly. 'These are the pupils in my poo-coloured eyes we're talking about?'

'I was trying to win back some of the ground I'd lost to that teatowel. I'm thinking more topaz now, or tiger's eye. You're lovely.'

I summon the strength from somewhere and duck

under his arm.

Outside the long windows, the light has faded to nothing and the moon is rising: a great Toffee Penny of a moon, still wearing its golden cellophane, shining over the pinprick lights of an urban evening. I feel like I'm floating on the haze, high up here above the town. Bullet-holed Kev takes pictures; people talk to Jem and peer at my hand like forensic pathologists studying a murder victim. I hardly listen, bombed out by the smell of dope and the effect Jem is having on me.

The lift back down the block seems smaller than ever. I hold my fingers carefully away from my body and try to think about anything but the figure lounging against the steel walls of the lift beside me.

'Why the zombie stance?' he inquires, amused.

'I don't want to smudge it.' I still find it hard to believe that the skin on my hand genuinely hasn't been flayed off.

'The sealant will hold it for a while. Anyway, Kev got plenty of good shots, which is all that matters. You'll have to smudge it eventually. I'll smudge it for you, if you like.'

The implication scorches like a red-hot iron. He grins as he catches my reaction.

'I'll do your collarbone next time,' he offers.

My hand was bad enough. Two hours of this guy's brush on my collarbone and I'll be a wordless wreck.

'Who says there'll be a next time?'

'I do,' he says as the lift stops. 'Can I kiss you yet?'

'No!'

He takes my unpainted hand and pulls me down the bleach-flavoured corridor to the double doors and out into the evening. The cool air smacks me in the face like a big glassy glove.

'Not exactly romantic, is it?' he says, looking at the waterstained concrete and over-full wheelie bins nearby. 'We'll find somewhere else for that kiss.'

'You're very sure of yourself,' I say, trying not to sound as breathless as I feel.

'Call it optimism.'

The moon is already starting to lose its golden edge as it pulls away from the earth's grip. The shadows are confusing, part streetlight and part moonlight, striping the broken tarmac below our feet. I order my fingers to detach themselves from his but they aren't listening.

'Do you have a boyfriend?' he asks as we walk.

Say yes and all this will go away.

'No.'

'Did he dump you?'

'Other way round.' What is this, truth or dare? I've caught Jem's habit of telling it straight. I haven't even told Tabby that.

'Did you love him?'

'I just said I dumped him, didn't I?' I snap, groping for focus.

'Doesn't mean you didn't love the guy. Just that you had your reasons.'

We walk on in silence for a while, which is just as well

because I am trying not to cry. As we reach the road that will lead us back down towards the Gaslight, the town lies at our feet like a glittering carpet. The moon shines large and bright over our heads.

'Aphrodite's moon,' Jem says, turning to me. 'Isn't that what they call the really full, fat ones?'

The view spreads behind him like a spangled magician's cloak. *Bloody moon*, I think with ecstatic dread as he leans forward to kiss me. *Bloody Aphro-bloody-dite.*

He's hardly started when he pulls back like I've electrocuted him. His eyes are wide.

'Whoa,' he says. He sounds shaken.

I have that panicky sensation I had when I was fourteen and kissing a boy for the first time. That need to appear confident with absolutely no experience to back it up. If used incorrectly while kissing, tongues are little better than slugs. Have I just done a slug?

'What?' I ask nervously.

He mutters something I can't hear, gathers me back into him and kisses me harder. The kiss is deep and full and, frankly, lush. I soften and mould myself to him. If I'm honest, I practically start climbing him like one of those ropes in an old-school gym.

A chuckle from the shadows breaks the spell. I fling myself out of Jem's arms like a spring-loaded sucker toy as Studs walks into the glow of a street lamp, fists thrust deep into the pockets of his denim jacket.

'Jem,' he remarks, grinning. 'Doing fine, I see.'

Jem is having difficulty focusing on the change in circumstances. I hunch myself into my clothes, wishing and *wishing* that my hair wasn't so distinctive. It's hopeless.

'And Deli-la-lah,' whistles Studs, suddenly recognizing me. 'Naughty girl, messing with this one.'

'You know each other?' Jem says, surprised.

'Depends how you define "know",' I mutter.

'Delilah and me got a mutual friend,' Studs says, smiling slyly.

Recovering, Jem exchanges a complicated palm-and-knuckle routine with Studs that speaks volumes: the kind of routine you come up with when you're ten and hone for years until it's second nature. Any fool can see that these guys have a history. Studs winks at me and vanishes again. There's no denying he has that melting-into-the-shadows thing down.

My heart hardens. How many cars have Studs and Jem robbed together in the dark of night, sneaking around, spraying their territory like skunks?

'Kiss me again,' Jem whispers, sliding his warm hand under my hair to rest on my neck, bringing me back to him.

I bat him off and run down the hill, keeping in the glow of the streetlights. The moon feels like it's burning my skin. It's only when I reach the safe haven of the High Street and fling myself on the almost-departing forty-two bus that I realize something crucial.

I haven't given him Sam's number.

'Lilah! It's nearly ten o'clock! Where have you been? You haven't answered your phone or *anything*. I've been worried sick! How did it go?'

I wonder how to explain the evening to Tabby as I kick my shoes off.

'Not brilliantly,' I say at last, sinking on to my bed.

'Did he say he wouldn't do it?'

'I . . . forgot to give him the number.' I hold the phone away from me as Tabby squawks. 'I'm sorry!' I say at a safe distance. 'I got distracted, OK?'

'I left you at the Gaslight nearly five hours ago! What have you been *doing*?'

'Tab, please don't go on,' I beg. 'I've just walked back from town and my head and feet are killing me.'

'You walked? Are you nuts? Lilah, it's over a mile and it's *dark*. Why didn't you get the bus?'

'I did! But the bus driver threw me off because I didn't have any cash on me to buy a ticket so I went to the cash point to get some and catch the next one but just like at M&S my stupid card wouldn't let me take any money out. I felt like a medieval peasant walking home from the market because he'd sold his donkey by mistake.'

'Why didn't you call me? I could have asked Dad to fetch you in the car!'

'I didn't know how to tell you I'd messed up,' I improvise lamely.

'You said you'd fix this . . .'

51

'Jem promised to call Sam and explain,' I tell her, pleating my crumply duvet cover between my fingers. How he's going to do that without Sam's number is something I'll worry about later. 'I tried to message him the details about ten times throughout the evening but he kept saying, "Later, I've just got to paint one more teensy blood vessel on the back of your hand and will you kiss me" and all this stuff about moonlight and I *forgot*.'

There is a long pause.

'What?'

I just want to put my head under my pillow and sleep until Wednesday.

'Can we talk about it tomorrow?' I mumble. 'Love you. And sorry. Again.'

I switch my phone off and crash out, fully dressed. At some point in the night I have the kind of dream you don't even tell your best friend about. I'm human, OK? You try getting through the kind of evening I've just had and then deciding: 'Right, where's that ice-pack, I'm going to sleep on it and dream about road maps and plumbing.'

I press the button again. Nothing.

'Get a move on, love,' says a voice behind me in the queue.

I stare at the cashpoint, willing it to spit my life out. 'It just swallowed my card!' I say in dismay.

The grizzled guy in a workman's hat behind me shrugs. 'You finished?'

I hesitate. If I move away from the cash machine, I'll never see my card again. The next person's transaction will lie over the top of mine, like a Rottweiler on a trapdoor.

'What's up?' Tabby stands over me, head hunched into the woolly scarf she wears round her neck.

'Your mate's holding up the queue.' The grizzly workman's eyes flick over our student gear. 'Some of us have to get to work this morning.'

'But—'

Tabby pulls me away from the cash machine. The queue moves up; the grizzly guy punches numbers on to the keypad with calloused fingertips. I watch, hoping the machine is broken. But no: fat ten-pound notes come crinkling through without a problem. Folding the cash and sliding it into his back pocket, Grizzly Guy eyes me narrowly, as if I am after his PIN number.

'I'll buy you lunch,' says Tab, marching me across the street to college. 'Not that you deserve it. I can't *believe* you got with the bar guy last night.'

'I didn't set out to kiss him,' I say crossly. Losing my card is all I need today. 'Unlike *some* people I could mention.'

Tab leans against me in silent apology and I pat her with my painted hand. The fake veins and arteries are still pretty freaky, even though I left half of them on my sheets in the night.

My phone shrieks like a boiled cat in my jacket pocket. After failing to hear any of Tab's calls yesterday, I've turned it up deliberately loud. Unknown number. I hit the green button.

'Whatever you're selling, no thanks.'

'I was going to say, good luck with Keynes,' Jem says.

I am so shocked I can't speak.

'I went home and Googled him last night. Interesting guy, if massive moustaches and the cause of a boom-and-bust economy are your bag.'

'How did you get my number?' I stammer.

'I texted myself on your phone last night when you were half-asleep. You know. Just in case you forgot your very important promise to your mate about giving me her boyfriend's number.'

Tabby is watching, hawk-eyed. *Is it him?* she mouths. I nod. My mind is racing like the Grand National round a small suburban garden.

'Why did you run away last night?' he asks. 'We were only just getting started.'

The heat in his voice almost scorches my ear off. I hang up and stare at my phone like it's a bomb.

'What did you do that for?' Tabby demands. 'That was your chance to give him Sam's number!'

'I panicked!' I say helplessly.

My phone rings again.

'I really want to kiss you again, Delilah. And you still haven't given me your mate's boyfriend's number.'

I can feel myself flushing. 'I . . . I'll text it.'

I message Sam's number and turn off my phone as quickly as I can. Then I shove it deep into my bag where I plan to forget about it all together.

'Did you—'

'I sent the number, OK? Can we now stop talking about this?'

'Welcome to Friday, ladies!' Oz bounds up the college steps towards us with his arms extended and his bag bouncing on his back. 'Delilah Jones, will you be my date in Chemistry? I can't think of anyone I'd rather go with.'

Tabby is still looking at me with anxious puppy-dog eyes. Reminding myself how much she relies on me, I give her a hug. 'Jem'll call Sam and sort everything out,' I tell her in my most bracing tone of conviction. 'Trust me, your lippy will all be kissed off by lunchtime.'

'I'm not wearing lippy.'

'It's a figure of speech,' I say patiently.

Tabby looks dreamy and disappears off down the long corridor to the Arts Department, her clumpy boots echoing on the lino.

'Do you think Tab will ever kiss me?' Oz asks, watching her go with the thousand-yard stare of a lovelorn sheep.

'Move on,' I advise. 'There are hundreds of unattached girls here to suit your wide-ranging tastes.'

'But I think I love Tabby,' says Oz earnestly. 'Seriously, Delilah. I've never felt like— hel*lo*.'

A girl in a very tight tank has just swayed past us.

'You're breaking my heart, Osgood,' I say.

'Are all girls as sympathetic as you?' Oz grumbles, pulling his eyes from the tank girl. 'Coz if they are I'm going to turn gay. What the hell have you done to your hand?'

Chemistry is a lot more fun than Economics. I scrub my hand as clean as I can at the big sinks at the back, then stir and mix and measure and note stuff down. It soothes me, proves how the world – a world I am learning has way too many shades of grey – can sometimes just be straightforward black and white. It is, in scientific parlance, the dogs.

I want to kiss you again. There was a focus in Jem's voice that makes me nervous. I need to avoid him from now on or he'll try it again for sure. And then where will I be? Making all the old mistakes again, that's where.

The class starts winding up. Kids are taking off their goggles, formulae are being scrawled on the whiteboard for us to copy down. I make a few final notes in the margin of my pad and stuff everything into my bag. My fingers close on my silent phone.

I switch it on cautiously. A message flashes up.

His phone was off. Will try later. Gaslight tonight?

I delete it before I do something stupid like answer.

'He couldn't get through,' I say, the minute I see Tabby, looking wan by the chillers in the canteen at lunch. 'He texted to say he'd try again.'

'How do you know he's telling the truth?' Tabby wails.

I always mean what I say. I think of Jem exchanging greetings with the most untrustworthy guy in town and feel confused.

'I don't,' I admit.

My phone beeps.

Please?

'Can lunch be quick?' I say, deleting the message and switching my phone off. 'I need to go and see someone about my bank card.'

'I've only got three quid on me so it'll be as quick as one

57

egg sandwich each,' says Tab. 'Do you want me to come to the bank . . .'

Her voice trails off, her eyes fixed on the canteen door. Sam has come in, talking and laughing with a doe-eyed girl whose blond hair almost reaches her bum. Several other guys are with him, trying to get in on the conversation.

'Who's *she*?' I ask, so struck by her curvy figure, confident manner and gleaming poker-straight hair that I forget any kind of sensitivity.

'Maria.' Tabby's tone of voice indicates *Maria* is perfectly interchangeable with *Witch Knickers*.

I look at the girl again. She *seriously* lucked out in the hair lottery. 'Don't lose faith. They're only talking,' I soothe. 'I'll do the bank thing on my own, it's fine. See you after college, OK?'

'Jem had better call Sam,' Tab wails after me as I head for the street. 'Or there'll be murder in the corridor this afternoon!'

The personal manager that has been assigned to me is finally saying goodbye to an old lady who's been yakking at him ever since I arrived at the bank fifteen minutes ago. It's weird being in here on my own. I feel cowed, like I am in the head teacher's office for setting fire to the staffroom. Not that I've ever done anything like that, of course, unless you count that time with the Bunsen burner and the corner of the supply's lab coat.

I sit on the mauve chair in front of the manager's desk and smile nervously. He looks back at me with all the emotion of an egg as I stumble through my situation.

'Do you know your account number?' he asks when I've finished.

'I normally look on my card only I can't do that now, can I? My name's Delilah Jones though and I live at twenty-three Wyvern Court and my security question is Marie Curie – that's the name of my fish, but you probably don't need to know that?' I know I'm waffling but I can't seem to stop.

He looks impassively at me. 'We have that information.'

'Oh. Well, this is my branch and everything so you'll have my details on your computer,' I stumble on. 'When can I get my card back?'

'Assuming everything's in order, it'll be a different card,' says the manager, tapping his keyboard in a bored fashion.

I think a little sadly about the nice picture I had on my old one. Then I frown.

'*Assuming* everything's OK? Are you maybe assuming that it isn't?'

'Can you tell me how much you have in your account?' he asks, still tapping.

'I had about four hundred pounds in there a couple of weeks ago. I earned it at the lido in the summer,' I say, feeling the need to explain myself.

'You have exactly four pounds and twenty-three pence in your account. According to the records, you have tried to access non-existent funds three times, hence the recall of your card today.'

I grip the chair. 'That's . . . that's not right. Four pounds? As in . . . as in four hundred *pence*?'

'Four hundred and twenty-three pence, yes.'

I reel. I've spent a fair bit recently, getting ready for college and so on – but I haven't spent *all* of it. Have I? There was my winter parka, of course. And eating out in France. And my new phone, lost forever somewhere in the Mediterranean. And – well, a bunch of other stuff. My heart sinks. Stupid, stupid, stupid. How can I have messed this up so badly? Has the Euro exchange rate short-circuited my head?

'Independence is more expensive than most students realize,' he says a little more kindly. 'It's easy for our inexperienced customers to lose track of their finances. I'll order a new card for you, but unless you put some more money in your account, you won't be able to use it. Your age means we can't give you an overdraft.'

'Oh,' I say, trying to control the wobble in my voice. Like 'Oh' covers even one *millionth* of the situation. 'I'll check it out and . . .'

I have to leave or I am going to burst into tears and no way is Egg Face seeing that. Flapping my hand in silent farewell, I back out of his office and make my way to the doors of the bank, where I take several deep, shocked breaths. I've spent four hundred pounds without noticing. I am totally skint in week one of my first year

60

at college. This is bad.

For one brief unwitting moment, I think of asking Dad to loan me some money. A millisecond later, I realize what a pointless hope *that* is. He made it clear that I was on my own, cashwise, when I said I wanted to go to college in the first place. I squirm to think of what he'll say if I tell him I've already managed to spend everything I saved. It looks like I'll just have to stick it out, prove him wrong about being as capable of looking after myself as a hamster in a plastic ball on the M25.

I need another job. It's the only way. Where do people find work in term time? They know people, they ask around. Who do I know? How can I find employment?

I try to calm myself down. I've seen something about job vacancies recently. Where? It flickers at the edge of my mind. A pinboard. A crusty brown carpet . . .

Oh rats.

I want to make it clear that the only reason I am heading for the Gaslight on an afternoon when I am supposed to be studying in the Science library is because I remember seeing a couple of jobs advertised there. Theatre jobs are most likely to fit around the twenty-four hours a week I need to put in at college this year, aren't they? Evenings and weekends? The job is the thing, I say to myself. I need money or I can kiss goodbye to uni and the kind of future I want.

Like chewing gum trying to get off a shoe as it heads towards a cliff, I look desperately in every single window that I pass on my way to the theatre, willing there to be some other part-time job – retail assistant, cleaner, shelf stacker – *anything* that will stop me having to go up those concrete steps at the bottom of the High Street and feel the crunch of that carpet and see Jem smirk at me from behind the bar, thinking that I've come running because he is irresistible. There is nothing.

Maybe I've got it wrong, I tell myself, wringing my hands at the theatre's double doors. Maybe I've mistaken a VACANCIES board for a FOR SALE one – you know the kind of thing: *red leather sofa £50; boy's bike £15 o.n.o.*

He is polishing glasses behind the bar, his glossy black head bent over his task. I tuck my telltale hair deep down inside the collar of my jacket, flatten myself to the wall, resist the urge to shout 'Cover me!' and inch towards the big brown corkboard beside the poster of *Cinderella*.

Wanted: bar staff. Evening and weekend work. Start immediately. See Val, catering manager.

I rest my head against the bit of paper that spells both my doom and my salvation and close my eyes. Just my luck. It's perfect.

'All right there, love?'

I peel myself off the board and stare into the mascaraed eyes of yesterday's blond lady. She smiles in recognition, shifting the crate of wine she's holding into a more comfortable position.

No choice.

'Are you Val?'

'Yes?'

'I've come about the job,' I whisper, keeping my back to Jem and the bar.

63

'You what?'

'The job,' I repeat even more quietly, hunching my head deeper into my parka, haplessly gesturing bar actions like pressing optics and pouring drinks. '*The bar job.*'

Val frowns. 'What is this, Charades?'

There is a chink of glasses being set down on the bar behind me. I stare pleadingly at Val, willing her to take pity and remove me to a quiet room where we can discuss things out of Jem's eyeline. Sudden understanding flares in her eyes as we both hear his footsteps crunching towards us, but it's too late. She pats me on the shoulder, like you might pat a frightened horse.

A wide white grin splits his face in two as he clocks me.

'Tonight not soon enough?'

'No teatowel today?' I say, looking into his flecky eyes with resignation. 'It lent your face distinction. I've come about the bar job.'

'Really?'

I lift my chin. 'I need part-time work that fits around college hours and I saw the job board last time I was in here.'

For a moment I think he looks disappointed. 'You're too young for bar work,' he says.

'My dad runs a pub. I mean,' I amend, 'he *used* to run a pub until the brewery closed it last year. I helped out sometimes. It's OK to be under eighteen if you're supervised by the licence holder.'

Val's eyes flick from me to Jem and back again. She

looks amused. 'I can offer five quid an hour plus tips, Friday nights five until midnight and Saturdays twelve noon for the matinée crowd until the first evening interval at nine. When there's no matinée, it's five until midnight, same as Friday. When can you start?'

My heart sinks. Surely it isn't going to be this easy? Jobs are impossible to get these days. How come this one is dropping into my lap like an egg rolling off a table?

'Whenever you want,' I mutter, aware that Jem's eyes are trained on me like blue-grey searchlights.

'Tonight would be good. Can you be here for five?'

'No problem,' I say, dying quietly inside.

Val wags a beringed finger at Jem. 'We need to train this one up for the Musical in a Month alcoholics next week. Keep your hands off her during work hours and we'll all get along just fine.'

My embarrassment levels rocket through the ceiling in a blaze of humiliation and roof tiles. Perhaps Val thinks she's doing me a favour – girl power and all that. She is plainly under the impression that Jem once ate me up and spat me out, and has decided to encourage me back into the gladiatorial arena to even the score. I am too mortified to tell her that I am the one who did the spitting.

Jem blasts me with his best stripping stare as Val hauls her crate of wine behind the bar. 'See you later, bar girl,' he says.

The look on his face leaves me in absolutely no doubt that he will ignore Val's warning the first opportunity he gets. I wonder if maybe I need to go away and practise dodging stuff for a bit.

'I called your friend's boyfriend again, by the way,' he calls after me as I flee. 'Spoke to him this time and got threatened with a punch on the nose. I'm guessing it didn't help.'

Poor Tabby. This is going to take more sorting than I thought.

'Thanks,' I say, stopping reluctantly at the doors. 'You didn't have to.'

'I said I would.'

'And your word is law?'

He smiles. My traitorous tummy does a flip.

Perfect job, perfect hours, perfect pain in the neck.

I arrive back at college just in time to witness a virtual replay of Sunday night, minus the kissing.

Tabby and Sam are standing centimetres apart on the college steps, glaring at each other. Sam is pale with anger while Tab is bright red. The pretty girl with long blond hair – Maria – stands close by. I can see the tension in Sam's shoulder muscles from here.

'You're a coward, hiding behind that slab of beef that calls himself a barman. You put him up to calling me, didn't you? I told him where to go.'

'Will you just listen to me, you stubborn arse?' Tab shouts. 'I'm trying to make this right!'

Sam swells up like the Incredible Hulk. I wonder if his

tight shirt might rip down the back and display his famous walnut muscles for all to see.

'*Don't* call me an arse—'

'I'll call you an arsing arse if I want to!' Tabby shrieks. 'I'm *sorry*, OK?'

Maria places a hand on Sam's arm. 'You guys need to calm down.'

Tabby rounds on her. 'Piss off, Barbie.'

There is a delighted intake of breath from the goggling onlookers, Oz included.

'Nice,' says Maria coolly. She smiles up at Sam. 'You coming?'

'Well I'm not hanging around here to be called an arse again,' Sam mutters. He looks defeated. 'You messed this up, Tab. Live with it.'

'You're an ARSING ARSEMINSTER ABBEY!' Tabby screams as Sam and Maria walk away down the High Street. They don't look back.

The crowd disperse in disappointment, leaving Oz and Tabby still standing on the steps. Oz puts his arm cautiously around Tab's shoulders.

'Good one,' he says. 'Arsing Arseminster Abbey.'

Batting him off, Tab rushes down the steps. I almost fall backwards as she throws her arms around me and weeps all over my parka.

'I've screwed up,' she hiccups. 'Totally and utterly screwed up. Maria's got him now and I think I want to die.'

I rock and soothe her, but she is inconsolable.

'Let's go and get doughnuts,' suggests Oz. 'Sugar's good for shock.'

'Great idea,' I say, stroking Tab's shuddering back. 'You're buying.'

Krispy Kreme is down Water Lane, off the High Street and near the river. Oz orders a box of six and we sit at a table near the back with a wodge of serviettes from the dispenser. It isn't long before we are surrounded by soggy paper napkins, crumbs and sugar. Tabby manages a Strawberry Gloss, leaving Oz and me to cope with the rest.

'Your lips match your eyes now,' says Oz as Tabby wipes strawberry icing off her mouth with a trembling finger.

'Tabs, ignore the insensitive elephant across the table and listen to me,' I instruct. 'You have to let Sam go. Find something to take your mind off him. Something new and challenging. The bad stuff will pass more easily if you're busy.'

Tabby gazes puffily at me. 'You mean, like do a missionary thing in Papua New Guinea?'

'Maybe not quite that challenging,' I say. 'You've got to keep up your college work and I don't think they do the same modules in Papua New Guinea.'

'I can't let Sam go!'

'Of course you can. Break-ups don't kill people.'

I try to hold her eye while willing her not to notice the Dave-shaped shadows lurking behind my eyelashes. Oz sneaks the last doughnut.

'I guess,' Tab mumbles at last.

I check my watch. Four forty-five. 'I have to go. New job starts at five.'

This seems to startle Tab out of her funk. 'You got a job? Your life is always so together, babes,' she sniffs. 'Doing what?'

Dodging a guy with North Sea eyes. 'Pulling pints,' I say out loud.

'Can we come?' asks Oz, rising from the table. 'Can you get us free crisps and beer and stuff? Where is it?'

'Take Tab home for me, Oz,' I say cagily. 'I don't want to leave her by herself. I'll call you in the morning, hon,' I add, kissing my soggy mate's salty cheek. 'We'll have worked out your Let Sam Go strategy by Sunday night. Totally doable.

'Trust me.'

It is an interesting evening.

For the first forty minutes of my shift Jem keeps trying to talk to me, so I shoot off on missions I've suddenly 'remembered' Val asking me to do. Stuff like cleaning the dishwasher filter with a very small brush and colour-coordinating the wine bottles in the fridge.

At around six-thirty, Val finds me in the cellar, where I am feather-dusting cobwebs. Her bracelets jangle as she places her hand on her denim hips.

'What next, polishing the barrels? I gave you this job assuming you could cope with an ex-boyfriend. You knew you'd have to work with him when you applied. Have I made a mistake here?'

'He's not my ex,' I say in mortification. 'He's – OK, so I kissed him last night, but that's it. He's totally not a problem.' Pulling myself together, I wave my feather duster around in a super-efficient manner. 'But the spiders down here, Val – they seriously ARE a problem. You could get Health and Safety on your back if they're not sorted. Dad's pub got into all kinds of trouble over it. If you ask me, that's why it closed.'

'You're embarrassed.'

'No!'

'Yes.'

I let the feather duster fall to my side. 'OK, yes, a bit,' I mumble.

'My son's a good lad,' Val says more gently. 'And you have to work together. So unless you man up, you can forget this job because it's not going to work. It's time to start doing what I pay you for, love. Serving customers.'

Tumbleweed seems to roll through the cellar in a gust of imaginary desert wind.

'I'm on my way,' I squeak.

Jem is spraying the bartop with something that smells of lemons and hospitals. He turns, aiming the spray nozzle at me like a gun.

'Stick 'em up or I'll disinfect,' I say weakly. 'The boss is your mother?'

He shrugs.

'But you call her Val!'

'Always have.'

'You didn't think to mention this before I told her we kissed?'

He smiles slightly. 'Sorry.'

Focus on the conversation, Delilah, not the smile. 'Would she really have docked your wages last night if you'd missed your shift?'

'She's running a business, not a charity. Did your dad pay you at the pub?'

'Yes,' I say. 'Not much but – yes.'

'And there were rules about not knocking off early or generally taking the mick?'

'I guess.'

'We have more in common than you think.'

I lace my fingers together. 'I'm sorry I've been avoiding you.'

'Girls don't usually run away when I kiss them,' he says wryly. 'One minute we were moonstruck, the next you were legging it like a greyhound. Was it Studs? That mutual friend he mentioned?'

'Yes.'

'And are you seeing this mutual friend?'

I stare. 'No! No, that's not— the mutual friend's the guy I dumped.'

He looks confused. 'So why was it a problem?'

'My ex was seeing someone else the whole time we were together. Studs was there when I found out . . .' I swallow. I haven't had any practice in saying this stuff out loud. 'I didn't take it very well. I'm still not taking it very well, to be honest.'

The clouds in his eyes evaporate. He steps towards me. 'I've been going nuts, wondering.'

I raise my hand, placing it on his chest to stop him getting any closer, feeling his warmth radiating through my palm. 'I'm not looking for . . . any complications in my life.' I cringe inside as I say this. It sounds extremely naff. 'That's why I ran away. So I'm telling you now, please don't try and kiss me again or do anything to make me like you because I don't want to like you.'

'OK,' he says slowly, looking down at my hand. 'No complications. Check.'

I laugh, a combination of embarrassment and nerves.

He turns away to serve a cluster of customers who've suddenly come into the bar. I want to say something else, but don't know what. So I suck it up and get to work.

It isn't long before we are drowning in a blur of beer and Twiglets. I fetch glasses, fire the soda gun, count change, ring the till, change the music, change the music back, distribute beer mats, wring out bar towels, twist off Coke lids, take empty crisp boxes round the back, learn the knack of the hand-held swipe machine and the way the vodka optic dribbles sideways, blush and mumble my way past some of the friskier customers, scarf a packet of crisps for my dinner and grab precisely one visit to the loo. It isn't even that busy, punter-wise. Val watches me throughout; Jem, not so much. In fact, not at all.

'So much for the lull during showtime,' I gasp in the kitchen, wiping my sweaty forehead with my sleeve as Jem calls last orders.

'There's no show just now,' says Val.

'Oh,' I say, now feeling stupid on top of tired.

'We have the annual amateur Musical in a Month starting next week, with a performance around Hallowe'en,' she adds. 'That'll perk things up.'

Musical in a Month sounds as much fun as a harpoon through the neck. Mum did am-dram, leaving a toxic trail of high kicks, ambition and melting vinyl records in her wake. I still can't hear *Chicago* without breaking into a sweat. I try to focus on what Val is saying.

'Kids with stage ambitions and enough energy for long rehearsals come from the college. They get in a couple of pros to give it some weight. The theatre lends costumes and props and expertise. It's good publicity working with amateurs, and big business for the bar at a quiet time of year.' She smiles a little evilly. 'Think you can take the pace?'

I give a fixed smile. 'No problem.'

By the time we have put the dishwasher on for the final load of the night, it's close to midnight. Val gives me my money and I pull my coat from one of the kitchen lockers, heading wearily for the door.

'Tomorrow at five!' Val calls after me. 'Don't be late!'

Jem is waiting for me on the steps.

'Thought I'd walk you wherever you need to go,' he says.

'There'll be a bus in five minutes,' I say, feeling stupidly shy as I point at my bus stop opposite. 'It takes me to the end of my road. I'll be fine.'

He rubs his jaw. I have a terrible urge to rub it too. Maybe even kiss it a bit, on the part where the stubble gives way to the softer skin on his neck.

'Guess I was the only one that felt it,' he says.

'Felt what?' I ask nervously.

He frowns. 'Like the moon was inside me.'

I open my mouth like a poleaxed goldfish. He turns away, head down, pushing back inside the theatre doors and out of sight.

'Babe, it's me,' I say through Tabby's bedroom door the following morning, unfeasibly bright and early. 'Your mum let me in. I know it's Saturday first thing but she says you're going out later and we have to talk. I brought you tea.'

Tabby peeps blearily out from under her duvet as I flip on the light and crash into her room, putting the tea on her bedside table.

'Wher time zit?' she croaks. 'Wass happened?'

Where to start? The beginning, I decide. It's going to sound crazy however I do this, but beginnings at least prove there's some kind of order in the world.

'Remember me telling you about making out with that French guy in the holidays? About the incredible brain-frying kiss and the moon?'

Fumbling on her bedside table, Tabby finds her glasses and slides them on. She's starting to look more awake. 'Lilah, in what way is this urgent? First thing in the morning, a wee is urgent, not a chat about kissing. On the subject of which . . .'

'The French guy Laurent,' I resume the minute Tab returns from the bathroom. 'He spun me this line on something called Aphrodite's Kiss in the sand dunes. A load of donkey doodah about—'

'I know about Aphrodite's Kiss,' she interrupts.

I freeze. This is exactly what I don't want to hear.

'You do?' I say weakly.

Tab extracts a bit of sleepy dust the size of Wales from one eye. 'I'm studying Classics, babe. We talk about Aphrodite a *lot*. Not that she's been much help lately,' she adds bitterly.

'Tell me,' I order.

'According to the legend, Aphrodite first gave the Kiss to a huntsman in the foothills of ancient Athens by the light of a full moon,' Tabby says with a yawn. 'The Kiss drove him gloriously, happily mad. But life is fickle, and Aphrodite didn't stick around.' Her voice wobbles, but she steadies herself. 'The huntsman caught the eye of a girl in the market place and gave her the Kiss instead. The girl instantly fell in love with the huntsman. Then a soldier with nice biceps passed through Athens and gave the girl a pretty bead necklace, causing her to thank him in the traditional manner and do the dirty on the huntsman. Cow. And basically the Kiss is supposed to have spread from there, leaving a trail of love and agony in its wake.'

So far, Tab's version of the story tallies with what

76

Laurent told me. This is NOT GOOD.

'It's all a big fat lie,' I prompt her.

'I guess,' Tabby says, looking wistful. 'Why is this important?'

'Something Jem said to me last night.'

Her eyes narrow. 'You saw him again? More kissing?'

'I went to the bank yesterday, learned I was broke, got a job at the Gaslight bar because seriously it was the ONLY job I found, embarrassed myself with his mother, worked myself to a shred beside him last night, end of story,' I say in one breath.

Tabby reaches for her tea. 'Sounds more like the beginning to me.'

'I told him I don't want anything else to happen,' I say impatiently. 'It was all massively Jeremy Kyle. And then he said . . .' I pause. This is still extremely weird. 'He *said*, when we kissed, he felt like the moon was inside him.'

'That's so romantic,' gasps Tab.

She's missing the point. 'Tabby,' I say, 'the thing is, I felt like that when Laurent kissed *me*. Like the moon was shining inside me, sort of cold and bright and intense. I can remember thinking it in *exactly those terms*. It was a full moon both times – when Laurent kissed me, and when I kissed Jem. Don't you think that's a weird coincidence? Both of us describing – feeling – a kiss in that way?'

Tabby ponders this. 'Maybe you read it somewhere?'

'That's what I was wondering,' I say. 'Can we check for quotes online?'

We start scrolling through variants on 'kiss', 'Aphrodite' and 'moon' on Tabby's phone. ('Not *that* kind of moon,' says Tab at one point. 'Honestly, my *eyes*.') A couple of academic websites pop up; so does the British Museum.

'I was thinking more along the lines of gossip mags and *New Scientist*,' I say, feeling worried. 'I don't read this stuff.'

'How about movies?' says Tabby, scrolling on. 'Elizabeth Taylor is supposed to have given Aphrodite's Kiss to Richard Burton.'

I think back to a recent *Grazia* retrospective I read a while back, about Elizabeth Taylor and Richard Burton. 'Not ringing bells,' I say, a little uncertainly.

We suddenly hit gold. An Australian Classics professor has written an entire thesis on the subject of Aphrodite's Kiss and uploaded the lot. There is silence as we both read what we can – me on Tabby's laptop, Tab on her phone.

'This weirdo's tried tracing it,' I say after a few moments' rapt silence. How could a theoretically intelligent person be so gullible? 'He says it went from Ancient Greece to Egypt – he's quoted some source about Anthony and Cleopatra – to Rome . . .'

'Italians!' Tabby says with excitement. 'It explains a lot about Italians.'

My best friend is supposed to be putting me *off* the idea that there's something in this.

'Tabby, it isn't true,' I insist.

'The guy's a *professor*,' Tab points out. There's a look in her eye that I don't like. 'Professors don't publish theories without evidence. All the other academics would laugh themselves sick. Where did it go next?'

I scroll on and on, knowing this whole weirdness to be a massive heap of dungballs and yet somehow unable to tear my eyes away. 'Apparently it pops up in Venice in the eighteenth century— no way, *Casanova*?'

'See? Italians again!' Tab is now hovering over me, still-undrunk tea in her hand.

I scroll faster and faster. Venice, London, Naples, Sicily, back to Rome. I reach a bit about Richard Burton and my skin goes clammy.

'. . . in Burton's own words, recorded shortly before his death in 1984: "When I kissed Elizabeth Taylor for the first time that day in Rome, it was as though a light had gone on inside me. As if the moon had poured through my skin and taken hold."'

By the time we finish reading Professor Aussie Crackpot's thesis about the whole myth-made-flesh thing, my brain has been through the tumble-dryer and come out again the wrong shape for my skull.

'The last known record of the Kiss was the South of France!' Tab starts bouncing on the bed like a crazed kangaroo. 'That's how your Frenchman caught it! Delilah, you are a legend. *An actual Greek legend!* Actually, not you, you passed it on . . . Jem! Jem now has the Kiss! He—' She stops bouncing abruptly. 'Sweet mother of all marzipan, I know how to get Sam back.'

This has 'wasp in your swimsuit' written all over it.

'Tabby . . .' I start in warning.

Sliding off the bed, Tab grips my jumper, hauling me up from where I've been sitting at her desk. Red spots of colour have flared in her cheeks. 'I have to get with Jem again.

Then I'll have the Kiss – oh my God, *historic* – and then I'll waylay Sam at college and give the Kiss to him and he'll forgive me and come back to me and we'll be the most famous lovers in the universe just like Richard Burton and Elizabeth Taylor!'

She clearly hasn't had enough sleep.

'No,' I bleat.

'Delilah, you were meant to bring the Kiss to me like this so that my life stops being awful,' she says feverishly. 'When Jem kisses me and I then kiss Sam, Sam will actually *feel the moon inside him*. Only an idiot could fail to fix a love affair when they've got Aphrodite on their side. OMG, the sex!' Her cheeks brighten even more, and she clutches herself a bit. 'When we finally have sex, it will be Greek-god awesome! I really, *really* need new knickers.'

She looks so sweet and excited – so like the Tabby of old – that I have to smile. This is mad, but anything is better than her previous soggy-cotton-ball-of-misery approach.

'Oh,' she says suddenly as she fixes on me. 'Will you be OK if I kiss Jem again? I promise I'll only do it once. Once is all I need.'

'Of course I'll be OK!' I protest, laughing loudly. 'Are you crazy? I don't *like* him! Don't you know me at all? We only had one kiss, one moment of insanity, and I'm not going there again. N-O-T.' I make vague 'As if, do I look mad to you?' gestures with my hand.

'Brilliant!' she says happily. 'So I'll come and visit you

81

later at the Gaslight. My technique at the college party worked fine so I'll do the same thing again. I—'

'Tabitha!' her mum calls up the stairs. 'Have you packed yet? We're leaving in half an hour.'

My best friend gasps in horror. 'Oh poop, we're going to lunch with my aunt in Southampton and staying the night – I totally forgot. Tomorrow? Monday?'

I wrench myself out of the peculiar bog of discomfort that is suddenly clogging me up. *Come on Delilah*, I think. *Tabby needs you to fix this*. And it comes to me in a marvellous haze of sequins and jazz hands. The vision I am having almost obscures Mum in her *Chicago* outfit. Not quite, but almost.

'Your Auntie Delilah has the perfect solution,' I announce. 'When does she not? There's an am-dram thing auditioning at the Gaslight next week. Calls itself Musical in a Month. Loads of college students go in for it. You're into musical theatre, you'd love it. Lots of opportunities to put your Aphrodite theory into action. When it all turns out to be a load of rubbish – and it will, trust me – it could work as your "keeping busy" challenge. The one we said you needed in order to let Sam go. And we can see each other while I'm working. Is that win-win or what?'

'You're my guardian angel,' says Tabby in bliss. 'Phone me later with details. And help me find clean socks. Oh, and my suitcase. Auntie Nora's doing roast pork for lunch and if we're late the crackling will be soggy.'

* * *

At the Gaslight that night, I locate a poster advertising Musical in a Month. WHAT AN ADO! it says. AUDITIONS TUESDAY 7PM! There's no website, no email address, no Twitter tag, nothing anchoring it to the real world at all. Tab is going to love it. I tap her a message. My phone interprets my intentions in its own special way.

Tues 7pm auction
What a dodo Gaslight xx

> Auction for dodos? What? xxxx

Suction What An Ado

> Do you mean audition?? xxxx

Stupid auto cat rectal
CALL ME 2MORON

> omgggggg, dead from laughing xxxx

'Are you into that stuff?' Jem says behind me.

I feel my ears going scarlet. Will they always do that now, every time I see him? Last night's uncomfortable conversation looms in my memory as I shove my phone in my pocket. 'It's for a friend. The one you . . .you know.'

For a wild moment I wonder if he can read Tabby's insane plan through my guilty eyes. But he merely nods and heads for the kitchen.

'Hey,' I call after him, unable to stop myself from asking. 'You know the moon thing you said last night?'

He stops and scratches his head. His black hair somehow gets cooler. 'I'm trying to forget I said it out loud.'

'I've been thinking about it,' I say, hoping I sound casual. 'Did it really feel like the moon?'

He looks puzzled.

'Sorry, stupid question – who goes round swallowing the moon and then making comparisons,' I say hurriedly. 'I mean, did you read it somewhere? Like, a quote to try on a girl?'

'I don't do that.'

'Have you said it or felt it before? About kissing?'

'Can we stop this conversation?' he inquires. 'It's a bit too weird for me.'

I am blushing a fiery red all over now. 'Ready for work if you are.'

The rest of the evening goes smoothly enough, considering. I fetch and carry, get through three rolls of paper towels, develop a blister on my heel, unblock a sink, try not to admire Jem's shoulders too often and generally earn my wages. At midnight, Val rings the till and I tuck my earnings into my purse with beer-scented fingers.

This time Jem crosses the road with me and props himself up against the bus shelter, hands in his pockets and ankles crossed like he isn't going anywhere anytime soon.

'You don't have to wait,' I say after a couple of minutes. I pull my parka more tightly around myself. 'I told you yesterday, the bus'll be along in five minutes.'

'You did, didn't you?' he says, like he's just remembered. 'Oh well, five minutes can feel like a long time when you don't have someone to talk to. It can feel like, oh, hours.'

He smiles at me blandly.

'Were you watching me last night?' I say, rising from my plastic bench.

'I have better things to do at midnight than watch bus stops,' he assures me. 'But I happened to see the timetable when I came in today. Buses on this route stop at eleven-thirty.'

I sink down on the bench again.

'Why did you lie about there being a bus?' He sounds curious rather than annoyed.

'I . . . didn't know.'

'You know now. And yet here you are again.' He gazes at the litter blown into one corner of the bus shelter and the spatter of something orange and nameless on the kerb. 'Can't see the appeal myself. I can ask Val to give you a lift home if you want.' He looks down the road. 'I'm guessing you live in the same direction as us, unless your actual bus stop is somewhere completely different and this is just another scheme to get rid of me.'

I know about the buses. Of course I do.

'You make me uncomfortable,' I say, blushing furiously as I wish him a hundred miles away.

'Aha!' He clicks his fingers. 'She speaks the truth. You make me uncomfortable too.'

'Please go away.'

'Going,' he says obligingly. He heads back across the road towards the theatre. 'Watch out for the wolf,' he calls over his shoulder as Val comes out through the theatre's double doors and clicks open a small green car parked close by.

'What?' I shout after him. He's talking in code now?

'It's a shame if no one listens the one time you scream for real.'

My embarrassment keeps me warm for almost an hour. Just as well, as it takes about that long to walk home through the cold and dark. Up in the night sky the moon is on the wane.

What business is it of his, if I choose to fib about the small stuff? I think as I pound along, my blood surging self-righteously through me.

So blinking what?

Tabby calls me on Sunday.

'Auditions on Tuesday only gives me two days to prepare,' she says, sounding panicky. 'I don't know any songs from *What an Ado!* If I download the film, will you come over and watch it this afternoon with me?'

I loathed *Much Ado About Nothing* most of the way through GCSE. Beatrice and Benedick were OK, snapping and snarling while trying not to fancy each other, but Hero? What was with the shame spiral? She drew the short straw with the whole better-off-dead thing. Oh, and don't get me started on all the lurking behind trees and comic turns by uncomic night's watchmen. It wasn't a show Mum ever did, so I don't know the songs. However, I can pretty much guarantee that turning it into a musical won't have improved it. I arrive at two with a heavy heart and a bag of popcorn I bought on the way over.

'Oz is here,' Tabby informs me as she opens the door. 'I bumped into him earlier. Apparently he's mad about musicals so I invited him to join us. Go on up. I'll get us some drinks.'

I go upstairs and push open Tabby's bedroom door. Oz jumps up from the bed, looking guilty.

'Were you just sniffing Tab's pillow?' I ask.

'Uh,' he says, 'if I said no, would you believe me?'

I check him out, up and down. 'Looking good today, Osgood. New shirt? Is that aftershave I can smell?'

Oz wafts his hand around his head a little anxiously. 'Too much?'

'I didn't have you down as a musicals kind of guy,' I say.

'Never watched one in my life. Don't tell Tabby.'

Tab comes in, her arms full of Coke and packets of crisps. 'Don't tell me what?'

'Don't tell you what a massive fan of *What an Ado!* Oz is,' I say blithely, as Oz makes horrified faces at me behind Tabby's back. 'He's quite embarrassed about it. He knows all the words, to all the songs.'

'Really?' Tabby looks excited. 'Which are the best ones?'

Oz flaps about like a dog in a swamp. 'Uh, the, uh, love duet is great. And . . . and . . . so's the one when they, uh . . .?'

'Don't look at me,' I say, enjoying myself. 'I've never seen the musical, I've only read the play. Which part do you think Tab should go for, Oz?'

Tabby chucks us both a can of Coke as the titles

start up, saving Oz from any more floundering. He gives me a Chinese burn as she slides the curtains closed. I kick him back.

It's an old film, dating to when movies of musicals lured the crowds from their radio sets and knitting and showed them a glossy vision of Hollywood in full song. The musical numbers are pretty good, and on one or two of the really fast ones, I wind Oz up by asking why he isn't singing along. But the storyline is still a shocker.

'Brilliant,' squeals Tab as a Hollywood orchestra brings the whole thing to a whopping snog-fest of a conclusion. 'Right?'

'The best,' Oz agrees, looking relieved that it's over.

'It was a bit . . . retro for me,' I say. Hero was as pathetic as ever, trilling away like a dappy blond canary. I'll never get past her pretending to be dead because she didn't have sex. I'm sorry, but there it is.

'The show *was* written over sixty years ago,' Tabby points out, catching the look on my face. 'But the songs are amazing. I love how it's about two people who love each other while pretending to hate each other.'

'I liked that bit too,' says Oz.

'She's never going to kiss you,' I tell him when Tab has hugged us both and shooed us into the street with promises of meeting up at college the next day. 'However many bad musicals you commit to memory.'

'I know,' Oz sighs. 'But what am I, if all the life I have is made of cold reality, not dreams?'

I look at him in alarm. 'A scientist last time I looked.'

'If scientists didn't have dreams,' he points out, 'Isaac Newton would still be sitting under that apple tree rubbing his head and vowing to dig up his orchard on Health and Safety grounds.'

Audition day hits in an all-singing, all-dancing supernova. I come with Tabby to give her courage, although there are a hundred other places I would rather be. Oz is supposed to join us, but after a massive party on Monday night is fit for nothing but a beanbag-and-PS4 combo in the comfort of his own bedroom.

'Whose party?' I ask with interest when he calls me.

'I have no idea,' he croaks before hanging up.

The Gaslight is organized chaos. Or maybe disorganized chaos. I'm not sure how you tell the difference. The big foyer is loud and bursting at the seams with actors and singers blasting death-laser eyes at each other as they line up outside the auditorium for their chance to perform and bag a role in the show. We join them. I don't look at Jem shooting soda into a line of glasses for a gaggle of scared-looking auditionees, but Tab does. He is, after all, the main reason that she's here. I'm still not sure how I feel about this.

'He really is hot,' she sighs. Her hand goes to push her glasses up the bridge of her nose, then falls away again as her fingers discover for the tenth time that she is wearing contacts. 'I know kissing him last week ruined my life but then I look at his shoulders and think it was maybe worth it. Don't you just want to chew them?'

'He's not a dog toy,' I say. 'Move up.'

The line of hopefuls moves towards the auditorium doors. We can both hear faint warbling already going on inside.

'That's good,' Tabby says, listening. 'What's she singing?'

'"Bad Baby Bea",' announces a spotty lad of around eighteen just behind us. I remember the song from the film and can't help a shudder. Beatrice – the best character in the entire show – has annoyed everyone by being brainy and female, so her cousin the hideous Hero rewards her by singing about what a naughty wittle girl she was when they were kids.

Tabby looks crestfallen. 'Oh! I'm doing that one too, only my version doesn't sound anything like as good.' She lowers her voice. 'Lilah, wouldn't it be easier just to kiss Jem now and run?'

I propel her closer to the doors. 'You can do this. You have a gorgeous voice, fat and fluffy like a warm bread roll. The waiting is the hardest part.'

The spotty lad busies himself warbling like a nightingale as if he isn't eavesdropping.

'You love singing, dancing and acting,' I remind her as we shuffle along. 'You always got the main parts in our school shows.'

91

'Apart from the year I broke my nose and hid in the school toilets for two weeks till the bruising went down,' Tabby says, biting her lip.

'Apart from then. Even someone like me who doesn't know one end of a piano from another can see that you're in with a chance,' I say persuasively. 'And you'll have loads of fun doing it. Apparently this place turns into Social Central when the am-drams are in.'

Mum starts singing something from *Les Misérables* in my head. I push her firmly out.

'Voice?'

'Yes, I have one,' says Tabby, eyes on Jem's shoulders again.

The red-haired woman with the clipboard looks over her glasses. 'What voice are you?' she repeats.

'Oh!' Tabby adjusts her top nervously. 'Sorry. Mezzo.'

'Do you have a top B-flat?'

'F's my best,' Tabby says. 'G if someone treads on my toe.'

'It's a different language,' I say, bemused.

We shuffle on. I think about cows being herded into an abattoir and consider the merits of vegetarianism. I can't imagine how Tabby is feeling.

'I don't think I'm going to get a part,' Tab moans.

'You won't know until you try, will you?' I tell her as calmly as I can.

'Did you know actual proper *agents* come to this show, looking for singers to represent?' Tabby tells me, teeth chattering. 'Imagine if I get spotted.'

She shoots one more anticipatory glance at Jem before we pass through to the velvet darkness of the auditorium.

A frightened lad is on the stage, blinking in the bright spotlights. I'm guessing we just missed his singing.

'Maybe he couldn't do it,' Tabby mutters. Her confidence is draining away like bath water. 'Maybe he just opened his mouth and quacked like a terrified duck. That's what I'm going to do. I know it.'

'Thank you,' says an old man with military hair sitting in the gloom. He looks like a cross between Simon Cowell and one of those round papery seed-heads you get on autumn roadsides. 'Next!'

The lad lollops off with relief written all over his face. He is replaced by a big woman the wrong side of forty who starts belting into 'I Dreamed a Dream' before she's been asked to begin. Tabby winces.

'Next!'

Shuffle, shuffle. Bolster Tabby's courage, shuffle some more. I'm exhausted already. It's a relief to sit down as Tab finally climbs on to the stage.

As soon as the song starts, the Tabby I know melts away and someone new takes her place, someone soppy and pathetic, and even though I wish she was trying out for any other part but the virginal viper, I swell with pride as she sings.

'*Bad Baby Bea, burned down a tree when she was three . . .*'

I wonder what the tree did to annoy Beatrice. Her uncle, Hero's dad, probably never let her climb it.

'*Bad Baby Bea, always scraped her knee and then blamed me, When Daddy came a-calling, Bea was quite appalling, oh-so-loudly bawLING . . . Bad Baby Bea!*'

'Very nice,' says the director after a ripple of applause spreads through the theatre, led by me. He makes a couple of notes. 'Can you read for us now?'

Tab reads the bit of script she's been given, breathy and Marilyn Monroe-ish. 'I'll do what I can, if it means helping my cousin to find a husband. Whether she'll keep him or not is out of our hands!'

I remember the scene from the film. It was one of the first lines to set my teeth on edge, and made me want to shout at the screen: 'Burn your petticoats and run!'

'We'll be in touch,' the director says. 'Next!'

Flushed with success, Tabby trips off the stage. Literally. Leaping to my feet, I rush down the nearest aisle to help her up. For someone who just smashed an audition, she looks as white as paper.

'It's OK, no one noticed,' I lie as I pull her upright, tugging her clothes back together as subtly as I can. 'They were too wowed by your voice. You were amazeballs up there, babe. Really incredible.'

'No,' she stutters.

'You're so ready for this. Trust—'

'Behind you,' she whispers.

Sam and Maria are standing by the doors of the

auditorium, sheets of music in their hands. Maria is glaring. Sam's eyes are glued to his ex-girlfriend like a pair of hypnotized ping-pong balls.

'Oh *fish farts*,' I say in horror.

This is SO not part of the plan.

Tabby sits at a table with her head between her knees. I wait as Jem fills a large glass with orange juice, tapping my fingers grimly on the bar top and trying not to think about moonlight or bodypainting or wolves.

He pushes the drink across the bar top, flicking his eyes at Tabby. 'Bad audition?'

'Good audition; bad timing,' I say fretfully. 'The angry boyfriend and his new girlfriend were auditioning too.'

Behind me, Tab moans.

'Val told me how popular this show was with college music students but I didn't think it through to this level,' I say, gnawing my lip.

'Why is it up to you to do the thinking?'

I wish he would leave this to me.

'I told you before,' I say a little sharply. 'This situation is my fault.'

He nods. 'Oh yes, I forgot. You were there, pushing her lips towards mine at the college party. Funny how I didn't notice you at the time.'

His words make me feel uncomfortable. 'You don't understand.'

'I understand very well, Mother Duck. At what point are you going to encourage your duckling into the pond to swim for herself?'

I am getting annoyed now. 'I came to the bar for a drink, not psychoanalysis.' I'm pleased with how this sounds as it comes out of my mouth. 'In the truth according to Delilah Jones,' I continue, 'Sam and Maria in Tabby's show constitute a problem. Is that OK with you, Dr Sigmund Freud?'

'Nice use of the third person,' he says. 'Would Delilah Jones like anything else to go with Delilah Jones's drink?'

'Delilah Jones would like your head on a cocktail stick,' I respond sweetly.

'It would have to be a very big cocktail stick.'

I can't help it. 'To fit a very big head.'

He leans his elbows on the bar, bringing his face way too close to my own. 'You know what you are?' he says in a whisper. 'A control freak.'

I gape at him. 'You can't say that. That's just . . . rude.'

'It's the truth,' he answers, rocking back on his heels again. 'And you know how I feel about the truth.'

What the . . . That's just . . . I can't even finish a sentence inside my own head to describe what he's . . .

'Are you saying you've never lied about *anything*?' I say furiously.

'Of course I have.' He takes his time counting the money I've given him into the till. 'I might even tell you what, one day.'

The doors to the auditorium swing open. I spin around to see Sam and Maria step jubilantly on to the crusty carpet. They are mid-kiss. It's a miracle they don't fall over each other's feet. Luckily Tabby is still gazing at the carpet, her head now in her hands.

'Angry boyfriend's looking this way,' Jem observes.

Over Maria's head, Sam's eyes flit away from Tabby via a simmering glare at Jem. I feel a flash of hope that improves my mood. Maybe not all is lost.

'You think he was looking at Tab?' I say, hardly daring to hope.

'Was he pleased to see her in the auditorium?'

'He couldn't take his eyes off her. But that was mainly because she fell off the stage. Does that count?'

'Totally. Your friend is looking hot today. Then again,' he adds, checking Maria out, 'the replacement's hot too. Dude's in a tough position.'

I'm annoyed with him again. 'Thank you for your understanding approach to the problem,' I say a little sourly.

'Any time.'

I take Tab her drink. She knocks back two-thirds in one go.

'What now?' she asks in a trembly voice.

'Stick with the plan.' It seems the best approach. 'You know, Sam was scoping you out just now, straight after he and Maria . . .' I pause and rephrase – 'He was checking you out big time, plus incinerating Jem with his gaze. He's not over you yet. You just have to regroup.'

She looks at me with enormous eyes. 'Sam and Maria are officially together now. Did you know?'

I think about the suction-pump action I just witnessed by the auditorium doors. 'You told me yesterday.'

'I can't do a show with them in it,' she groans. 'It's hard enough seeing them together at college. She puts her hand under his T-shirt in Music Theory.'

'Don't be so wet,' I say, determined to jolt her out of this. 'Is this the girl who once ran topless down Leasford Hill? Who can limbo like a gymnast? Who can breathe through her eyeballs?'

'I can't breathe through my eyeballs,' Tabby protests. 'I can just make a weird squeaky noise.'

I take a slug of her orange juice, bang the glass down. 'Don't you realize, it's actually better if Sam's in the show? You can kiss Jem right under his nose. You'll drive Sam crazy with jealousy and he'll come running back with Maria looking on, helpless in the face of your mutual passion. Your reunion will be monumental. Everyone knows that make-up kissing is the best kind. And make-up kissing with the full welly of Aphrodite's Kiss behind it? You'll knock him off his feet.'

Tab's eyes flicker. 'You don't believe in Aphrodite's Kiss.'

'But you do.'

She drops into my lap like a ripe plum from a tree. 'Oh my God,' she says in wonder. 'This could be epic.'

I pat her on the shoulder. I have done what I can. 'Now finish up your drink and let's go.'

Tabby knocks back the remainder of her drink and stands up, smoothing her outfit down her tummy and tugging her skirt down to a moderate length. Her fingers stop as she clocks Sam and Maria at the bar, metres away from us. Sam glances across semi-casually. There is an agonising pause.

'You're Sam, right?' I say brightly, deciding to get things moving. 'We haven't met properly. I'm Delilah.'

'And I'm the guy who kissed your ex-girlfriend,' Jem puts in helpfully across the bar.

'I know,' says Sam in a voice as thin as finely-sliced ham.

Maria pokes him in the arm. 'Here's your Coke, Sammy. Let's get that table.'

'Your audition sounded good,' says Sam, looking at Tabby again.

'The director seemed to like it,' Tabby says in a remarkably airy voice. For extra points, she shoots a smouldering look across the bar at Jem. 'I really hope I get a part.'

'I'd give you one,' says Jem.

'Unfortunately it's not up to you, Shoulders,' says Tabby flirtatiously.

Sam looks like a rabbit teetering on the brink of Niagara Falls.

'Babe,' says Maria in a loud voice from a corner table. 'I'm over here.'

Sam does a sort of head-ducking thing at me and Tab, fires another poisonous look at Jem and goes to join his girlfriend.

'You were cold, Tab,' I say wonderingly. 'Like ice. I didn't know you had it in you.'

'Nor did I,' says Tab, sounding a little dazed. 'Do you think we should leave now? You know, go out on a high?'

'Absolutely,' I say.

Linking arms with her, I propel us both across the carpet. I'm not sure why I turn my head back as we reach the double doors, but I do. Almost instantly I wish I hadn't.

Jem is resting his arms on the bar top, his eyes fixed appreciatively on my best friend's backside.

'I don't think kissing Jem tonight is such a great idea,' I begin as a specs-free Tabby fixes her lippy in the mirror two days later in preparation for her first Musical in a Month rehearsal. To her amazement but not mine, she's bagged the role of Miss Prissy-pants Hero and has been called to the Gaslight tonight at seven for a read-through. Sam and Maria are Benedick and Beatrice. The evening that lies ahead promises fun for all the family.

I don't know if I'll be allowed in, not being in the show myself, but Tab and I have decided that if I need a reason for my presence I will simply say I work there. It isn't a lie, although nor is it technically true on Thursdays. Jem would be proud of me.

'He's friends with a drug dealer and his eyes were all over your bum on Tuesday. I think you should just gun for Sam,' I continue. 'I don't think he'll take a lot of persuasion.'

Tabby caps her lippy with a firm popping action. 'I'm sticking with the plan, Lilah. Time check?'

Something about my friend seems different tonight. Like she's discovered some kind of superpower. Not for nothing is her character called Hero.

'I'm serious about this, hon—' I say.

'Chill out, will you?' Tab interrupts a little crossly. 'We already discussed everything and you said you were fine with it. You can't turn round and change things now. For the hundredth time, Jem's just a means to an end. The more I read about Aphrodite's Kiss – and I've been reading a *lot* – the more convinced I am that there's something in it.'

'AND you need a full moon,' I go on doggedly. 'The next one's not for three weeks.'

'You don't actually *need* the moon. Not according to the stuff I've been reading. It just sharpens things up. A hot guy like Jem isn't going to hold on to the Kiss for long, so if I don't get in there quickly, I'll lose it to someone else and then where will we be?'

I'm not conveying this very well.

'I'm *worried* about you,' I persist, following her through the swinging doors and back into the college corridor. 'Jem's an operator. Before you know it, he'll be having sex with you outside by the theatre bins.'

Tabby looks aghast. 'What kind of girl do you think I am?'

'A lovely girl,' I say hurriedly. 'A pretty, kind, naïve girl – and I mean that in a really nice way.'

She glares. 'Don't patronize me, Delilah. Having sex with Frenchmen in sand dunes doesn't give you the right to dictate my love life.'

I feel like my teddy bear has just grown fangs. 'W . . . what?'

She marches through the main doors and on to the street.

'Hey!' I say furiously, following her. 'First of all, I *didn't* have sex with Laurent. You don't rush into these things. After Dave—'

Tabby swings back to face me. 'OK, so Dave was the perfect boyfriend but in the end he *dumped* you, Delilah. Was it because you tried to run his life too? You never did explain.'

'You *asked* me to help!' I splutter.

'And now I'm telling you to stop! I'm sixteen, I have a plan, and I need to take control of my life my own way, however dumb it seems to you or to anyone else.'

We stare at each other. My first thought, irrationally, is how much Jem would be enjoying this. So much for the tree and the bicycle. *Mother Duck.* Tectonic plates shift, creak and settle.

'So,' says Tab more quietly. 'You still coming to this rehearsal or what?'

'Why should I,' I mutter. 'My advice is clearly not wanted.'

I stay by her side. We walk towards the Gaslight in silence. Two parts of my brain are wrestling like snakes in a trap. *I've created a monster*, complains one part. *Get over yourself*, states the other, with considerable scorn. *You're not God.*

I catch her by the arm as the Gaslight comes into view. 'Just . . . don't get carried away,' I say lamely. 'Eyes on the prize.'

Tabby squeezes me in a bone-crunching hug. 'I'm sorry, Lilah,' she says, sounding appalled at herself. 'I shouldn't have said all that. It's just – for once in our lives, we don't agree about something. Are you OK?'

No, but hey.

Lots of people are milling around the Gaslight lobby – old people, middle-aged people, normal people. The director is talking to a cluster by the auditorium doors. Sam and Maria are by the bar, chatting to the red-haired clipboard woman from the auditions while Val pumps beer and distributes peanuts and bottled water. Others are starting polite little conversations with each other about the show.

Tab scans the room anxiously. 'Jem works on Thursdays, right? You met him here this time last week, right?'

'Ah,' I say, remembering with a mild flash of relief. 'He does a half-shift arrangement so he can do his body-painting on Thursdays.'

Tabby deflates on my arm like a sad balloon.

'He'll be back by nine,' I add.

'Nine's too late! I need to boost my confidence *before* we start rehearsing!'

The spotty kid who was behind us at the auditions comes over. He looks directly at Tab's chest. 'Hi,' he says. 'I'm Warren and I'm playing Claudio.'

Tab lifts her bag to shield her cleavage. 'Er . . . hi.'

'See you both later.' Warren adjusts the collar on his unpleasantly transparent T-shirt and wanders off.

'By "both", did he mean your boobs?' I ask.

'That guy's playing *Claudio*? Just my luck. I should have come in a hoodie,' Tabby moans. 'But I didn't think Jem would look at me in a hoodie.'

I want to laugh but I don't dare. 'You wanted a confidence boost.'

'That wasn't it,' she mutters.

'Tabitha!' The director is hobbling towards us. 'Welcome to the company. You're going to be tip-top as Hero.'

'Hi Desmond,' says Tabby, looking pleased and flustered as she shakes his gnarled hand. He smells of cigarettes and hair oil.

'I work here,' I supply on cue as he looks at me.

Nodding politely and flashing me a set of yellow tombstone teeth, he turns back to Tab. 'Read-through starts in five minutes in the auditorium.'

'Better get in there and nab a place as far away from those two as possible,' says Tab, shooting a dark look at Sam and Maria as the director moves away. 'Please say you'll stay until we break at nine? I can't do this without you there to back me up.'

With a huge and heroic effort, I mentally slice two hours off my night and choose not to remind her about the whole 'I'm running my own life' thing she threw at me half an hour ago. 'That's what friends are for,' I say.

My old phone is too slow for Instagram, so after rifling through the magazine rack on the wall, I find a dog-eared edition of *New Scientist* and settle down on the sofa by the double doors to wait. It's a pleasant enough way to spend an hour or so, when I can stop the more troubling thoughts from taking over my brain. Tabby doesn't know the half of it.

'Hey.'

I pull myself from the underwater world I've been reading about. Jem is looking down at me with half his face missing. Behind him, the lobby clock states that it has just gone eight-thirty.

'You're early,' I say, gazing at the flaps of zombie skin that appear to be peeling off his cheek and revealing the bones beneath.

'I'm usually back around now unless something else intervenes. Nine's just the cut-off point. What are you reading?'

I am remembering a little too clearly how I intervened last Thursday evening. 'An article about deep-sea squid sex,' I say, still staring at his face.

Jem guffaws.

'It's interesting,' I insist, wishing I'd chosen to start a conversation about something else but doing the best with what I have. 'The male lies upside down and back to front on top of the female, and holds on to her head with his tentacles to stop her eating him while he fertilizes her. They only discovered this a couple of years ago because the squid live so deep underwater.'

He looks enchanted. 'Are you serious?'

'No. I just go around making up random cephalopod sex facts to impress half-zombies.' Bantering feels easier than normal, thanks to his beautiful face looking like a road accident.

'You're pretty funny for a hot chick.'

'You're entirely hilarious for a dead guy.'

He sits down on the sofa, the unpainted side of his face towards me and his leg warm against mine. He studies the magazine in my hands. 'What else is in there?'

The banter god abandons me like a dog on a motorway. 'Just nerdy science stuff,' I mumble.

'Impress me.'

I swallow and wish he wasn't sitting so close. 'A global mercury treaty. A four-stranded version of DNA that may have something to do with cancer.'

'How many strands does DNA normally have?'

'I've never met a guy who asks questions like you do,' I say helplessly. 'Are you genuinely interested, or just annoying?'

'I spent more time out of school than in it.' Idly he picks up one of my curls and twiddles it round his fingers. 'It's only after something's gone that you realize you may have missed out.'

It isn't fair. How can he look like a nightmare and yet still be this hot?

'What are you doing here anyway?' he asks, still twiddling. 'Val give you an extra shift without telling me?'

'Tab's first rehearsal. Moral support,' I say, unable to speak in proper sentences.

'And are—'

'Angry boyfriend plus new girlfriend are here as well, yes.'

He replaces the curl on my shoulder and absently starts stroking my earlobe instead. 'So what's the plan? I'm guessing you and her have a plan.'

I stand up. 'The plan is that you don't do stuff like stroke my ears.'

He raises his hands apologetically. 'Totally subconscious. Sorry.'

I order my heart to stop thumping. 'Do you plan to terrify everyone when they get out of the auditorium or are you going to wash your face?'

Tilting his head, he examines his reflection in the plate-glass window behind the sofa. 'I don't suppose this show has zombies in it?'

'Might improve it,' I say. 'But sadly it's directed by an old man for an audience with an average age of sixty-five. You're more likely to send them all screaming for the doors than commissioning you to do the make-up.'

'Better put my pretty face back on then.' He gives me a slow half-skull smile as he unfolds himself from the sofa. The effect is horrific.

'Any good-looking women in the cast more likely to fall for my boyish charms than you?' he asks when he is upright.

I probably should mention Tab here. I don't.

'Depends how choosy you are,' I say, folding my arms across my chest.

'Get back here, Jem!' Val calls. 'We have ten minutes to change a barrel before all hell breaks loose.'

Jem does a surprising thing. Encircling my wrists with his fingers he pulls them downwards, placing my arms back by my sides; unlocking me.

'We're not all like your ex-boyfriend, you know,' he says.

As he heads for the bar, people start coming into the lobby, checking their watches: partners, family, friends, all

111

rolling in for a first post-rehearsal drink with the cast. In a matter of minutes, the auditorium doors crash open and a herd of people gallop towards the bar like pigs towards a feeding trough. The volume of noise goes through the roof.

'Lilah, it was brilliant!' Tab is before me, her eyes glowing. She is clutching a book of music. 'I've got the *best* songs. And the dialogue is really funny once you get past how wet Hero is. And the others are all lovely, apart from Witch Knickers and Warren who's totally as creepy as we thought. Desmond's actually directed *Les Mis*! The repetiteur is the red-haired lady and she's called Honor and she's awesome! I can't believe we've only got a month to put it together. Desmond wants us three times a week from next week, plus extra rehearsals for soloists.'

Jem is serving efficiently, all evidence of facepaint gone. Already a cluster of girls are colonizing his end of the bar. 'I won't ask what a repetiteur is,' I say, because it's important to muster something resembling conversation for my best friend. *We're not all like your ex-boyfriend, you know*. 'Do you want a drink?'

'I'll get it,' Tabby says meaningfully.

The action at the bar is as good as a show itself. Sam is already nursing a Coke at a table. Warren is at the end of the bar trying to look down Maria's shirt while she flirts with Jem. Tabby is being bounced around like a pinball, dropping out of the pressing crowd and jumping back in again with renewed enthusiasm for the game. Desmond the director and Honor the vocal coach are comparing notes with a bottle of red wine and no doubt a nice selection of heart pills. Two good-looking dark-haired guys are clearly into each other over a shared bag of Monster Munch. Older members of the cast sit together by the fruities, nursing pints of bitter and glasses of wine and considering their raucous comrades with curiosity. I feel left out.

'Pineapple juice,' Tabby gasps ten minutes later, plonking a half-slopped glass in front of me. 'I've got it too. It's meant to be good for the voice. Sam's looking completely miserable, don't you think?'

'Warren alert,' I warn in a low voice.

Warren's T-shirt is more transparent than ever, thanks to the large, fresh sweat patches front and back. 'Can I join you?' he asks.

A kind of madness descends on me like a mist. 'I haven't seen my girlfriend in two hours,' I say, and take Tab's hand. 'We'd like some privacy if you don't mind.'

'Lilah, you're so naughty,' Tab giggles as Warren blushes and leaves. 'I'm now going to get a reputation as the cast lesbian. I couldn't get anywhere near Jem just now. Sam being here's making me really nervous. It feels like I'm being unfaithful all over again every time I look in Jem's direction. I don't know how I did it at the college party.'

'Alcohol,' I remind her.

'That must have been it. I'll have to start smuggling vodka into rehearsals in my water bottle.' She brightens at the thought. 'Not a bad idea, actually. We're rehearsing Thursdays, Fridays AND Saturdays from next week – that's good, isn't it? When you're on the bar you can keep everyone else at bay while I try Jem again.'

'Sure.'

The lack of enthusiasm in my voice makes her frown. 'I'm really sorry about earlier,' she says again. 'I don't know what came over me, mouthing off at you like that. Nerves, I guess. I'll make it up to you, I promise.'

'You were right,' I say.

Tabby looks taken aback. 'I was?'

'I think,' I say, staring at my pineapple juice, 'that I like being in control of stuff. Even when that stuff's nothing to do with me. That's not good. Next time I do it, kick me.' I look up at her again, needing reassurance. 'Tell me honestly. Do you think I think all guys are like Dave?'

Tabby looks puzzled. 'In what way?'

'I mean, out to break my heart?'

Her face clears. 'Oh! Yes.'

'Totally not true,' I say, feeling alarmed.

'You two were over months ago,' Tabby says. 'How many guys have you kissed since then?'

'If you'd . . . I know what . . . Forget I asked,' I say, sinking back into my pineapple juice.

Of *course* I don't think all guys are like Dave. But it's a basic fact that when Studs is in the equation, some are more like Dave than others.

I take a deep breath.

'On the subject of Dave, Tab, there's something I should tell you—'

'Patricia Luard. How do you do,' booms a big lady who has suddenly appeared at our sofa. She plumps herself down next to Tab with a certain amount of force, so Tabby and I both bounce gently upwards. 'Desmond's always frightfully keen that the company mingles, so here I am. Mingling. Eunice and I – that's Eunice over there, floral blouse – Eunice and I have been doing Desmond's shows for donkeys.'

'You do the show for donkeys?' repeats Tabby in surprise.

'Sometimes,' Patricia agrees, slapping her knees. 'Half of them forget to turn their hearing aids on; another twenty per cent are snoring by the second scene. Someone died once. Mind you, that year we had a shocking lead soprano. EUNICE! Meet and greet!'

The polar opposite to Patricia, Eunice is petite and slim and dressed in the aforementioned floral blouse plus a soft beige cashmere cardie.

'Tabitha, isn't it?' Patricia continues after Eunice has been introduced. 'Lovely bit of casting. You'll make a splendid Hero, although I'm sorry she's wetter than the Pacific Ocean. Who's your friend?'

'This is Delilah,' says Tabby.

I give a rictus smile as Patricia launches into The Song. 'Ah, dear Tom,' she says as she brings the chorus to its usual toe-curling conclusion. 'One of the best lovers I ever had.'

Tab chokes into her pineapple juice. I almost do the same.

115

'Don't shock the youngsters, Patricia,' says Eunice in a high, pleasant voice.

Patricia offers up the kind of wink that almost dislocates her eyelid. 'Warren tells me you two are lesbians?'

Patricia and Eunice are unexpectedly fun. I don't ask if they met Mum during all their years of amateur dramatics because they probably did and I don't want to go there much. Eunice tells us she never married but once travelled on a camel across the Sahara. Patricia was widowed in the hurricane of 1987 when a falling tree smashed her rich husband's car in half. I'm impressed by their real-sounding lives. I've never met old people like this before. I might have met a few more if Mum had stuck around. Dad doesn't do parties.

'Let me buy you both a proper drink,' Patricia says.

'We're only sixteen,' says Tabby timidly.

—'It's high time you were corrupted then, isn't it?'

Close to two hours later and we are on the same sofa. Tabby is definitely drunk and I am feeling woozy. Loads of the am-drammers are still in the bar. Maria is ordering Fanta refills; Sam is chatting to Desmond the director; Rich and Henry the Monster Munchers are looking cosy in a corner by the auditorium doors. Warren has disappeared. After an unpromising start, this has turned into an excellent evening.

'More drinks,' Patricia announces at half-past ten. 'It'll be last orders soon.' She considers Jem at the bar. 'Shame the barman's young enough to be my gardener.'

'Lilah likesh him,' Tabby slurs. 'Kished him a few dayshago.'

We have sorted out the lesbian thing. They have both promised not to tell Warren.

'You kissed him too!' I protest, flushing.

'An' I gotta do it again. Gotta get Aphrodite's Kiss. Gotta get Sham back.' She aims her forefingers at me in a sloshed-gunslinger kind of way.

'*More drinks*,' Patricia repeats, banging the table.

'Better not.' There is the small matter of Dave that I still need to discuss with Tab. In my new state of self-awareness, I know that if I don't do it tonight, I might not do it at all.

'G'on,' mumbles Tabby, propped up on the table with her face resting against her cider bottle.

'We've got college tomorrow,' I say. I sound as square as a piece of processed cheese.

'Tosh,' Patricia says. 'It's Eunice's round. Eunice! Don't forget the peanuts!'

The bank tries to contact me on Friday morning but I ignore the call, partly because my head is killing me and partly because my cheeks still burn at the memory of my interview with Egg Face last week. I don't know how people drink and then have normal days afterwards. As far as I can tell, it's impossible.

I don't need a bank account, I have decided. Cash is easier to keep track of, provided of course that no one nicks it, or makes you spend it on bottles of cider and packets of Hula Hoops like Patricia and Eunice last night. I have a cheese sandwich and a glass of water for lunch at college because it's the cheapest option. It's hard work, keeping the cheese sandwich down.

'Sounds like a top evening,' says Oz as we sit on the college steps after lunch, preparing ourselves for the final push that will get us to Friday night. 'Can I come next time?'

'Yes, please come Oz,' says Tabby. 'You can flirt with Maria while I—'

She stops. We haven't shared the Aphrodite Plan with Oz. It's a bit too weird. Even Tab can see that. Besides, it would probably break his bouncy little heart, to hear about her intentions of re-kissing the guy who dashed his hopes at the start-of-term party.

'Just . . . flirt with Maria,' Tabby fudges. 'So I can concentrate on, um, talking to Sam. Next rehearsal is in a week's time.'

'I'll do my best, assuming my social services aren't engaged elsewhere,' Oz says. 'Delilah, any chance of—'

'No free crisps,' I say firmly. 'I've only worked there two nights.'

He recalibrates. 'How about we get into training and drink there tonight?'

'I'm *never* drinking again,' I declare. 'And no disrespect to my place of employment, but outside rehearsal nights you'll be hanging with a bunch of pinstriped bad boys fresh from the nearby insurance office.'

'Get *down*, girlfriend,' says Oz, doing a wrist-flick finger snap that almost takes his eye out.

'It's too bad your weekend nights are all workworkwork, Lilah,' Tabby complains.

'Got to make the money somehow,' I say as lightly as I can.

My massive over-expenditure still hurts. I remember something to cheer myself up a bit.

'You'll like this, Oz,' I say. 'My French friend Fatima emailed me this morning. She's coming to visit in a couple of weeks.'

I've known Fatima since Year Ten, when we started emailing each other as part of an inter-school language project. I'd email her in English and she'd email me back in French. Being the kind of girl that Fatima is, I swiftly learned more rude French expressions than my French teacher could translate. In return, Fatima learned a lot of random science facts, including a first-hand account of how to burn an almost perfect hole in a living-room carpet.

'I stayed with her this summer,' I go on. 'This will be her first time in England. And unless we fix up end-to-end parties for her, she'll announce that England is boring and catch the next flight home.'

'Hot or not?' Oz asks.

I frown at him. 'I'll pretend I didn't hear that, you sexist pig. She'll be a brain surgeon before she's twenty-five, assuming she hasn't started running a small South American country in the intervening period.'

'I like her already,' Oz says. 'Leave everything to me. I may only have been at this place for a couple of weeks, but I'm already the go-to guy.'

'You were so lucky to get Fatima on that project, Lilah,' Tabby says. 'I got Didier the Invisible.'

I snort. 'He never returned a single email, did he? You had to make up his life for the project.'

Tabby giggles. 'I turned him into a surfer dude with an

opera-singing mother and a Dalmatian called Oui Oui.'

'How did I miss this project?' Oz demands. 'Was there coursework?'

'You didn't do French GCSE second time round,' I point out.

He looks relieved. 'You know more about my life than I do. OK, ready to make up for lost time. When's she coming?'

'Just before half-term. She'll be here for Tab's show.'

Tab looks a little greener than she already is. 'I'm spending this afternoon's free period learning my lines. Well, that and probably throwing up in a library bin. I feel like an old pair of pants. There is *so* much to learn.'

'And there are *so* many parties to organize,' says Oz happily. 'This French girl will have parties coming out of her delicate little ears.' He pauses. 'They are delicate, right?'

He's one to ask. I let him sweat on the question. It coincides with an urgent need to heave.

Jem is whistling at the till as we load up the change in the bar on Friday afternoon. The sound goes through my head like a fire engine. My hangover has mostly gone, but I still feel threadbare and very, very tired.

I go into the cellar to fetch up a crate of J2O and order my thoughts. It isn't easy. In my exhaustion, I can't avoid the fact that I have a crush the size of an elephant on this guy.

He's friends with Studs, I remind myself. He eyed Tab's

bottom the other night like a fox checking a chicken for plumpness and all-round digestibility *and he is friends with Studs*. I can't let the Lust Labrador win.

Coming up from the cellar, I dump the crate on the bar top while avoiding his eyes.

'I want to ask you something,' I say.

'As long as it's not about moons again.'

'How do you know Studs?'

He rips the excess receipt paper off the top of the swipe machine. 'I've known him since we were eleven. We started hanging out from the first detention we ever shared, when we got done for tagging the science block.'

'Touching,' I say. I am heavy on the sarcasm.

'He can be an idiot but he's basically OK.'

'You know he deals drugs?'

Jem's eyes get a shuttered look about them. 'That's why he's an idiot.'

I shouldn't be surprised that he knows this, although there's a part of me that's disappointed. 'Do you see much of him?'

'Why am I getting the third degree?'

'Do you?' I persist.

'We hang out a couple of times a month. We have each other's back.'

'Even when he deals? Goes against your tell-it-straight approach, don't you think?'

Jem loads the fridge with the J2Os. 'Studs knows how I am so he doesn't tell me anything he doesn't want me to know. It's your turn to talk now. Tell me about your ex.'

The trouble with trying to make a conversation go in one direction lies with how, when it goes somewhere else, you're like an ant when a leaf falls into its path. Every part of your brain is focused on the *other* conversation, the conversation you *want* to have, so invariably the conversation you *actually* have turns into a bad-dream-dance-show disaster.

'I don't want to talk about him,' I say stiffly.

'Who did you catch him with? Was it someone you knew? That's always the worst.'

'I SAID, I don't want to talk about him,' I repeat.

And then I talk about him.

'He was with his girlfriend, if you must know. They'd been together for years before he talked me into going out with him. Apparently I was a blip.'

The panicky sense of earth shifting beneath my feet hasn't got any less, even though it's been a while since the Big Reveal. And right now, I feel more disorientated than ever. I really, *really* should have practised on Tabby first.

'A blip?' he repeats, pulling a face. 'Nice.'

His sympathy doesn't help. I feel the size of a gnat.

'I'm going to see if your mum needs help unloading the dishwasher,' I mumble.

He is waiting for me when I come back with eight clean wine glasses dangling among my fingers and thumbs like long glass bells. They tinkle gently against each other.

'Is he called Dave?' Jem says.

I feel like he has just smashed the glasses in my hands and gashed me with them. 'You know him?' I ask, shocked bloodless.

'I've come across him a couple of times. He's done it before, with other girls. Studs is his dealer, right? Actually, don't answer that.'

OK. OK. Breathe. 'What do you mean, he's done it with other girls?' I manage.

He is looking deep into my poo-coloured eyes. 'Do you want me to stop talking about this?'

'What do you mean, *he's done it with other girls*?' I repeat.

'Put the wine glasses down,' Jem instructs, looking slightly alarmed. 'On second thoughts, give them to me.'

I let him remove the wine glasses from my fingers. My body has gone into shut-down and is refusing to do anything I am asking of it.

'Studs has intervened before,' Jem says, setting the glasses on a shelf. 'He doesn't like the games Dave plays. I'm guessing he gave you a message telling you to meet the guy at so-and-so place at blah o'clock. You turned up and caught him with his girlfriend. I truly am sorry.'

A dam bursts inside me. I realize, to my horror, that I have started bawling like a mandrake pulled from its pot. Jem's arms come around me and he holds me like you maybe hold a half-drowned kitten when you pull it from the water butt, gently and carefully while trying not to get too wet.

'Why do I get the feeling you've never talked about this

before?' he asks over my head.

I howl more loudly and bury my face deeper into his T-shirt. His arms are warm, and as long as they are there, the demons cringe and keep their distance.

'Keep crying and the customers will all run away,' he says.

I pull away from him, wiping my nose most attractively on the sleeve of my jumper. True enough, a couple of anxious-looking punters are taking an acute interest in the pantomime posters stuck on the pinboard. 'I have to . . .' I point hopelessly in the direction of the toilets.

Oh hecky peck, I think, limping to the bathroom to wash my face. He is as hot as a chilli pepper while I am a brainless, hungover fool with no more street sense than an ant.

I am in so much trouble.

I don't know how I get through the evening. He is always there, directing me from bottle to barrel, sending me down to the cellar and out round the back, filling this and priming that and emptying the other. I know he is doing it to keep me occupied and away from the wasps' nest in my own head and I know I ought to feel grateful. All I feel is a terrible combination of longing and shame. Vulnerability doesn't suit me.

At midnight, I notice one of the bar regulars waiting at the back door: a sweaty-faced guy in a bomber jacket and a habit of smoothing what is left of his hair back over his head.

'Pay Delilah and lock up, love,' says Val, tossing Jem the keys. 'Be good.'

'One of her better boyfriends,' Jem says as his mother's laughter drifts back at us through the closing door. 'Though you wouldn't think it to look at him.'

My self-absorption subsides. 'Your dad . . .?'

'Went years ago.' He is looking right at me, and his gaze is clear and cool and soothing. He understands too much.

'Mum went too,' I tell him, staring back. 'Five years now. America. She wanted to act on Broadway. Delusional.'

I am leaking tears again like a human colander. Jem gives me some space, going about the bar switching appliances off and locking things away. When he rings open the till and tosses me a brown envelope containing my evening's wages, I tuck it into my pocket and swipe my wet cheeks with my hands.

'You ever had a theatre to yourself?' he asks.

I shake my head. Theatres haven't been my favourite places since Mum chose them over me. Something tells me that's about to change.

He jingles the keys temptingly. 'Want a tour?'

We begin in the long members' room at the top of the building. We don't switch on the lights, accustoming our eyes to the dirty streetlight-orange pooling through the long wall of windows instead. It's strange, being in here by ourselves. I look around in the semi-darkness.

'A theatre should be full of people,' I say into the silence. I walk the length of the room, measuring it with my feet, arms out to the side to maintain my balance. Twenty paces, forty paces. If I concentrate on counting I can perhaps forget that I'm all alone with someone I fancy to the point of madness, with a set of emotional defences lower than a Dachshund's ankles. 'What's a theatre without an audience? That's what Mum used to say.'

He sits on a nearby sofa and links his arms behind his head. 'You've got an audience of one.'

'Sorry about the performance I gave earlier,' I mutter.

'Forget about it.'

I make it to the end of the room without falling over. Crossing the carpet I stand at the long windows and rest my elbows on a chest-high window table, gazing at the black river and the dark tops of the trees against the glowing brown sky. There is no moon tonight. I put my chin in my hands, watching the trees go *shush-shush-shush*.

'He had a car,' I tell the window. 'Great clothes. I was going out with a guy half the girls would have given their hair-straighteners for. Everyone started looking up to me, coming to me for relationship advice, sex advice, life advice. I may not have had money, or designer gear, or expensive holidays, or a mum but I had him.'

'Only you didn't,' Jem says.

There was a time and a place for his truth thing.

'Do you want the rest of this story or not?' I demand. I steady myself at the window by putting my palms down on the table. 'When I caught him with Louise, I didn't know how to tell anyone. I decided it was better to have my perfect boyfriend dump me than have me catch him with his actual girlfriend, so that's the story I told.' I pause. 'Does that make any kind of sense?'

'Nope.'

'I knew you'd see it my way,' I say drily.

'Are you going to tell your friends, now you've told me?'

'Probably. Maybe. Some day.'

'Liar.'

We are both silent for a bit.

'Remember that lie you asked me about on Tuesday?' he says into the darkness. 'I said I'd tell you one day. I think one day just came.'

'Shock me,' I say, rolling my eyes. 'You shoplifted a Mars Bar. Left the TV on standby all night.'

'I killed someone. Want some peanuts?'

Leaving some money balanced on top of the members' bar till, he rips open a bag of dry roasted nuts, tips half of them into his mouth and then approaches me, nuts held out like an edible shield, eyes almost impossible to see.

'Want one?' he offers cautiously.

I have moved back from the window as if the glass has just vanished, leaving nothing between me and a forty-metre fall. He is close enough now for me to make out his eyes. There is no humour in them at all, just ghosts.

'What happened?' I ask when I can formulate the words.

'I was thirteen, driving a car around the Watts Estate. The car hit a guy and his dog. I lied to the police about it. Said I was somewhere else.'

My throat feels as dry as dust. 'Makes my boyfriend stuff look pretty lame,' I say, swallowing.

He rubs his head fiercely. 'Hey. Not your fault. I've had

129

a thing about truth ever since.' He concentrates on ferreting out the last peanuts from the little bag, then drops the wrapper in the bin. 'It doesn't help the guy who died. It doesn't help me much either. But it's the best I've got.'

We make our way through the theatre dressing rooms, the private boxes, the lighting and sound desks and assorted cupboards of interest. I know that I can say nothing to make him feel better about what he's told me. Small talk feels wrong. The only option left is silence. It is weirdly comfortable in its loudness. Like we are underwater, looking at sea urchins and coral reefs, companionable and wordless.

We enter the auditorium via the lobby door which leads straight into the wings of the theatre. Mum isn't in my head for once because, for now anyway, that space is occupied by someone else.

Jem flicks on a bank of spotlights as I walk to the centre of the stage, listening to the echo of my feet. The shadowed seats soar up and away from the light, receding in form and definition, and my shadow splits in eight different directions beneath the spots.

'Speech.'

It's the first thing he's said since the members' room.

'All the world's a stage, and something something something something,' I declaim obediently. Dust motes dance about my head, silent as fairies.

He crosses his feet at the ankles, balancing them on the

backs of the stalls in front of him. 'Louder, Dame Judi.'

'Where the hell have you been, Bond?' I return, warming up. This is kind of fun. 'You wait until the PM hears about this.'

A half-smile breaks across his face. 'A moving performance. The voice of a generation.'

His words make me think of one of Mum's favourite songs. It died on the gas fire but I still hear it on the radio sometimes. *'People try to put us down,'* I sing a little hesitantly in a voice that croaks like a pond full of frogs.

'I would lie about you having the voice of an angel if I could, Delilah Jones.'

'People try to put us down,' I repeat a bit more forcibly.

'Talking 'bout my generation . . .' he concedes after a moment.

He knows it. I point a finger at him. *'Just because we get around . . .'*

'Worst Roger Daltrey impression I've ever heard. *Talking 'bout my generation . . .'*

'Things they do look awful cold . . .'

'Talking 'bout my generation . . .'

'Hope—'

I stop, horrified.

'Hope I die before I get old,' he supplies. 'It's OK. Keep singing.'

'Only if you come up here with me,' I say, blushing.

He jumps on to the stage with a passable impression of Pete Townshend whirling his arms around and smashing his guitar up. I sidle out of his way, giving up my croaky lyrics with increasing gusto.

We grow dizzy with a kind of escalating madness, singing until we have no breath left, dancing to the music in our heads. Jem attempts a caterpillar and ends up with his shoulders covered in fluff from the floor. I mosh around the middle of the stage until my hair looks like one of those huge woolly dogs you get at Crufts. It's ludicrous and amazing and entirely nuts.

'Drug police!' I gasp, pointing at the silent auditorium doors. 'Hide the stash!'

'I won't go down for this!' Jem bellows.

We both do a massive leap into the orchestra pit, one of those jumps that gets freeze-framed in bad pop videos.

'We'll have to disguise ourselves before the rozzers nab us!'

He whirls back on to the stage, running through the great black curtain. When he runs back again, he's holding it about his head like an old-fashioned nun.

'Who is this Mary Joanna you speak of, officer?' he says in a high voice. 'No one of that name has entered this convent.'

'You are lying through your butt, sister,' I shout, levelling an imaginary gun at him.

'And you are farting through your teeth, girlfriend!'

I almost choke myself laughing. 'I have never met a nun with such a filthy tongue!'

Two fingers peek out from beneath his nun's chin and

flick at me. I grab them before they vanish behind the curtain again. 'I don't care how many hit records you've made, it's life imprisonment for you, lad. Lass. Creature from the planet Zorg,' I puff, wrestling with his hand.

We grin at each other, blazing with the knowledge that we have pulled back from the maw of the sea monster among the corals. His palm fits mine perfectly.

'Where next, Mother Superior?' I say, dropping his fingers reluctantly and making a show of stashing my gun in my belt.

'The psychiatric ward.' He tips his head so the curtain drapes coquettishly over one side of his face. 'You'll find it marked Props and Wardrobe.'

The props room is like Aladdin's cave, covered in velvet hangings, stuffed with costumes encrusted with gilt and paste and ribbons, shelves covered in helmets and suitcases, shields and walking sticks. Scenery towers around: palm trees, a ship's prow, castle walls.

If anything, we get giddier. We fence for a bit with two swords that wobble pleasingly every time we jab each other in the stomach. Hardly knowing where to begin with the costumes, I try on a pantomime dame frock, a pirate's outfit and a pretty golden dress with wings. Jem dresses up as the Emperor of China in a long satin robe, then lies down watching me as I run back and forth with a fairy wand that I've found, drunk on gauze and glitter, satin and silver.

'I'm going to try the Peter Pan outfit next,' I say, wriggling out of the fairy dress and dashing for the green leggings hanging on a nearby rail. 'You be Captain Hook.'

Jem shoots out his hand and catches me by the ankle, bringing me tumbling down beside him on a heap of fur-edged Dick Whittington robes. I realize with a sudden rush of delicious shock that I am in bra, pants, socks and nothing else.

'Do you have any idea how sexy you are?' he says.

The cold satin of his emperor robe on my hot skin liquifies my insides. I stare into his eyes with their huge pupils, now so close to mine, and fiercely wish that I'd thought to remove my socks. He shifts on to his elbow, keeping his eyes on my face. I can't look away as his fingers circle my belly.

'Does this count as a complication?' he says.

'Complicate it some more,' I beg.

He kisses me, his hands skimming me, his hair against my skin, the smell of him up close and everywhere. The ball sails high, high into the air – and the Lust Labrador gallops joyously after it into the sea, tail thrashing, water glinting, barking at the big bright moon as it fills me to bursting in that windowless room.

We lie nose to nose, Dick Whittington robes wrapping us up in a big fur cocoon.

'Crazy evening, huh,' I mumble.

'Certifiable.'

I study his expression in the half-light, trying to see the shadows. 'How do you live with it?' I ask. I want to understand.

I feel his body tense. 'I live. I tell the truth. That's it. We shouldn't have got in the car. My life, boiled into one sentence.'

I pause. *We?* 'Who was with you?'

He is silent. The answer dawns like a little winking diamond.

'You were driving with Studs,' I breathe. 'Weren't you?'

'He was driving.'

I prop myself up on one elbow. Is it wrong to feel this

delighted? A man *died*. 'Then it was his fault, not yours!'

He won't look at me. 'It's not that simple.'

'Someone told me the other day that I should never take responsibility for someone else's life,' I say. How can he be so blind? 'Tall guy, likes wearing teatowels, I forget his name . . .'

'It's not the same.' He rolls away from me and stares up at the single bulb swinging above our heads. 'I took a life. It doesn't compare.'

I feel a chill. I need him to look at me again. This thing that I am feeling – confidence, I suppose – is still very fragile.

'Can we talk about something else?' he says, still staring at the lightbulb.

'No.'

He turns back with a slow smile. 'Are you sure?'

That should fix things – him looking at me with his beautiful stormy eyes, his mouth knowing and a little bruised. I scrabble for the feeling, but it's like grabbing smoke.

'You are beating yourself up over someone else's mistake,' I say, forcing myself to focus on the conversation.

'I know what I know,' he says.

It suddenly hits me like a thunderbolt in boxing gloves. *The Kiss.*

I hurtle to my feet.

Jem sits up. 'You OK?'

My heart lurches at the sight of him sprawled among the

furs: a proper, full-on, no-messing Aphrodite lurch. If I have the Kiss back, I am basically screwed. All I have to do is look at him and I am a howling wreck. Open. Vulnerable. All my favourite things.

What am I talking about? *The Kiss isn't real.*

'I have to go,' I say, mildly hysterical. I grab my clothes, then try and fail to flatten my hair. I have a nasty feeling it's not the only thing that's beyond repair.

'How are you getting home?'

'I'll walk.'

'Don't be stupid. It's late.'

'I can't afford a taxi because I am *broke*,' I hiss. 'The bank's after my blood, they keep ringing me up, and *I don't know how I got here because this was never the plan*.'

'Stay here,' he says in a soothing voice. 'I'll walk you home at sunrise.'

'Tell me something.' The question comes out angry. 'Why did you leer at Tabby the other day?'

He looks taken aback. 'For her ex-boyfriend's benefit, of course. To kick him into action.'

This feeling scares me and I've messed up with Tabby all over again. 'I just – I have to go,' I say in desperation. 'My dad will notice if I'm not in my own bed in the morning.' I back towards the props-room door, clutching my bag before me like a shield. 'Which door can I use?'

'Everything's locked.'

'Then we need to unlock it!'

'Delilah, what's going on?'

I almost stamp my foot. 'I told you not to be nice to me!'

'Hey,' he says, frowning. 'You gave me the go-ahead. Complicate it some more, you said.'

'You have no idea how complicated this has just become!' Almost gibbering, I open the props-room door. 'I need to go home.'

Silently we make our way out to the lobby and the great glass doors. He unlocks them and makes a little bow.

'Your escape route,' he says.

I guess I deserve that.

'Jem, I—'

But he's closed the door behind me.

I spend most of Saturday morning in bed, cursing my stupidity. Then I ring Val.

'I'm sick,' I mumble. 'I'm really sorry to let you down but I won't be able to come in tonight.'

'I knew I shouldn't have left you two alone,' she says. 'What's he done?'

She is almost as perceptive as her son.

'Nothing! It's nothing to do with Jem. I – I threw up in the night and I think I might . . .' I push the phone aside and make some convincing retching noises. 'Sorry,' I whisper. 'I don't want to puke over the regulars.'

'Stay where you are,' Val says with a sigh. 'There's some nasty things going around. If you're still ill on Friday, you're fired.'

I hang up, not entirely certain that she's bought my

story. However, it looks like I won't have to face Jem for a few more days and I still have a job. The week will be tight, but I'll just have to bear it. I punch my pillow in impotent rage. Stupid, stupid, *stupid*.

My phone rings cheerily.

'Hi babe. I just made a hair appointment. I'm revising my look to wow Jem. I thought I might come to the bar tonight and try my luck.' Tabby pauses. 'He didn't kiss anyone last night, did he?'

Never have I felt my dishonesty so acutely. 'I didn't see him with anyone new,' I say with a squirm.

'Phew. My appointment's at two this afternoon. Meet me there? You'll be able to tell me if what I'm planning is the worst idea I've ever had. I need your expert opinion as usual. Love you.'

She is pacing outside the salon when I arrive.

'What do you think?' she asks, thrusting the magazine at me.

The picture she's circled shows a model with a peroxide pixie-cut. I blink, unable to picture Tab as a blonde at all.

'Are you sure?' I say. 'The colour too?'

'I'm not sure at all,' she sighs, pushing open the door to let me into the salon first. 'But Sam must like blondes because he's going out with Maria. And Jem got with *you*, and you're blond.'

'I think you might be better going red, because of your colouring. I mean,' I add a little bumblingly, 'it's your choice, obviously. But that's what I'd do if I were you.'

The stylist agrees with me. 'Red or a deeper chestnut brown, love. Blond will make you look like a corpse.'

Tabby goes with a henna rinse. The pixie cut emphasizes all the best bits about her face. She tips her head from side to side, smiling at me in a pleased kind of way. 'Red's not bad on me, actually,' she says. 'Is it?'

'It's gorgeous,' I say truthfully.

'You want me to get my straighteners on that lot, love?' the stylist asks me, eyeing my cloud of hair as Tab goes to pay.

'No she doesn't,' says Tab without looking round.

We push through the doors, back out into the glimmer of the late September sun.

'When do you have to be at the Gaslight?' Tabby asks. 'Do you think it would be weird if I rocked up with you? I might stand more chance of catching Jem before the competition pours through the doors.'

'Can we go for a walk up the Hangers?' I ask.

She looks strangely at me. 'The last time we went for a walk up the Hangers, you told me you'd started your periods. What are you going to tell me now?'

People push past us on the pavement, hurrying about their lovely, uncomplicated, truthful lives. As if I'm not nervous enough, I start worrying about Val or Jem spotting me when I'm supposedly at home puking my guts out.

'Can we walk or not?' I demand.

We head over the town bridge and up through some

residential streets, leaving the town behind as we make for the Hangers: a stretch of woodland at the top of Leasford Hill. Tabby knows enough not to press me until I am ready to speak, and as speaking requires breathing, I don't begin until we reach the top and collapse on a nearby bench. The humps and bumps of the North Downs spread before us like the underside of a mighty green pine-covered eggbox.

'It's like this,' I say.

I tell the Dave story from start to finish. I probably add more detail than strictly necessary, but it is suddenly important that Tabby should know *everything*. How he picked me up outside school at the end of the Christmas term by leaning on the horn of his car until I looked at him. How he tried to take my virginity in the back of the same vehicle and how I almost impaled myself on the gear lever by mistake. And finally, the dreadful day of reckoning, when I learned in the most humiliating way that I wasn't the only decent fibber on the block.

'Whoa,' says Tab, into the silence which follows my extensive speech. 'Did the gear lever, you know . . .?'

'That's it?' I demand, blushing furiously. 'I tell you I've been lying to you all this time and Dave was stringing me along and you want to know if my first attempt at sex was with a gear lever?'

Tab starts laughing. She claps her hand across her mouth and snorts through her fingers. Then she gives up, puts both hands on the bench, grips on tight and roars.

'You'll never want my so-called expert opinion on

anything ever again,' I mutter.

Tabby pulls herself together. 'Of course I will. You're still way more experienced than me, even if your first time . . .'

She is off again.

'It didn't happen,' I say quietly. 'After the gear lever I sort of lost the will. Dave lost interest in me pretty quickly after that.'

This makes Tabby worse. 'Oh, ow,' she gasps, clutching her sides. 'Good job you were in a sand dune with Laurent, I hear French cars have . . . gear levers that . . . that stick out fro . . . fro . . . frontways.'

Truth or bust. 'I didn't do it with Dave but I nearly did it with Jem,' I say in a rush. 'Last night. In the wardrobe. At the theatre.'

Tabby stops laughing. She boggles at me. 'Tell me you're not serious.'

'I don't want to lie to you any more, Tabs,' I say helplessly. 'It's totally true. And I am having a *huge* freak-out about it.'

'You had sex?' Tab gasps. 'In the theatre?'

'I said *nearly*,' I point out. 'I didn't . . . We didn't . . . but for the first time in my whole life I think I actually . . . *wanted* to. I think maybe I would have but he said we'd have plenty of time for that and so . . . we didn't.'

'OMG,' Tabby says faintly. 'What was it like?'

There is so much to say and I can't say any of it. It's too private and too strange. Nothing prepares you for the *intimacy* of it: not books, not films, not conversations with your girlfriends and most definitely not the bananas in Sex-Ed. And I'm not just talking about the physical stuff. It turns out that your soul gets as vulnerable as the rest of you, and there's nowhere to hide.

'I've known him for barely a week,' I say, swerving Tabby's question. 'I've made a total mess of things.'

'Don't go all twentieth-century on me, babe. You nearly

143

had sex.' Tab looks at me with awe. 'You're a nearly-had-sex goddess.'

This isn't going the way I had imagined at all. 'Aren't you mad at me?'

'Why would I be mad?'

'*I kissed him,*' I say patiently. 'With a capital K for Aphrodite.'

Her hand flies to her mouth. 'Wow! I forgot about that.'

I am incredulous. 'This Kiss thing is your total reason for existence right now. The show, the hair. And you *forgot?*'

'I'm so busy learning my words and songs for the show that I don't think about it all the time. A lot of the time, yes. But not all of the time. And I guess . . .' She checks her watch . . . 'not at four forty-three this afternoon.' She looks at me with compassion. 'Are you now totally mindless with love?'

Yes, I think hopelessly. I am flayed like a Victorian tiger skin. Gutted like a fish dinner. 'Of course not,' I say out loud. 'All feelings can be controlled, with or without imaginary goddesses. Our own brains manufacture them after all. You get through these things. I got past Mum. I'm getting past Dave. I'll get past Jem.'

'That is actually quite good,' says Tabby slowly.

I feel pleased. 'I thought so too.'

'Not your speech. The fact that you have the Kiss.'

'Wait, what?' I say, caution in my voice. 'Why?'

She beams. 'You just took out the middle man! Now

I don't have to glam up for the Gaslight. I don't have to queue with the other girls at the bar and make you miserable because you like the guy I'm trying to get with. I don't have to live in fear of the Kiss going somewhere else because it's right here in front of me. Everything just got very simple.'

She looks expectantly at me.

'No WAY,' I say.

'Kiss me,' she orders.

'Be serious.' I look around. 'We're in a public place.'

Tab has already taken off her glasses and is looming in, eyes closed.

I scoot back on the bench. 'Have you gone completely insane? You're prepared to kiss me in broad daylight for the sake of a legend?'

'You're the one who had to bring me up to the Hangers to tell me how you got this so-called legend back.' She puts her hands on my shoulders. 'If you didn't believe there was something in it, you wouldn't have bothered. You would have let me think everything was going to plan. You could have let me kiss Jem and move on to Sam. You could have consoled me when Sam rejected me with some "It was never real anyway" advice. But you didn't. Explain *that*.'

I can't.

'See?' Tabby says with satisfaction. 'Now, I'm guessing it has to be a proper kiss, not just a peck.' She breathes on her hand, sniffs. 'Breath, check. Lesbian chic . . .' She pats

145

her new hair – '. . . check.'

All my powers of reasoning fall away before a true, honest-to-goodness fear. 'What if you fall in love with me?' I squeak. 'What then?'

Tabby pauses, inches from my mouth. 'I won't,' she says uncertainly.

'This is Aphrodite we're talking about!' Somehow I have forgotten that I don't believe in any of this.

'It's a risk I'm prepared to take,' Tabby says. 'It's only me that's taking it, after all. The person who receives the Kiss is the one who deals with the fall-out. Now, do your best to fancy me.'

'I can't,' I splutter.

'Yes you can. Focus. I have nice new hair. I have lovely kissable lips.'

I feel her kissable lips on mine. It isn't too bad, although it's all a bit . . . I can't help remembering the feel of Jem's rough chin, his stubbly cheeks between my palms, the hungry switching from side to side amid the sense of blood whooshing everywhere in a godlike tumble-dryer of nerve endings, and making unfavourable comparisons.

Tabby pulls away with a loud kissy *pop*. Her fingers go to her lips. Her eyes have a major thousand-yard stare going on. I feel sick as I wait for her verdict.

She drops her fingers. 'That was the most unsexy kiss I've ever had.'

Wanting to whoop with relief, I whack my best friend in the shoulder. 'I've never had any complaints before.'

'You were just too . . .'

'Smooth?' I supply, grinning.

'Smooth,' she agrees gloomily. 'Do you think Aphrodite's homophobic?'

I put my arm around her. 'Maybe you caught it, but just didn't *feel* it because it was girl-on-girl.'

'So Aphrodite *is* a bigot!'

'She's hardly going to be that. The Greeks practically invented homosexuality.'

'Have I got the Kiss or not?' Tab demands.

'All I know is that you haven't fallen in love with me and that makes me happy because frankly, my life's complicated enough,' I reply, still smiling like a loon.

'Maybe Jem kissed someone else before kissing you the second time.' Tabby gets up from the bench and starts pacing. 'Or maybe you're right and I *have* got it but I just can't *feel* it. I don't KNOW.' She looks tragic. 'We've lost it, haven't we?'

'I think we lost it some time ago, if I'm honest,' I say. 'Around about the time we started believing Australian Classics professors.'

Something moves behind us. I swing round.

Warren is fussing with the collar on a small shivering white dog on the path. He gives an unconvincing start. 'Oh! Hi Tabitha and er . . . Hi. Didn't see you there. Just, you know, walking the dog.' He waves at the scenery, which is starting to fade into evening gloom. 'Nice up here, isn't it? Very . . .' He pauses. 'Romantic.'

I rise from the bench. 'How long have you been there?'

He looks vague. 'Couldn't fix Isambard's collar on properly.'

The dog's collar looks in perfect working order to me. Warren walks off, tugging poor Isambard along and casting veiled glances back over his shoulder at us.

'That is SO embarrassing,' Tabby says.

I am still feeling too cheerful about Tabby's lack of passion to care overly about Warren.

'I have to do rehearsals with him!' she wails. 'He already told Patricia and Eunice, and that was just based on what you said at the first rehearsal. Now he's actually seen us kissing. What if he tells the whole cast? What if he tells *Sam*?'

I start laughing. I am feeling as light as a feather. I've told Tabby everything. There is nothing to hide any more, except for the way I feel about Jem.

'First we lose the Kiss, now I'm officially gay,' says Tab disconsolately. 'How is any of this going to help me get Sam back?'

'We'll work it out,' I say. 'Just promise not to kiss me again.'

My phone squeals a message at me. Still laughing, I pull it out.

Did you say the bank was after you?

'Jem?' says Tab, catching my expression.

I nod, wondering how text messages can effectively snip through a person's vocal cords.

'What does he say? Does he want to see you again?'

I clear my throat. 'He's just checking my credit rating.'

Tabby looks confused. 'Is that code?'

I show her the text. 'Doesn't bode well, does it?' I say, trying to sound airy. 'Not "Babe can't stop thinking about you". Just "Are you in trouble with the financial services?"'

Tabby looks worried. 'And are you?'

I wave my hand impatiently. 'They keep ringing me up. Haven't they got anything better to do? I'm not *using* my account.'

'What are you going to do?'

Try not to cry for starters, I think. My heart is thumping unpleasantly. I flattered myself that he thought me worth more than this. Then again, why would he? I ran away from him last night like my shoes were on fire.

'I'm going to save up enough money to get me through till the end of term,' I say. My voice feels thick. 'Find another job so I don't have to see him ever again. Change my name and emigrate to Mexico.'

'Listen Lilah,' Tab says in an anxious voice, 'boys are terrible at communicating their feelings. Maybe this is his way of telling you he loves you.'

'If that's the case, Valentine's Day will be a riot,' I say.

I start texting something witty and non-committal back, but remember just in time that I am supposed to be ill. Then I tap out something about puking, but can't bring myself to send *that* because it's a bit gross and I know he'll see right through it. Sighing, I settle for the only thing I can think of, typing extra carefully to avoid auto-correct horrors.

It's a real wolf.

'I won't ask,' says Tab, looking mystified as I hit send.

'Probably best,' I agree.

By keeping my head down, working on my Economics presentation to the point where I can ace *Mastermind* on JM Keynes, and restricting myself to home-made sandwiches and water from the drinking fountain at lunchtime, I stretch my pathetic half-income all the way to Thursday night. I'll have to scrounge lunch off someone tomorrow but I've done that before.

'You do understand why I'm not coming tonight, don't you?' I say as Tab fixes her hair in the college toilets before her second Gaslight rehearsal.

'He's horrible for not texting you since that weird banky one at the weekend,' she says, tweaking her fringe and playing with the bits around her ears. 'I'd avoid him too.'

'It's not just that,' I say. 'There's only so many drinks I can expect Patricia to buy.'

'Don't worry, I do honestly understand. I'll be fine by myself,' she assures me. 'I've done one rehearsal with these guys now, so I kind of know who to avoid.'

'Warren,' we say together.

'And Maria,' Tabby adds. 'Still the biggest cow in town. She's so full of herself, she thinks the agents will be lining up on show night and begging her to join them so they can make her a West End superstar.'

'What about Sam?'

'If I've got the Kiss, I'm officially impossible to resist.' Tabby gives her hair one last tweak and sighs. 'But it's a big if.'

'You're impossible to resist anyway,' I tell her. 'Just ask that girl you kissed last weekend.'

Oz is outside the toilets by the main college pinboard, scrolling through a tablet. The phone in his top pocket is winking, heavy with messages.

'It's rehearsal night, Oz,' says Tabby when she sees him. 'Fancy it? You did say last week how you wanted to see Patricia and Eunice's legendary drinking abilities for yourself.'

'Can't,' Oz says. 'I'm organising a party at the Fire Station tonight. Tomorrow?' His phone rings. He whips it out. 'Yup? Yup. Yup. Yup.'

Boys lumber past us in the corridor, high-fiving Oz as they go. He nods at them all, phone still clamped to his ear, palms ringing out time and again.

'Who are they?' I ask as Oz rings off with a final

'Yup' and slots the still-winking phone back into his pocket. 'You and me do all the same classes and I've never seen them before.'

'You don't need to know the punters by name.' Oz's fingers are poised over his tablet again. 'You need only know them by their ability to tell everyone about what's going down courtesy of the Ozmeister at the Fire Station tonight.'

'Why don't you take Lilah?' suggests Tabby. 'She needs a party.'

It's tempting. I feel an urgent need to be somewhere that isn't my room, and isn't the Gaslight, and isn't college. Somewhere to remind me that life ticks on no matter how hard I try standing still.

'Can't afford a ticket,' I say.

'Have one on me,' says Oz generously.

'You'll have to buy me drinks all night,' I point out. 'Not that I'm trying to put you off or anything.'

He pats his trouser pocket. It jingles. 'I can stretch to something for my favourite girl.'

'Go forth and enjoy,' Tabby says. 'I gotta go and sing songs.'

My best friend is right. I need a party. I can do the whole going-to-a-party-alone thing, because I'll be with Oz, and that isn't alone, is it?

'You're on,' I say. 'The Fire Station? By the old Co-op?'

'You can't miss it,' he promises. His phone starts ringing again. 'There's a real fire engine parked outside.

153

I'll see you on the door around nine.'

Walking to and from home to save on bus fares may be tightening up a few of my looser muscles, but it badly eats into the evening. By the time I get to my front door, it's almost seven o'clock. I have about an hour to have a shower, do something approaching party make-up and find something to wear for Oz's gig that includes sensible walk-all-over-town shoes but doesn't shout NERD.

I come downstairs again just over an hour later, a little breathless, in my everyday Vans and a cute flippy yellow dress I bought back in June when I had money. The dress is a bit summery, but walking to the bar, dancing and walking home again will keep me warm enough.

I have flushed cheeks and a faint line of perspiration around my hairline by the time I reach the Fire Station. A line of people snakes down the pavement past the old fire engine, tarted up to the skies for what is plainly the hottest ticket in town. How does Oz do it? I gaze down the line towards the doors, looking for his familiar pyramid of hair, hoping I won't have to join the queue.

I spot him by the doors, talking to the two bouncers. With a stab, I recognize one of them as Kev, the bullet man from the bodypainting collective. I wonder nervously if Kev being here means that Jem might be too. I wonder how I feel about that, and decide that I haven't got a clue.

'Delilah Jones, you look like an adorable omelette,' Oz beams. 'This is Kev.'

Kev is quite handsome without the bullet wound painted on to his cheek. 'We already met,' I say. I wonder if he remembers me.

'Jem's girl?' he says. 'Never forget a face.'

I am proud of myself for not flinching. 'Not Jem's girl, just his canvas. Not doing the collective tonight?'

'This pays better.' He jerks his head towards the doors. 'Get in then, before I have to ask you how old you are. Gotta get this queue moving.'

He shoots a beefy hand into the crowd clustered by the door, seizes a lad by the lapels and deftly chucks him out of the line. 'I already kicked you out once, kid,' he shouts. 'Don't make me do it again.'

Oz shepherds me right through to the bar. 'You going to be OK? I'd hang out only I need to be on the door and . . . you know. Around.'

My eyes widen. Flying solo is one thing. Flying solo without a wing man is something else entirely. I'm not sure I'm up to it at all.

'I'll be fine,' I squeak. 'I'll probably find someone to talk to. I really appreciate this, Oz, honestly. The ticket, the drinks.'

Oz looks relieved. 'Just put in a good word for me with Tabby whenever you can.'

He still hasn't got the message, bless him. 'All the words in the world won't make her fancy you,' I say as kindly as I can.

'Humour me.'

He leaves. I squeeze my arms in at the bar and order a bottle of something blue because everyone around me seems to be drinking it. It tastes vile, but it is free and gives me something to do with my hands. It's weird standing here by myself. I smile tentatively at a couple of people, but they look right through me and carry on with their conversations. Glancing around the room, I try singling out familiar faces, people I can barge up to and join. Several from college – a number from school –

And Louise.

Blood thunders to my face. Dave's girlfriend is standing moodily in a corner by the dance floor. I flick my eyes around like a rat in a trap. If Louise is here . . .

'What the hell is that mouthwash?'

With her hair caught up on top of her head and her face painted like an extremely beautiful tiger, the angry redhead from bodypainting – Ella – is beside me, looking aggressively at my bottle.

'I don't know,' I say, unable to say much else. I am relieved to be having a conversation with someone, but my brain is clattering around my head in clogs. 'Tastes terrible though.'

'I saw Kev on the door,' she says. 'He said you were here. Jem with you?'

I shake my head. How quickly can I get out of

156

here? I haven't seen Dave yet, but that doesn't mean he isn't lurking.

Ella takes a moody glug from a can of lager she's holding. 'He wasn't at the collective tonight. I thought he took his art seriously. Seems I was wrong.'

'He does take it seriously.' I can feel myself going cross-eyed with the effort of looking at Ella and scoping out the bar for Dave at the same time. 'He wants to make a career of it. Do films.'

'So why wasn't he there tonight?'

She glares at me as if Jem's absence was my fault.

'Why should I know?' I demand, fed up with the interrogation already.

Seeing a tiger laugh rates pretty high on the freakometer. 'Sorry, I don't mean to take it out on you,' she says. 'Delilah, right? Next time you see him, give him a kick from me. If he's serious about this, he can't miss sessions.'

Louise is approaching the bar. To my horror, Ella is beckoning her over. They know each other. Sometimes I hate this town.

I finish my drink and put the bottle down. 'I have to—'

It's too late.

'Lou, you remember Jem?' Ella says. 'In our year, completely gorgeous when he bothered to show up? This is his girlfriend Delilah.'

As introductions to your ex-boyfriend's girlfriend go, it isn't bad. Deciding not to correct Ella on the girlfriend bit,

I start breathing more normally and try to act like I get introduced this way all the time. Louise runs her almond-shaped eyes up and down my dress.

'Hi,' she says coolly.

The giddy combination of adrenalin and blue stuff kick me in the head. 'No need to pretend we don't know each other,' I say. I lean towards Ella conversationally. 'I used to go out with Louise's boyfriend by mistake.'

Louise bursts into noisy tears that run down her perfect brown cheeks and smear her mascara. Ella looks from me to Louise and back again with a combination of interest and glee. And it suddenly occurs to me that perhaps I'm not the only one who's been put through the emotional mangle by the D-word. All these leaps of self-knowledge are a bit dizzying.

'I am so sorry,' I say, appalled. 'I didn't mean to make you—'

'He dumped me a couple of days ago.' Louise takes the serviette Ella is proffering and blows her nose. 'I put up with a row of little tarts like you and now he's dumped me like . . .' She looks at the snotty serviette and chucks it down on the bar in disgust.

'This is awkward,' Ella drawls.

I don't know how to feel about this astonishing piece of information. Horrified? Embarrassed? Ecstatic?

Louise looks at me with loathing, then heads for the toilets as fast as her maddeningly long legs allow, stumbling across the dance floor with one hand held to her face. Something I never thought I'd ever say rises to my lips.

'Do you think Louise is OK?'

Ella snorts. 'Call me psychic, but I'm guessing not. Boys spread misery wherever they go. Girls are where it's at, Delilah, believe me.'

When Ella turns her tiger-striped face towards the bar, I am off like a hare on a dogtrack.

'Going already?'

I summon a smile for Kev on the door, smoke issuing from the heels of my Vans. 'Somewhere else to be. Say bye to Oz for me.'

My brain is bouncing with impossible speed from one thought to another. What's happened between Dave and Louise? Has he met someone else? After several lacerating seconds of jealousy, I indulge in fantasies of being the cause.

I move on. Why haven't I heard from Jem? Should I be worried that he didn't turn up to his bodypainting thing? I give myself a mental kicking even as I feel the pulse of Saturday night in my guts. I ran from the theatre because I was scared. I'm a coward.

How do I feel now? How does *he* feel? He doesn't feel like calling me, I know that much. Maybe he didn't do his bodypainting thing because of me too. But that's laughable. Then because . . . because . . . I have no idea.

The clerk on the thought counter shouts 'NEXT!'

Money. How to get it. How to survive on it. Always money. I hate the stuff. No one ever warns you how hard independence can be.

My phone rings, bringing some relief. I take it out – and stop, my answering thumb in mid-air. The screen is telling me something I can't quite believe. A name I haven't seen on my phone since the day I bought a new one. A new one which was washed into the Med and has since been replaced by the old one again, complete with old contacts still in place.

I hit the green button and lift it to my ear. 'Dave?'

'Hey, babe. How's it going?'

I am incapable of small talk. My heart rate is off the scale. 'What do you want?' I manage.

'No need to be unfriendly.'

'What do you want please, Dave?'

'You know,' he says after a moment. 'A chat.'

'A chat,' I repeat. 'What do you want to chat about?'

'Stuff.'

'Why now?' I am clutching the phone so tightly I can feel my knuckles seizing up. 'Why, specifically, do you want to chat about stuff now?'

'You busy?'

161

I'm going to hang up. I *am*.

'I heard about you and Louise,' I blurt.

'Who told you?'

'Louise did. Just now. At the Fire Station. Is it true?'

'You at the Fire Station now?'

I hold the receiver away from my ear, wave it at the silent streetlit world, then return it to the side of my head. 'Doesn't sound like it, does it?'

'You with anyone?'

'You still haven't said what you want to talk about.'

He is silent.

'Chat time's over,' I say.

'Don't hang up,' he replies quickly. 'Can you meet me? Now?'

I feel his question like a kebab skewer through my stomach. 'No,' I say, and turn off my phone.

I shake for the last ten minutes home. My world is a box of matches, scattered in one mindless I-opened-it-upside-down moment.

He is waiting in his car at the end of my road as I turn in, one elbow hanging out of the driver's window. His face looks thinner, his blond hair longer. It doesn't suit him.

'Dee,' he says in greeting.

'What are you doing here?' I implore.

He drums his badly bitten fingernails on the side of the car. 'Good to see you too. What's the Fire Station – forty minutes from here? I guessed you were walking so figured I'd wait till you showed up.'

Too confused for anything else, I walk slowly round to where he's popped open the passenger door and slide inside. The familiar smell of the car assails me. Vinyl, motor oil, hash. He moves to kiss me.

'Don't,' I say sharply.

Shrugging, he starts the engine.

I reach over and pull the car key out of the ignition. 'Don't do that either. We're not going anywhere. Why are you here?'

He takes his time answering me, patting his pockets for something. Now I can see him up close, he doesn't look good. His eyes are red, his skin patchy. Pulling out a ciggie, he lights it and inhales.

'I'm sorry I messed you around,' he says. 'That's what I wanted to say.'

'Oh,' I say. 'Well, I'm pretty sorry too. But it's over now. I'm over it.'

There is a pause.

'You got a job at that theatre, Studs says.'

'And?'

'Nothing. Just – that's cool.'

We sit in silence as he smokes. I am feeling increasingly bewildered.

'You're better off without me,' he says after a while, gazing out of the windscreen. 'So's she. Louise.'

He is starting to weird me out. 'Is this some kind of verbal suicide note, Dave, or are you angling to write for *Hollyoaks*?'

163

'You always were funny,' he says, with a half-smile.

He flicks the filter out of the window and, reaching over, opens the passenger door again for me. I flatten myself to the seat so as little of me touches as little of him as possible.

'That's it?' I say, looking from him to the open car door and back again.

He lifts his car keys from my hand. 'Thanks. You know, for listening.'

Mystified, I stand on the pavement and watch him drive off, his rear lights boring into me like a pair of red-rimmed eyes after a heavy night.

'Delilah?'

I rouse myself from stupor. 'Hmm?'

'You're up.'

I shuffle my papers slowly. Jem and Dave have been popping in and out of my head in turn like crazed cuckoo clocks.

'Er,' I say, looking at the class. 'I'm here to talk about cuckoos. Sorry, what? Not cuckoos, I'm here to talk about Keynes.'

'I'd prefer to hear about cuckoos,' says a girl on the front, through the wave of laughter rippling through the room.

'Keynes,' I repeat. My flipping *toes* are blushing. 'John Maynard Keynes. Maynard like the wine gums.'

More laughter.

'Cuckoos and wine gums aren't the most orthodox way to start a presentation on one of Britain's most important economists,' says the teacher. 'Does this get better?'

Everything goes out of my head. My pile of notes might be written in Urdu for all I understand. The only thing I can think of is Jem saying *Interesting guy, if massive moustaches and the cause of a boom-and-bust economy are your bag.*

'He was gay,' I say hopelessly.

The teacher sighs. 'You've had two weeks to get this ready, Delilah. We'll discuss it after class. Sit down.'

I sit and stare at my pile of papers, my little Post-its marking bits that I was most proud of. I even have photos.

At the end of the class, I thrust my perfectly serviceable presentation at the teacher and flee for the canteen, not daring to look back at his puzzled face.

'That was like a car crash in there,' Oz says, catching up. 'What happened?'

'My brain died,' I say shortly. 'And I saw my ex-boyfriend last night. It's safe to say that the two things aren't unconnected.'

Oz rubs his eyes. 'Give me details but keep it low. My head's like a brick today.'

'Buy me a sandwich first?' I implore.

Oz coughs up for a BLT that I want to kiss him for. 'Why are you so broke all the time?' he says at the till. 'I thought you had a job.'

I'll be seeing Jem tonight – talking to Jem tonight – for the first time since running out on him in the darkness of the theatre. I am beyond scared.

'I do,' I sigh. 'But it comes at a cost.'

Tabby waves us over from a table in the corner. I've hardly sat down before I am wolfing the BLT like a starving dog.

'Patricia and Eunice told Warren off for pestering me at rehearsal last night,' she says gleefully.

'Dave's not going out with Louise any more,' I say, when the sandwich has gone and I can draw breath. 'And I saw him last night and he was *weird*.'

'And Maria and Sam rowed,' Tab goes on. 'I did the song where I sing and flirt with Warren, which is the hardest thing in the world because he grosses me out so totally – and I *think* their row happened straight afterwards so like, maybe I was the cause?'

'And I'm now totally confused,' I groan.

'I love how girls talk AT each other,' says Oz.

'What?' Tab and I say to one another at the same time.

'Dave,' I repeat. 'I saw him. The long-term girlfriend I caught him with? I saw her too. They split up. Talk about confusing.'

'Delilah,' Tab says, 'Dave was a two-timing rat. What's confusing about that?'

I fix her with a meaningful stare. 'Jem hasn't called me so he's obviously not interested.' This hurts, but I have to put it out there because it's true. 'Dave on the other hand *did* call me. Maybe he broke up with Louise because of me.'

'You haven't seen the guy in months. Why would he do that?'

'It's still a maybe,' I say stubbornly.

'You don't want to get back with him, do you?' says Tabby disbelievingly.

I don't know what I want. Oh, hold on – yes I do. I want a world back where everything makes *sense*.

'*You* want Sam to forgive you for cheating on *him*,' I protest.

'One kiss is totally different! You were in a *relationship*.'

'This is like watching a tennis match,' Oz says. 'Only without a replay button.'

'I'll talk to Oz if you're going to be unhelpful about this, Tabby,' I say, annoyed. 'Oz, if a guy is interested, they call you, right? And boys have been known to dump current girlfriends for old girlfriends but not tell them right away, right?'

'Oz,' says Tabby. 'Do guys row with their girlfriends about their ex-girlfriends when they see their ex-girlfriends flirting with weirdos even though they're all just acting?'

Oz looks flummoxed. 'All of a sudden I hold the key to the Holy Grail of Guy Thinking? The only relationship I've had lately that's lasted to its natural conclusion is between me and a packet of Doritos.'

'You're no use,' I say crossly.

A girl stops at our table. 'Hey, Oz! Great party last night.'

Oz blossoms like a flower. 'I like to spread the love. Do

you like to spread the love? Do you want to spread some in my direction?'

But she's already gone. Oz looks despondent and eats more crisps.

'Lilah, we're rehearsing in the bar tonight because they're set-building in the auditorium,' Tab tells me. 'You can watch during your shift and tell me what you think is going on between Sam and Maria. You're always giving me stuff to do to take my mind off Sam. I'm returning the favour with you and Jem.'

'I don't need my mind taking off Jem,' I say. Hasn't she been listening? 'I need my mind taking off Dave.'

'Whatever. Just watch. Eyes on stalks. Read the signs. Tell me afterwards. Yes?'

'I'd come to offer moral support, only I'm busy,' says Oz with his nose in his phone. 'The gigs just keep coming.'

'Will you watch Maria and Sam tonight?' Tab prompts me. 'Please?'

I am feeling forgiving after the BLT. I can be cool, non-committal, occupy my downtime observing Sam and Maria and pondering the conundrum of Dave. Act totally cool around Jem.

'No problem,' I say with firm resolve. 'No problem at all.'

'What do you mean, he's not here?'

Val shrugs. 'We'll just have to manage with two of us tonight.'

I feel ridiculously angry. All afternoon I've been psyching myself up to this. All through study period I was going over how I'd say hello, right through to something funny about the side-squirting optic. I put on make-up in the college toilets, and washed it off again, and put it on again. And he's not *here*?

I try to catch Tab's eye, but she and Eunice are setting out chairs. Warren is talking to Sam with his eyes on Maria's breasts. The other cast members are milling around the lobby like sheep in a high wind, trying to find places to sit down.

'IF we can begin,' says Desmond the director with a loud cough.

'So where is he?' I ask Val.

She raises her hands. 'I haven't seen him for a couple of days.'

'Was he here last night?'

'I haven't seen him *for a couple of days*,' Val repeats patiently.

'So you don't know where he is?' I persist. 'He hasn't called?'

'He's eighteen, love,' Val says, rubbing her temples with both hands. 'He can do what he wants. But I'll tell you this. When he does turn up, I'll box his ears off the sides of his head.'

Several punters drift in, look at the assembled chairs and people, assess Honor at the piano in one corner and Desmond the director's waving arms, and disappear into the street again. Only a few of the regulars run the gauntlet of the close-harmony singing, retiring to a corner of the bar to watch over the tops of their pints.

'They'd better have built that set by next week,' Val grumbles as the chorus gets into full swing on a fast track called "A Weddin' and a Beddin'". 'We may be short-staffed, but we still can't afford to lose business.'

I go about the usual jobs of priming the pumps and emptying the bins, my brain scaring itself on the subject of Jem. Is he lying at the bottom of Leasford Hill with a broken neck? Face down in the canal? Does this town even *have* a canal? Hell, it has a river. Is he face down in the river?

I take out my phone, tap in a message and press send before I can think it through too much.

You OK?

Maria saunters over with her purse out. Her eyelashes are absurdly long and lush. I squint at them, trying to work out if they are falsies.

'Fanta for me. No Jem tonight?' she asks, peering over the top of the bar in case he's hiding down by the wine fridge.

'Doesn't look like it, does it love?' says Val.

I start dutifully watching Sam as per Tab's instructions. He is drinking Tabby like a cool glass of water as she laughs about something with Patricia. *He still likes her*. He just needs . . . a little push in the right direction.

'You want a Coke, babe?' Maria calls, looking back at Sam.

Sam starts guiltily. 'Uh, sure. Thanks.'

'There will be plenty of time for refreshments later, Maria,' says Desmond. He pulls out a bottle of pills and necks a couple. 'We have the whole of Act Two to cover this evening, an act with *plenty* for you to do, so I would appreciate your attention.'

'Silly old fart,' says Maria, in a not-very-subtle voice. She sweeps her blond hair over one shoulder and returns her hard blue-eyed gaze to me. 'One Coke, one Fanta.'

I am already siphoning the fizzy stuff into two glasses: one brown, one orange. 'Two eighty,' I say, pushing them towards her.

'I'll take the vodka shot off your wages tonight, shall I?' says Val as Maria carries the glasses back to her chair, handing the brown one to Sam.

'What vodka shot?' I say, a little shocked at her apparent ability to see round corners.

'The one you put in the lad's Coke. Trying to cause trouble?'

There's no point in denying it. 'Just trying to make things right where they've gone wrong,' I say cautiously.

Fortunately, my boss seems amused. 'You'll be telling me he's eighteen next. I suppose a vodka shot's money in the till. *Your* money in the till. So I'd say we're square. Besides,' she adds, looking at where Sam is morosely drinking his Coke, 'I quite fancy seeing a smile on that lad's face before I die.'

I hit Sam with a couple more singles before the mid-way break thanks to Maria's total disregard for the director's repeated demands that she leave the bar alone. It's costing me a fortune. The cast rips through the songs, hammering so hard at "A Weddin' and a Beddin'" that by the time they reach the break I have it jumping around my brain like frogs on a trampoline.

'Well?' Tab pushes eagerly through the crowd at the bar. 'How's it looking? What's Sam been doing? Seen anything I should know about?' She glances around. 'Where's Jem?'

'Not you too,' Val says.

'Absent,' I say as Val moves down the bar to serve the

clamouring hordes. 'And no, I don't know why and I haven't had a message and I'm feeling spooked that he's not here because of me. I wasn't very nice to him when I left on Saturday. He's disappeared, and no one—'

'Hey shexshy,' Sam says, popping up a little blurrily next to Tabby. ''Nother Coke pleash.'

Tab looks astonished.

'I recommend a glass of water to go with it,' I say, giving Sam the Coke I prepared earlier. 'Too much high fructose corn syrup can mess with your digestion.'

Sam sinks the glass of water I offer and wipes his mouth with the back of his hand. 'Tabbywabby,' he says suddenly, nudging her in the shoulder as he lines up his fourth vodka and Coke of the evening. 'Did I ever tell you how pretty you are?'

'Whisky, Delilah,' says Patricia, muscling in between Sam and Tab. 'Lots. With ice.'

"*What's going on?*" Tabby mouths at me, nodding so vigorously at Sam that her head looks like one of those bobbing woodpeckers you sometimes get on pencils.

'I'm loving this show,' says Sam, swinging round to the assembled cast. 'Ishn't everyone loving this show? We love you, Desmond. We love you, Honor. We love you, Tod Shnorter dude that wrote this stuff.'

'Tod Slaughter,' says Maria, narrowing her eyes.

'Shwat I shed. Shnorter.'

'That boy needs to sober up,' comments Eunice, sipping a glass of red wine at the end of the bar.

'Let me top that up for you, Eunice,' I say. 'On the house.'

'I'm watching you,' says Val without actually looking up.

At this rate I'll spend my entire evening's wages on other people's drinks. Still, if I achieve the objective of reuniting Sam and Tabby, it will be worth it.

'Desmond would like a large glass of water,' says Honor, squeezing up against the packed bar. Behind her, the old director is sitting at a table mopping his head with a large spotted handkerchief. 'And I'll have an elderflower cordial.'

'Last of the big spenders,' Val mutters at me, pushing a pint glass of water and a bottle of elderflower juice towards the vocal coach.

'Get OFF me,' Sam says loudly.

Maria is trying to tug him towards the double doors. 'You need some fresh air, Sammy. You're not well. You have one of your biggest numbers after the break. Your concentration's totally off.'

'I'm ferpectly well,' Sam announces. 'Get your armsh and your teeny tiny fingersh off me. I want another Coke.'

'Bladdered,' observes Patricia, her whisky halfway to her mouth.

Sam's a lot drunker than I was expecting. A single shot of vodka seemed too small to cause much damage, but maybe four was a mistake.

Maria gets him as far as the box office. He suddenly gives her a bad-tempered shove, lurches sideways and ricochets off a nearby pinboard. Notices and a couple of brightly coloured pins flutter to the ground. Maria loses her balance and lands on the sofa, the one I sat on at the first rehearsal when Jem curled his fingers in my hair.

'Sam, what are you *doing*?' Tabby demands, rushing over. The rest of the cast watch in fascination.

'Tabbywabby,' mumbles Sam again, brushing a flyer for a donkey sanctuary off his shirt front and reaching for her. 'Kish me.'

Tab heroically ignores him. 'Are you OK?' she asks, helping Maria back to her feet instead.

'I'm fine,' says Maria, thin-lipped, tugging her dress down and trying to straighten her hair. 'But I have a few questions for your curly midget friend on the bar.'

'She'sh not a midget,' says Sam with a hiccup. 'She'sh lovely.' And he throws up copiously down the closed box office window.

I should definitely have stopped at three.

'I'm on it,' I squeak as Val glares at me. I fetch a bucket, a cloth and a squeegee bottle of disinfectant and enter the vomit zone.

'Shorry,' Sam mutters as he sinks on to the sofa, rests his elbow on the armrest and buries his face in his hand. Shoving Tabby away, Maria sits down beside him and pats him gingerly.

I want to put my arm around Tab as she stands there, all alone on that horrible brown carpet, but I am mopping sick off the ticket desk. I have a feeling my intervention wouldn't be appreciated anyway.

'Break's over!' calls Honor.

175

With a collective sigh of regret, the cast drifts back to their chairs to resume the rehearsal. Maria helps Sam to the toilets with a pinched expression on her face. Tabby moves silently back to a chair beside Eunice as I finish my mopping and cart the bucket back to the kitchens.

And Desmond the director stands up, riffles the pages of his score, makes a strange bleating noise, clutches his chest and falls to the ground with a boom.

'Of course it's not your fault,' Tabby says for the millionth time as we mount the Gaslight steps on Saturday evening. 'He's *ancient*. Had a heart condition for years.'

'But if I hadn't pulled that stunt with Sam and the vodka—'

'That, as we have established, is totally irrelevant. Desmond was purple in the face about Maria and the bar refills already. It would have happened whatever you or anyone else did. Anyway, he's obviously going to get better or Honor would have cancelled tonight's rehearsal and most likely the show as well.' She pauses, halfway up the steps. 'Do you think Sam will be here tonight? I wonder how he's feeling?'

'Like death in a blender, probably,' I groan.

'He told me I was pretty. He asked me to kiss him. Should I have kissed him?'

'And had your reunion kiss forever etched on your memory as tasting of puke? No.'

'Oh *why* is Maria still with him?' Tab cries passionately. 'I swear, she doesn't even *like* him that much. Did you see the disgust on her face when they left last night?'

'Sam's basically a decent guy, popular at college, nice-looking, good singing voice, wears muscle-enhancing shirts, blah blah,' I say. 'Maria's not going to give up that easily. Plus she probably enjoys annoying you. It's hard when your boyfriend goes woozy over his ex in public.'

Tab gives a snort of laughter, then stops. 'Is it bad to have enjoyed that?'

'Darling Tabbywabby,' I say, 'it's as evil as evil can be.'

She squeezes my arm. 'Anything from Jem yet?'

'Ooh,' I say, and point at the sky. 'Pigs.'

'What?' says Tab, looking up.

Last night was bad, but tonight is guaranteed to be worse. Sam will probably threaten to report me for assault by alcohol – assuming he's here and not nursing a killer hangover – and Tab's director is three-quarters dead in the Royal Surrey Infirmary. With or without Jem, I am looking at an evening in Fun Central.

Honor is pale, the gathering cast subdued. Sam, white as paper, is sitting with Maria, who is holding his hand ostentatiously and playing with her hair with her free fingers. Rich and Henry – who play Don Pedro and bad guy Don John – are sitting even closer together than normal. Patricia is uncharacteristically silent; Warren too. I make my way behind the bar as Tabby takes her seat beside a red-eyed Eunice. A hopeful glance in the empty kitchen tells me Jem isn't back. My spirits sink even lower.

'Two things to report,' says Honor when everyone has taken their seats. 'One, Desmond's condition is stable but not improving. Two, I will have to take a decision next week on whether doing this show is still realistic without Desmond in the driving seat.'

There is a horrified hubbub. It's hard to tell what some of the hard-core members of the cast are more concerned about: their director's health or the fading chance of their moment in the spotlight. I mechanically polish the glass in my hand. If the show is under threat, so is my job. Without the show, the bar will be less full and Val will have no further need of my services until panto season – and maybe not even then. How am I going to survive?

'Desmond would want us to continue,' says Eunice. She is looking particularly rough and her cardie is buttoned up wrong.

Honor looks harassed. 'That's easy to say but hard to achieve. Desmond knows precisely how to make the most of the two weeks remaining to us. Being so well-known for his work in musical theatre, he is also the reason people come to watch the show. Without him, we will struggle to sell the tickets that we need to make this viable.'

'Rubbish,' Patricia says, roused to speech. 'People come for the tunes, for the flash of nostalgia. For the romance, for the fact that tickets are only a tenner. We can still do this if we stick together!'

There is a smattering of applause.

'You don't understand, Patricia,' Honor says. 'Word is out that Desmond's off the project. And the Peacock Theatre in Woking has just pulled *Me and My Girl* and are staging *What an Ado!* in two weeks' time instead.'

'Those Machiavellian backstabbers are after our audience!' shouts Henry.

'What have I missed?' says Jem behind me.

My stomach drops like a severed elevator to see him standing there like a very real, very wide-shouldered, dark-blue-T-shirted sex-god Colossus – even with the enormous disfiguring bruise running down the side of his face.

'You look like you've been in a car accident,' I say when I can speak. '*Have* you been in a car accident?'

'Good, isn't it? Took several hours.'

He gives a small smile, and winces at the pressure it puts on the tight skin around his eye. We look at each other, brown on grey-blue, as the air thickens with the long, silent week that has passed. I can't decide if I want to kiss him or kick him.

'Paint doesn't puff up your face,' I say. 'Unless you're allergic. Are you allergic?'

Why does that matter? my brain screams. *You're doing this ALL WRONG.*

'Who said anything about paint?' he says.

He bends down to heave up the trapdoor leading to the cellar. I catch him by the arm. He feels firm and warm and real. It's so very hard not to melt like cheese on a radiator.

'That's *it*?' If I don't sound loud and angry, I'll know I'll sound pathetic and needy instead. 'You've been off the radar for an entire week and that's all you're going to say?'

'I can add "ouch" if you like,' he says, looking at my tightly gripping hand.

'Why didn't you answer my text?' I say in a small voice.

He straightens up, the trapdoor clattering open between us. 'What text?'

'The one I sent last night, asking if you were OK.'

He looks surprised. 'I didn't get it.'

My phone is *ruining my life*.

Cast members shuffle about gloomily on their chairs, turn pages, whisper together as Honor goes on about being flat here and sharp there.

'I got the one about the wolf though,' he says. 'You really should go see your bank.'

Oh good. The bank thing again. Just what I need to hear at this, my most vulnerable moment. Not trusting myself to speak, I go back to cleaning glasses.

Tabitha sends me a startled glance as she registers Jem in all his bruised magnificence standing beside me at the bar. Within moments, Maria is resting her slim arms on the bar top so that her bangles jingle against the wood. Her cheeks have a pretty flush to them.

'So,' she says to Jem. 'What happened to *you*?'

'A fight, funnily enough,' he replies, fingering his cheekbone.

I detect a hint of sarcasm, which cheers me.

'Very macho.' She flicks a glance at me that brims with dislike. 'I want to lodge a complaint.'

'About what?' asks Val, coming out from the kitchen.

'Her.' Maria jabs a finger at me. 'Lacing my boyfriend's drink with alcohol last night.'

'I don't know what you mean,' says Val blandly.

'Maria,' calls Honor, tapping her music stand.

'Sam's underage, you know,' Maria continues, ignoring the summons. 'It's illegal, what she did.'

'So was your double vodka,' Val counters.

I glance up from the glass I've assiduously been polishing. Maria looks like someone has just chucked a bucket of cold water on her head.

'I wasn't drinking,' she says in confusion.

Val taps her nose. 'I don't like dropping my underage customers in it. But my licence is at risk when kids like you get at the optics.'

'But I *wasn't*—'

'You need to be careful.' Val looks Maria up and down. 'The booze is already starting to make you fat.'

I watch with ill-concealed delight as Maria gulps like a fish at a fireworks display. Val drums her fingers beside the prominently displayed *Don't be offended if we ask your age* sign on the bar.

'What's it to be?' Val inquires.

'*Maria!*' calls Honor in exasperation.

'Fanta,' says Maria at last. 'Two.'

'That was brilliant,' I say, overcome with gratitude as Maria walks slowly back to her chair with two Fantas on a tray and a strong haze of 'outmanoeuvred' about her head. 'Thank you.'

'If it happens again, you're out,' says Val.

'Understood,' I say humbly.

I reach up on tiptoe to put the glass on its shelf. When I come back down again, I catch Jem looking at me, his elbows propped on the bar behind him.

I can't figure out his expression at all.

On Tuesday night I lie on my bed, staring at the tiny heap of cash on my bedside table. After Sam's vodka shots, Eunice's wine and my usual contribution to the household budget, I am out of pocket already. Reaching down, I pick up my Vans and consider the holes in both soles. I can't walk to and from college in heels or flip-flops. There's no way I'm doing it in my tatty old school trainers. How much will a decent pair of shoes cost?

Honor said she'd make a decision about the show on Friday. No more show, no more job. No more brown packets. No more Jem.

I put my so-called earnings in my bedside drawer, switch off the light and fail to sleep for several hours.

'I've cracked "Love Eternal", my solo,' Tabby announces at lunch on Wednesday. 'I was doing it last night with Honor and Warren and I actually got to the end without losing it by pretending Warren was Sam. The power of imagination is a wonderful thing.'

We both glance to where Sam and Maria are queuing at the food counters, hand in hand. Tabby blinks hard.

'I've got to find another job,' I say as I force the last bit of cheese sandwich down my neck.

'Too difficult working with Shoulders this weekend?'

I shake my head. 'I can't survive on what I'm earning, even with tips.'

'Jem looked awful on Saturday, didn't he?' Tabby says. 'Have you found out how he got that face?'

'He wouldn't tell me on Saturday and I haven't seen him since.'

'Did you want to jump on him every time he asked you to take out the bins?' she asks. 'Even though we did that snog experiment, I think maybe you've still got the Kiss. You're so . . . moony at the moment.'

'I had the old pesky jumping urge under control,' I say drily. 'But it wouldn't have been reciprocated even if I'd let it off the leash. I don't think we're . . . in the same space any more.'

'Self-protection,' says Tab, with the air of expertise that I've noticed she's developed lately. 'I've been reading *Cosmo* this week and it had this whole article about how guys self-protect. They act like your most basic arthropod, closing off all but the most essential levels of communication. In other words, they shut themselves up like snails. I've seen

185

it with Sam. You're seeing it with Jem. He likes you but he can't risk it because you've already rejected him once.'

'Twice,' I correct. 'If you count the first time we kissed.'

'Self-protecting,' Tabby confirms.

'I'm running just to stop falling over,' I sigh. 'And now, if the show doesn't go ahead, I'll lose my job altogether because Val won't need me any more. At least, not till panto season in November.'

'If Honor *does* cancel,' says Tab in her best grief-counsellor voice, 'it's not the end of the world. I'm sure your dad would help if you were really at a crisis point.'

I look wearily at her. With her regular weekly allowance from her entirely reasonable parents, she has absolutely no idea what my life is like.

'Have you actually talked to your dad?' Tab prompts, all optimism. '*Really* talked to him?'

'About what? Dad hates the fact I'm at college. He gets fifteen quid a week housekeeping off me at the moment, and he makes it clear that's way under the going rate.'

'But you're going to be a *scientist*! You'll end up researching something really important, like . . . like rabbit fertility, or thermal underwear fibres, or . . .'

Not being a scientist, Tab swiftly runs out of career options.

Am I? I'm seriously starting to wonder. It'll take five years of studying from this point – minimum. We're still in the free part, and I'm already thinking about jacking it in. 'Try telling him that,' I say.

Oz plonks his tray between us. 'Party tonight at this place by the station,' he announces. 'I need bar staff. You up for it, Delilah?'

If Oz was a bone, I would lunge like a bloodhound. 'Oh my God – a hundred times *yes*,' I say. I have homework, but it will have to wait. 'What are they paying?'

'Four seventy-five an hour.'

Slavery rates. 'Why don't I donate my blood while I'm at it?' I complain.

'If a donator donates, shouldn't a blood donor *done*?' Tab muses.

'Four hours' work, cash in hand,' says Oz persuasively. 'That's nineteen quid all in, plus tips. It's at Aphrodite's Moon.'

Tabby spits out her Coke.

'*Where?*' I say.

'The Greek place by the station.' He looks from me to Tab. 'I take it that you know it? They do—'

'Great mezze, I know.' Weird has nothing on this. 'What time?'

'Eight.' Oz frowns at Tabby, who is gurning at me like a madwoman. 'Am I missing something?'

'Nope,' I say. 'I'll take the job.'

Even on a Wednesday night, the student body needs amusing – and apparently has the cash to do it. The music is pumping, the queue snaking out the bar's half-glass door is as long as last week's party at the Fire Station. The name of the bar hangs mockingly over the door, complete with a half-naked Aphrodite dancing in a brightly painted moonlit glade.

Niko the bar owner is delighted to see me.

'Flirt with the punters. Pile it on thick. Tell them about Aphrodite's moon. You know about the moon? Very powerful. Sends people crazy with lust.'

'So I've heard,' I say, doing my best to ignore the way he's waggling his eyebrows. 'Where do I put the empties?'

'Keep them coming, Delilah!' Oz shouts, beckoning for beer over my head as the evening gets a nice tight grip on the swaying sociability of the crowd.

I serve and serve and serve, and wonder if I am the only person under eighteen in the whole of Surrey that doesn't have money to burn. Val would kill for mid-week custom at the Gaslight like this.

Tab appears through the sweaty, heaving crush. She glances up at the bar name. 'It's a sign, you know,' she confides.

I flip off a Coke lid against the bottle opener with one hand and siphon lemonade with the other. 'Yes,' I agree. 'A badly painted sign that makes me want to heave every time I see it. Five thousand years since the Greeks civilized the world, and all us girls get for it is an immortal half-naked nymph. Who's the goddess of brains?'

'There's a goddess of wisdom,' says Tab. 'Athena.'

'There you go. Why can't we have a few bars called Athena's Wisdom, covered in wall paintings of brainiacs hanging out solving the world's problems?'

'Athena doesn't sell beers,' says Niko as he swoops past.

'I think it's the *other* kind of sign.' Tabby takes the lemonade and shovels ice into it. 'That the Kiss hasn't given up on us yet. That it's still out there, fired up and dangerous. Oh boil a brick, Warren's here.'

Warren waves across the dancefloor just as a cross-eyed, red-haired peacock emerges from the toilets and starts dancing with him. He looks as if he can't believe his luck. Just behind the peacock, a figure in bright white trainers with winking diamonds in his nose is leaning against the wall, observing the crowd with shark's eyes.

'Who is *that*?' Tab says, looking at the glittery peacock in awe.

'Ella,' I say, feeling the familiar clench in my gut when Studs is around. He makes me think of Jem instead of Dave these days, which at least makes some kind of change. 'Bodypainter. Scary, kind of funny. And right now, higher than Mary Poppins' kite. There's no other explanation for that bump and grind thing she's got going on with Warren. Niko!'

The bar owner looks alert.

'I think there may be a problem in the toilets,' I say. I nod at Studs.

'Oi!' Niko roars, striding across the room in a flash.

Ella bounds to the bar. 'Hello Delilah,' she grins. 'You ever fancy girls?'

'Delilah's a lesbian,' says Warren, looming up behind Ella.

'First Jem, now this little bombshell,' says Ella with interest. 'You get more intriguing every time I see you, Delilah.'

Delighted by the painted girl's reaction, Warren thrusts out his chest and points at Tabby. 'She's a lesbian too. Delilah was kissing her on Leasford Hill last weekend.'

Ella presses beringed hands on either side of Tab's blushing face. 'Call me if you fancy a change, darling,' she whispers, and kisses Tabby on the end of the nose.

I watch it dawn on Warren that Ella's provocative dancing has meant precisely zip. 'Is everyone around here a lesbian?' he says in dismay.

'Must be your aftershave, Warren,' I say.

'Not in my bar!' Niko bellows. He has seized Studs round the back of the neck and is now dragging him towards the door, with Studs loudly protesting all the way.

'Isn't he the dealer guy from the start-of-term party?' says Tabby as Niko throws Studs outside like a builder chucking an old toilet in a skip.

'And my evening is complete,' I say happily.

'No drugs here,' Niko shouts at the crowd, slamming the door and dusting his hands down his shirt. 'Drink and enjoy!'

Tab looks at my glass of water as we make our way to our customary table. 'Not having anything today?' she says in surprise.

'Not hungry,' I lie. 'I'll get something later.'

'Good last night, wasn't it?' Tabby is in the mood for dissecting the previous night's adventures in detail. 'That Ella was terrifying, but there was something about her . . .'

'You *definitely* caught the Kiss off me,' I say.

Tab's eyes snap back into focus. 'Do you think this is what happens?' she says, looking genuinely amazed. 'You get the Kiss off someone of the same sex and it actually, you know – turns you?'

'You're living proof, babes.'

'Wow.' Tabby sinks back in her chair. 'Wow,' she says again.

'Ella is weirdly gorgeous,' I point out. 'If girls in crazy

make-up are your thing.'

'But even if I do – did – kind of fancy Ella, I still want to get back together with Sam,' Tabby says firmly. 'I'd just like to make that clear.'

'Crystal,' I assure her.

My phone beeps.

Chérie, call me, F xxx

'Fatima,' I say, perking up. 'How much is it to call France?'

'Text'll be cheaper,' says Tab.

I have about a fiver's worth of credit on my phone. Like everything else in my life, it needs rationing.

Babe, too broke to call.
Story of my life.
U still coming?

> **Like a chou-chou train ma chère tout**
> **le temps. Tell the boys to get ready**
> **for me. You like foie gras? Champagne?**
> **I will bring. xxx**

Prefer Carambar and pate.

> **I will bring. BISOUS xx**

'She'll be here a week on Tuesday,' I say with satisfaction, clicking my phone off.

'Is she really as mad as you say?' Tabby asks.

'Madder,' I say. 'We'll have a job keeping her entertained. You rehearsing tonight?'

'Yes. Assuming Honor's not decided to can us.'

I feel the customary wave of nausea at the prospect of unemployment. 'You'd have heard by now, wouldn't you?' I ask anxiously.

'I guess,' Tabby agrees, blithely unaware of how my stomach is tying itself into knots. 'Want to come?'

'Studying,' I say, shaking my head. 'You should try memorizing chemical formulae some time.' I eye the half-sandwich on her plate. 'You having that?'

'I thought you weren't hungry.'

'Shame to waste it.'

Dave is waiting on the college steps as I leave the building, pacing back and forth like a nervous stork in a leather driving coat.

'Oh,' I say, stopping dead.

He clears his throat. 'Dee, I wanted to ask you something the other day, but I bottled it. Can we go for a ride?'

Tabby is long gone, off to sing songs of submission to the manly ideal of the nineteen-fifties. I long to be with her. Even the pain of an evening with Jem curled back into his shell is preferable to five minutes with Dave.

His car is parked by the river. In the daylight it looks more knackered than it did in the orange sodium streetlights. It has been raining, and the paintwork is speckled with tiny wet diamonds of light.

He sounds almost eager as I slide reluctantly into the passenger seat.

'Where do you want to go?'

'I don't *want* to go anywhere with you,' I say. 'Just drive.'

I rest my head on the back of the seat and finish the remains of a tube of paprika Pringles stuffed into the car door as we head out of town towards Leasford Hill. What does Dave want with me? Why am I even in the car?

'It's like this,' he says when we have parked and the North Downs are spread before us, hazy and darkening in the rain. 'I need money.'

A lone runner in blue sprints past the car as I start laughing. Proper laughing. I hold the car door and laugh so much that I spray Pringle crumbs across the dashboard. Two dog walkers glance curiously through the windscreen.

'It's not funny,' Dave moans. 'I *owe* people. Nasty people who will castrate me if I don't pay up.'

'Trust me,' I say as I catch my breath. 'It's hilarious.'

'It's why I broke up with Louise,' he says pathetically. 'She was vulnerable, going out with me. I'm in a mess, but at least I'm by myself.'

'By yourself plus me, apparently,' I point out.

The irony is lost on him. 'You're the only one that can help me,' he says.

I shake my head, feeling so old and wise you could coat me in feathers and call me an owl. 'Believe me, Dave, I can't help anyone. I've got nothing for you.'

He pats the air like some kind of large, unruly dog. 'Just let me talk, OK? I'll talk and then you can talk.'

'I won't have anything to say.' I fold up the Pringles tube

194

and stuff it back in the door. 'But I won't stop you talking.'

Dave grips the wheel of the car like he's driving at a hundred miles an hour, not parked perilously close to a wasp-infested rubbish bin. 'I owe these people five hundred quid,' he blurts.

If the door hadn't been shut, I'd have fallen out of the car. 'Five . . .? Are you *insane*?' I gasp. 'What makes you think I have that kind of money?'

'I'm not asking you for money,' he says quickly. 'I'm asking you for help. They'll pay you.'

I frown, trying to keep up. 'Who'll pay me?'

'These guys.'

'The testicle-removers?'

He nods.

I rub the bridge of my nose, wondering how I've slid sideways into a gangster movie. 'What have you done?' I ask.

He groans and rests his head on the steering wheel. 'Too much stuff that I haven't paid for.'

He's an idiot. 'You're an idiot,' I tell him. How did I never notice this when we were together?

'I know. But there's a way out.'

He reaches under his seat and pulls out a large grey plastic brick. I stare at it. My evening is getting weirder by the minute.

'Is that what I think it is?' I say.

'Depends whether you think it's an elephant,' he answers, with a sad attempt at humour.

I take it. Stare at the buttons, the receipt paper, the little slot at the bottom for credit cards. It strikes me too late that I've just splashed my fingerprints all over it. My ex-boyfriend is *officially insane*.

'You're not seriously thinking of using this? It's like robbing a bank!'

'Robbing a bank with no security guards, no cameras, no beady-eyed witnesses. It's a whole different game. And this baby routes straight into the bank account of your choice.'

He is looking at the fake swipe machine like a man looks at his first-born child. It's scaring me.

'You'll go to *jail* if you use this,' I say as clearly as I can. I'm still holding it like it's glued to my hands. 'Where did you get it?'

'From a friend.'

Dave's taste in friends is shocking. But I know this already.

'Wait,' I say cautiously. 'You're showing me this because . . .?'

At least he has the grace to blush.

'Oh my God,' I say, realization dawning.

'It's just a simple switch,' he pleads. 'Do it at the Gaslight on a busy evening. A hundred quid for ten seconds' work, that's all it is. Make the switch for me, Dee. Please?'

A hundred quid isn't that much when you think about it. Two fifty-pound notes. I imagine the gangster suitcase, empty but for two sad and flapping bits of paper.

I thrust the horrible machine back at him, yank open the car door and start running back down Leasford Hill to reality, trying to ignore the wet from the rainy ground as it seeps through the holes in my shoes. I want nothing to do with what Dave is suggesting. Nothing at all.

I make it home an hour later, my hair frizzed up by the damp air, my legs freezing. My shoes are wet and my toes feel squelchy. Thoughts and feelings in my head are pushing and shoving for my attention.

I need the money. I would never do it to Val. I would be caught. I could do it in between Maria's endless Fantas and Eunice's peanuts. Jem hates me already, what's one teensy crime going to do to change that? I'm not a bad person. One hundred quid is more appealing when you picture it in clinking gold nuggets.

I'm *not* thinking about it, I think desperately. I'm just . . . thinking ABOUT it. *There is a difference.*

As I put my house keys on the hall table, I see a plastic bag leaning against the table legs. My stomach feels like it's full of ants as I peer inside, already knowing what it contains.

Half now / half later Dave has written, on a torn-off bit of the Pringles tube I finished. The whole bag smells of paprika crisps.

'Lad in a car stopped by twenty minutes ago with that,' Dad says as I creep past the living-room door, clutching the bag to my chest.

I pause in horror, one foot on the stairs. 'Did you look inside?'

He looks at me oddly. 'I couldn't give a stuff about textbooks. Put the kettle on if you're passing.'

I make him a cup of tea and retreat to my room, where I shove the bag under my bed. I feed Marie Curie. She boggles at me in her usual silent, orange way.

'Work,' I say loudly, pulling out my folder and slamming it on my desk, like the noise alone will hammer the facts I need into my head and push away the creeping thoughts.

My phone goes off.

'I need to ask you if I should wear my green jumper or my blue one for rehearsal tonight.'

Leaning one elbow on a list of empirical and molecular formulae, I take off my bust-up shoes and massage my toes. New shoes would be good.

'Talk me through both,' I say wearily.

Tab lingers on her description of the low-cut green jumper a bit longer than the tight-fitting blue one. When I advise green, she argues the case for blue, so I switch arguments, which brings her back to the green again.

'Rehearsal starting at seven?' I check when we have exhausted both options and she is as confused as she was at the start of the conversation.

'Assuming I ever get any clothes on. Any messages for Jem?'

'Tell him to kiss Maria. She blatantly wants him to. He can do it in front of Sam like a *Crimewatch* reconstruction.'

198

'I'm not sure Sam could cope with *two* girlfriends kissing the same guy in front of him.'

I rub my eyes. 'OK, scrap that. Anyway, he does his bodypainting thing on Thursdays. He won't be around much.'

'Is he good at the body art thing?'

'You saw what he did to my hand,' I say.

'I dreamed about Sam last night,' she tells me. 'He was singing to me, only I was on the top of this bus on the way to Ibiza and I was leaving him behind. I tried to stop the driver, but he was a dog so he didn't understand.'

Much as I love her, I need Tab to go away. 'I have to learn about the ratio of atoms in compounds, babe,' I say, hoping she'll take the hint. 'Will you try and get a decision out of Honor about the show tonight? I *really* need to know.'

When she's gone I set my alarm for one hour. I'll learn as many formulae as I can and then forage for food. There are usually a couple of tins of spaghetti knocking around in the cupboard. It isn't steak, but it will do.

My phone rings again. I snatch it up, irritated now. 'What?'

'Did you get it?'

'Yes, thanks,' I say. 'I passed it to the police.'

Dave sounds terrified. 'No way, Dee! You—'

'I'm joking,' I say shortly. 'I'm not doing this.'

'They said I could offer you up to a hundred and fifty quid. They're trialling these things, testing them out.

If yours works, they'll do more in the area. It's worth their investment.'

I'm pressing the phone so hard to my ear that my ear hairs are buzzing. 'No.'

'Dee, I meant something to you once. They'll kill me if I don't sort my debt out. You want that for me? You want my death on your conscience?'

'I thought they were only after your balls,' I say, and hang up.

On Friday evening I prowl behind the Gaslight bar, watching the doors of the auditorium like a cat waiting for the mouse convention to emerge for their half-time cheese. Honor is making a final decision about the show tonight. They're in there right now, deciding my future. That's what this is. No show means no job, no money, no college, no research work, nothing ahead of me but pulling pints and dreaming of what could have been.

'I'm guessing you know that if she cans it, there'll only be enough work for me and Jem?' Val says, turning the screws. 'I'm sorry love, but that's economics.'

Keynes is nodding sagely somewhere, an otherworldly wind riffling through his moustache. I nod, biting my lip. I can taste the blood.

'It'll be panto season in a month's time,' she says. 'Plenty then for a hard worker like you.'

A hundred and fifty would tide me over until panto season, with a couple of extra bar jobs through Oz along the way and the odd stroke of luck.

'Great,' I say, hopelessly. 'Thanks.'

Val pops out for milk as Jem strides among the tables, disinfectant in one hand and cleaning cloth in the other. The bruising on his face has gone down, and is now brown and yellow at the edges. Whoever did it really worked him over. I hope they have a couple of bruises of their own to show for it. I watch him for a bit, wondering if I'll ever see him again after tonight.

Coming up to the bar, he sets his squeegee and his cloth down. 'You look like a corpse,' he says bluntly.

I should have conditioned my hair this morning, I realize. It is standing out around my head like an anaemic microphone. My shirt needs a wash too. My mind hasn't been on shampoo bottles and laundry baskets of late.

'I saw you in a car yesterday,' he says. 'On Leasford Hill.'

I blanch. 'What were you doing there?'

'Running.'

I stare at him, feeling hunted. *Your deeds will find you out.*

'Who was the guy?' he asks. Ever so casually.

'No one important,' I manage to reply.

'Looked like maybe that ex of yours.' He studies me. 'Whoever it was, was making you laugh.'

I remember the runner now. The Pringles crumbs. Talk about timing.

'Been to the bank yet?' he says, with a sudden subject swerve that should make me feel calmer but doesn't.

I roll my eyes jerkily. I probably look like a terrified cow. 'I'll go in my own time, OK?'

I wish I'd never told him about the flaming bank. Right now I'm feeling like a kid caught shoplifting and I haven't even *done* anything. The air crackles. We are back in the wardrobe, talking of life and death, guilt and responsibility, and the scent of him is making me breathless.

I need to get away from him. I need to know what they are deciding through the double doors of doom. The two elements come together with perfect urgency as I half-run towards the auditorium doors, tripping over my bag in my haste. Opening the doors as quietly as I can, I enter the dark space.

The stage is lit softly, illuminating a beautiful set: an Italian courtyard, cobbles on the floor, a flight of stairs rising to some kind of balcony. The cast is sitting slumped in metal chairs beside an ornately tiled fountain.

'More!' Honor shouts, banging away at the piano.

No one is giving it much. The air of hopelessness is tangible. The voice coach rubs her face with long-taloned fingers. 'Give me a reason to keep this going, people. *A weddin' and a beddin', it's where we'll all be headin', although the bride is lookin' kind of pale . . .'*

'*A weddin' and a beddin'*,' drones the chorus in response, '*is something Hero's dreadin', and not for fear of treadin' on her veil . . .'*

'Can't say I'm looking forward to it much myself,' says Patricia.

I slide out again as silently as I entered. They won't be continuing after tonight. My granny could sing that stuff better, and she's dead.

The contents of my upturned bag lie spilled around Jem's feet beside the bar. Tampons, tissues, a hairbrush. The swipe machine is in his hand. I think haphazardly of a guinea pig facing a jaguar deep in the Amazonian jungle because that's the way I roll when I'm in a corner and there is precisely *no way out*.

'When exactly,' Jem says in a voice of dangerous calm, 'did you start keeping a spare card reader in your bag?'

I am so frightened by the sight of Jem holding the machine that I practically wet myself.

'What are you doing, going through my stuff?' I manage to say.

'You kicked your bag over,' he says. He rises slowly to his feet, waggles the incriminating gadget from side to side. 'What the hell is this?'

'I know it looks bad,' I begin, trying to get a grip on the situation. 'But seriously, I—'

He pulls his arm back and lobs the machine across the room. It skids on the crusty carpet, takes out a wastepaper basket, whangs into a fire extinguisher with the most appalling clang and breaks in half. He points at the bruise on his face, his voice way calmer than his gaze. 'I got this for you,' he says.

I stare at him, uncomprehending. 'What?'

'Go to the bank. Go to the bank. How many times do I have to say it?' He runs his hands through his hair, swears under his breath. 'You were about to rip off my *mother*, Delilah!'

I urgently need to explain. 'I *wasn't*—'

He is advancing towards me. 'Banks don't care if you've spent your own money. They only call when there's a problem. A *real* problem. *I can't believe you'd be so stupid as to add to that problem.*'

'I wasn't going to use it! I swear!'

My head is going BOOM BOOM BOOM. I can't think. The questions are still coming.

'You carry spare card readers around for fun? Where did you get it?'

'I wasn't going to use it!' I repeat helplessly. 'I was going to chuck it in the river after work!'

His expression suddenly changes. 'You got it from your so-called ex, didn't you? Dave, the guy in the car? The one that was making you laugh, the one you wept all over me for?'

He isn't listening. This is bad. I cover my face with my palms. THIEF is as good as inked on the backs of my hands.

'I can't believe I fell for you,' he says in wonder. 'I thought you were real, Delilah. What kind of idiot am I?'

There is a massive wrecking ball of misunderstanding crashing through the bar, choking everyone with dust.

'I know what you must think, but I wasn't going to use it,' I insist, shaking like tissue paper in a high wind. 'It was tempting, but I wasn't – things have been really hard lately, but I would never . . .'

He leans towards me, his voice low and hard.

'Liar.'

Hell isn't hot. It's a freezing, merciless space, bleak and dark and lightless, unbroken by anything but buses going the other way. I throw my phone into the first bin I pass on leaving the Gaslight. Chuck my holey Vans in the next one. All the screaming and shouting and pleading in the world, and Jem still looked at me like I was a heap of nothing. I showed myself the door before he could do the honours.

I make it home with shredded feet and get into bed in my clothes, and there I pretty much stay. Rigid with injustice and shrivelled with guilt at the same time. Dry-eyed. Thinking.

At least ten times over the weekend I sit bolt upright as a car pulls up outside, convinced it's the police coming to cart me off to jail. I didn't do it! I want to shout at the walls. I did *nothing*!

At times like this, it would be nice to have a mum that I can talk to. But I don't, so I keep staring at the walls and thinking. By Wednesday my sheets are starting to stink, but I can't find the energy to do anything about it. I can barely move.

'Someone to see you,' Dad shouts up the stairs on Wednesday afternoon.

Tab stops at my bedroom door, wafting her hand vigorously in front of her nose. 'It reeks in here,' she declares. 'What's going on? Why haven't you been answering your phone? Oz said today you haven't been in college all week.'

'I've been ill,' I say, not looking at her.

Picking her way gingerly through the mess on my floor, she opens my bedroom window and wafts her hands some more. 'Since when has illness stopped us talking to each other at least once a day?'

'I don't have a phone any more.'

'Why weren't you there when we came out of the last rehearsal? Honor canned us. Our sorrows got so drowned they grew tails and fish gills. Even Sam had half a shandy.' Tabby stops and visibly rewinds. 'You don't have a *phone* any more? What are you, dead?'

The mid-October air coming through my window is cool and a little damp. Reviving, somehow. I burst into tears. Tab rushes to put her arms around me.

'Is it Jem?' she asks.

This provokes a fresh storm of weeping. I tell her about

208

Dave's inane idea about the cash fraud and about Jem hating me forever.

'And the stupidity of it all is that it started with me doubting him and *his* friends,' I croak, gasping for air. 'And now he's doubting me and mine. He won't ever trust me again because he thinks I've lied to him and that's his worst thing. He got that bruise for me, he said,' I add with a feeble flash of pride.

The look on Tab's face cheers me up a little. 'He must really love you for a bruise like that,' she says. 'What happened? Did he fight Dave?'

'I don't know!' I wail. 'This should be the big finale when I fall into his arms and he tells me how he got his shiner by vanquishing the evil Nazgul for love of me and instead I'm lying here with my life in shreds!'

'Everything's a mess,' Tabby says gloomily. 'The show's been cancelled. Sam and Maria are still together. Warren tried to get my number on Friday night. Patricia is talking about moving to the Bahamas. Desmond's at death's door and Eunice is heartbroken. She's been in love with Desmond for years, Patricia says. The only good thing all week has been Oz. He's been so sweet that he's stopped me dwelling on the rest.'

I wipe my eyes. Yelp as I get a blast of my own breath reflected back at me off Tabby's shoulder.

'Give me a minute?' I say out of the corner of my mouth.

'You might need longer than that,' she says kindly.

I return after a long shower, having brushed my teeth till they bled, scrubbed myself from head to foot, conditioned every inch of my hair and tried my damnedest to wash as much of myself down the drain as I could. Dad will kill me for using so much hot water, but as I haven't showered in several days I figure I'm owed at least half an hour. The thoughts I have been having are starting to crystallize into something. I daren't look too closely in case the crystals break up again.

In my absence, Tab has stripped my bed, gathered my scatterings into manageable piles on my desk and chair and opened the other window for extra air. She fills me in on the details of Friday night as I hunt out clean clothes, and I hang on every word, waiting for the bit where she says: 'And then they found a bust-up fake card machine and called the police!' She doesn't. Jem has cleared up my mess and not reported me, which makes me feel worse than ever.

There has to be a way out of this. There must be something I can fix. Maybe not Jem's feelings for me, but *something*.

'What are you going to do now?' Tab asks.

'Go to the bank, I guess,' I say wearily. 'Give them a chance to tell me what their problem is. You never know, I might get some money back.'

'Oz said he'd take me out tonight to cheer me up,' says Tabby. 'Come with us?'

'I don't think he'd be too pleased,' I say.

Tab rolls her eyes. 'It's not like that.'

I gesture at the pile of papers on my desk. 'I've missed three days of class. I need to crack on with that.'

'So you're not quitting college?' she says, looking relieved.

'Not yet, apparently,' I say, a little wryly.

My best friend flops back on my bare mattress. 'You know what really stinks about the whole show thing?' she tells the ceiling tiles. 'The scenery they built for us at the theatre. They'll rip it down at the weekend, turn it into firewood. It's stupid to feel so sad about it, but I do. I should be more bothered about all the wasted work we've done learning the songs, and the words, and the dance steps. But it's the pointless scenery that gets me. Dead before it ever came to life.'

When she has left, I carry my old sheets downstairs, stick them in the washing machine and make my bed with some fresh ones. Then I do myself a ham sandwich, return to my room and sit down at my desk to gaze at formulae and think about things that aren't formulae at all.

I feel like a surfer in Hawaii, paddling out on a soggy tissue box towards the biggest wave of my life. But hey, it's *my* tissue box. Sink or swim, at least I'm giving it a go. And that's all I can do.

Oz beams as I slide into Economics just before lunch on Thursday. 'Wasn't expecting you in this side of Christmas,' he says. 'Tab said you looked like a bulldozer had flattened you yesterday afternoon.'

My new Vans have been trying to eat my socks for the last half-hour. 'I just unflattened myself,' I say, yanking them up. 'How was your date with Tab last night?'

'It was a friends thing,' he corrects. 'She said "just friends" to me about fifteen times, just to make sure I'd got the message. The other people at the bar thought she was my girlfriend though. So that was nice.' He gazes a little wistfully at the whiteboard, where the teacher is jotting down stuff about aggregate supply and demand.

The morning I've had still feels unbelievable. Explanations from Egg Face about rigged cash machines in town, a couple of faxes with my signature on, and just short of four hundred quid back in my account. Seriously. It feels like I just found a unicorn in Tesco's. And it's incredible what you can achieve when you ride through a busy morning on a unicorn's back.

'Can you lend me your notes to cover what I've missed this week?' I ask.

'Haven't made many, but you're welcome to what I've got. Too busy trying to sort next week's Hallowe'en disaster. I took my eye off the ball for a couple of days because I was behind on college work and now everywhere's booked. Can you believe it? Biggest money spinner of the year and no venue. Nightmare.'

I am almost taken out by a second brain tsunami in as many days. Cogs whirr and turn, wheels within wheels.

'Have you tried the Gaslight?' I say.

'That's no good, Tab's show's in—' Oz stops and backtracks. 'The show's off, isn't it? Do you think I could get a deal on hiring it if I move fast enough?'

'Oh, the show's still on,' I say as he fumbles for his phone. 'Kind of. But you'll probably still get a good deal.'

He looks surprised. 'Tab didn't mention that last night.'

'She doesn't know yet. Organize your party there, Oz. Fancy dress for Hallowe'en,' I instruct. 'I promise it'll be worth your while.'

He taps his head. 'Did the bulldozers get your brain too? No one's going to get bombed around a geriatric crowd of musical-theatre goers.'

I want to laugh. *This* is the kind of control I was born for. 'What's with the insults?' I say. 'Everyone knows how much you love musicals.'

He fixes his eyes on me suspiciously. 'What are you planning?'

'It's not totally a done deal,' I say, hoping I've hooked him. 'But you'll be the first to know when it is. Just promise you'll look into a Hallowe'en party at the Gaslight a week on Saturday. *Promise me!*'

'Fine!' says Oz, reeling at the intensity in my voice. 'Weirdo.'

At lunch, my new phone has three missed calls and five texts on it.

Delilah, what the jolly bollies? Of course I'm still keen to do the show. I'll half-nelson Eunice, get the word around. See you later, P

Exciting! *claps hands* Rich and I up for it, Henry xx

I'm afraid I'm no longer available; I have already started coaching pantomime in Canterbury. Honor

Won't strike the set until Sunday. Enough time? Trevor (stage manager)

Is Tab still doing it? Sam

I consider my newborn idea without the experienced Honor at the helm. OK, so she was the most obvious choice of director, but not the only option if we get creative. And if the past twenty-four hours have taught me anything, it's 'get creative'.

To give myself strength, I gaze at Sam's blatantly nonchalant text about Tabby. I can fix this. Maybe more besides.

'Oz just told me the show's back on,' says Tabby, practically throwing her tray of food at me in her excitement. 'What have you done?'

I show her the texts. I particularly enjoy showing her the one from Sam. She goes bright red with delight.

'But you hate the theatre! You hate musicals! Your mum—'

'With a few adjustments,' I interrupt, '*What an Ado!* could become my new favourite show.'

My new phone is ringing. I feel prickles rushing up and down my arms as I catch the name on the screen. This is my big fish, the key to it all. If I can catch it, my weird idea might have legs. And I know fish don't generally have legs.

'Delilah? It's Ella.'

'Thanks for calling back,' I say. 'I have a proposition.'

'I'll do it.'

'You don't know what the proposition is yet,' I say, startled.

'Life is boring without the occasional risk. Spill.'

'Can we meet to talk about it?' I ask. 'It's tricky to explain on the phone.'

'Collective starts at five. Come here and we'll talk.'

My carefully constructed plans teeter as I hear her words with a punch of dismay. Thursday night? The collective? Jem will be there.

'Oh, and make sure you shave but don't moisturize,' she adds. 'My usual model's gone to Amsterdam. You're going to be my canvas instead.'

I exchange panicky glances with a bug-eyed Tabby, who is listening in.

215

Ella sounds amused by my silence. 'That's my price.'

The plan has been sounding so good in my head all day. Even without Honor, it has still felt doable. Now it is starting to fray at the edges. I pray to all the gods I can think of that Jem will give the collective a miss tonight.

I shut my eyes. 'I have to be gone by six,' I say.

Ella texts directions, which is just as well. I can't remember anything about the walk to the Watts Estate with Jem four weeks ago, beyond a consuming sense of irritation. Twists, turns, a greenhouse. I stop at the viewpoint where we kissed, swallow and move on.

Darkness is starting to sink its teeth into the day when I reach the flat. A couple of people are mixing paints already, and the music is low. Ella makes me turn on the spot as she assesses my shape, making me feel like a pig in a butcher's shop.

'I'll do your back,' she decides.

'I didn't shave my back,' I say, worried.

'Glad to hear it. I'm not into werewolves.'

I pile my hair on the top of my head and undress from the waist up, holding my hands to my pathetically flat boobs. Then I lie down on a table she's covered with a towel. This will be like a massage, with luck.

'So,' she says, wiping my skin clean from the nape of my neck to the bones of my coccyx. 'What's the proposition?'

'They cancelled the amateur show at the Gaslight,' I begin. 'I'm trying to revive it. The theatre's agreed not to get rid of the set, at least until I can confirm things at the weekend, and I'm trying to put the cast back together. The theatre manager thinks I'm insane, but seems happy for me to give it a go seeing how she might still make money on something she thought was dead in the water. There's a problem with the director, but I'll find someone else.' I stop and bite my lip. 'I hope I find someone else.'

'Do you have any idea what you're doing?'

'No,' I confess.

I try to relax as her brush makes its way up and down my back. It's not as electrifying as Jem painting my hand, but it's very soothing.

'And I come into it how?' she says.

'I wanted to ask if you and the rest of the collective would do the make-up.'

She paints what feels like some kind of line down my spine. 'I don't do pantomime dames.'

'You do make-up though,' I say. 'Amazing make-up. I thought . . .'

I stop. Saying it out loud seems so unbelievably stupid.

'You thought what?'

Oh God. Press on.

'I thought we could do the show as zombies,' I mumble.

'Jem said it was a Shakespeare musical,' Ella says after a pause. 'Not a slasher movie.'

'It's based on Shakespeare's *Much Ado About Nothing*,' I say, encouraged by the fact that she hasn't laughed. 'I think we could reinvent it again. The songs are good. The story has its problems, but if you make everyone zombies then it gets ironic. The set and the costumes stay the same, but with zombies and a few re-writes on the lyrics and some heavy green lighting . . . it might be good.'

Ella snorts. 'Grannies watch musicals. I've noticed grannies aren't greatly into zombies. They're a bit true to life when you're half-dead yourself.'

'Grannies aren't going to come,' I say. 'Students are. Combine a zombie musical with a Hallowe'en party in the theatre bar – I've got someone checking that out – and you've got something. I think. I hope.'

A long silence follows. I can feel her brush making little stabbing gestures down my spine now, flicking and flicking and flicking.

'You asked Jem about the make-up already?'

'What's he got to do with it?' I say uneasily.

I can feel her eyes boring into my back. 'You tell me.'

'I haven't seen him for a few days. I'm not his favourite person right now.'

'Ah, love,' Ella says mockingly. 'Can't live with it, can't iron its socks when they're still on its feet.'

'Who said anything about love?' I protest. 'Love is . . . not this.'

'If you say so. The publicity angle could be good. Will we get paid?'

I think of the funds back in my account. If the show continues, I'll still have a job. 'Yes,' I say. 'But I can't promise much.'

'I'll talk to the others. We design the zombie look, yes? When's the show?'

Oh. My. God. This is *happening*.

'A week on Saturday,' I say with a combination of gratitude and terror at what I've started. 'And you can design anything you like, as long as it's zombie-ish. What are you painting on me anyway?' I crane my neck, trying to get a glimpse.

'Don't move or I'll smudge you.'

She focuses on the top corner of my back, painting something in what feels like an inverted triangle near my shoulder. I manage a sneak look at my phone, which I've stationed near my head. Four texts and two voicemails will have to wait until my body is my own again. Ten to six. He could be here at any minute.

'Is Jem coming tonight?' I ask, nice and casual.

'He'd better.'

'How much longer—'

'It takes as long as it takes,' she interrupts, with a flash of the scary girl I first met. 'Just lie still.'

It is an uncomfortable ten minutes. My feet are pointing at the door, so every time it opens my heart beats like an African drum, waiting for his voice.

I squeal at the blasting sensation of sealant.

'Get yourself over to Kev for the shots,' says Ella with satisfaction.

Shielding my breasts with my hands, I swing myself off the table and walk across the room to the camera set-up. It feels like one of those dreams where you're not wearing anything on your bottom half and your T-shirt's too short for comfort. At least Jem isn't here – yet.

Kev's face isn't painted today. 'All right, Delilah?' he says, waving his light-meter. 'Back to me, won't take a minute.'

I gaze steadfastly at the long white backdrop as he takes a few readings. The camera clicks and whirrs. I start working through the thousand things on my brain list that I still have to do to make *What an Ado About Zombies!* a reality, to take my mind off my virtual nudity. Lists soothe me. They remind me of numbers, formulae, immutable things that can fix the world when placed in the right order.

The door opens.

'About time you showed up,' says Ella behind me.

'Always with the pit-bull impression, Ella. Some of us have jobs.'

The blood whooshes into my face, round my ears, down my neck. I am reddening all over like a boiled cricket ball. Still facing forward, gripping my boobs like two fried-egg-shaped life-jackets, I pray for invisibility.

'Finished,' says Kev. 'Take a look if you want.'

My hands are the only things between my modesty and

the eyes of the person who hates me most in the world. I'm not up to looking at anything.

'Later,' I mutter, sidling towards the corner which holds my bra, top and hoodie.

Ella's voice is brimful of mischief. 'Avert your oh-so-wide eyes from my model, Jem. I imagine you've seen it all before.'

I dive behind a curtain and pull on my clothes as fast as I can, stuffing my bra in my bag. *Be cool.* His stormy eyes are hostile as I re-emerge. The bruising on his face has almost all gone. He folds his big arms across his chest like armour.

'What are you doing here?'

'It doesn't matter,' I mutter, brushing past him and doing my best to ignore the leap of heat in my belly caused by one tiny touch of his skin.

'Don't be vile, Jem,' Ella says. 'Delilah's—'

I blaze a message of pleading in her direction. She is quicker off the mark than Val, correcting herself smoothly mid-sentence.

'– leaving now.'

He grunts and heads for a space by the window, paints in hand.

Not forgiven then. I focus on Ella, trying now to transmit my thanks via traitorously watery eyes.

'Tell him about the show and the make-up,' I say in a low voice. 'Leave me out of it though.'

'What did you do to him?' Ella asks with interest.

'See you,' I say.

Shutting the door behind me, I concentrate on breathing for a bit. It is only as I head back down in the lift that I realize I still have no idea what Ella has painted on me.

Tears blur my vision most of the way back to town. As I make the turn on to the High Street, a big fat full moon peeps out from behind M&S, shining softly on me, lighting up the snot on my nose and cheeks like slug trails.

'Stop gloating,' I mutter at its shining face, and wipe my nose on my sleeve.

I have calls to make so I take out my phone. A new message from Ella flashes up, complete with attachment.

Ill unzip U any time

In the photo, I look much taller than I have ever pictured myself. A few escaped, darkish-looking curls lie on one shoulder. Below the curls I curve in and out again like a violin. A long zipper has been painted the length of my spine, silver teeth on a black ribbon. It is unzipped a couple of feet from the top and folded down on one side, revealing flesh, bone, ribs and the corner of a glistening heart.

I look more closely. The topmost edge of the heart has been chipped off, like a nick on the side of a china plate.

At eight pm, I'm in front of the reassembled cast for *What an Ado About Zombies!*, leaning against the long bar of Aphrodite's Moon to support my shaking legs. This is even more terrifying than my tragic Keynes presentation. Standing by the door, Oz gives me an encouraging wink.

'Thanks for coming,' I begin. 'It means a lot, especially since you've all bothered to come to this dive where the beer's not even very good.'

'Hey,' says Niko, prepared to be genial as I have brought more drinkers than he normally has on a Thursday evening. 'You don't like my beer, I got wine.'

'Bring out the bottles, Maestro,' Patricia booms. 'I'm buying.'

Cheerful conversations break out as Niko uncorks the retsina. Beneath the swinging bar sign of Aphrodite and her grapes, I reflect on the weirdness of a cast and how it can function as a single creature with one mood. One mood enhanced by free wine. I wish my mood would hurry up and enhance as well. I am cacking myself.

'OK,' I say, as the wine is passed around. 'First, the bad news. We don't have a director.'

Maria shifts in her seat and looks at Sam in annoyance. 'You didn't say she hadn't got Honor.'

'*Delilah* didn't get Honor, no,' Tab says, a little coolly. 'So *we* are going to choose someone else.'

'I could do it, I suppose,' says Maria with a show of reluctance. 'I directed a show at school once. It went pretty well.'

Patricia pours herself a generous glass of wine. 'Never directed anything in my life,' she says cheerfully. 'But I have this show tattooed on my broad backside so I'll give it a go.'

When Patricia wins the unanimous vote, Maria sinks back in her chair looking thunderous. I uncross my fingers and rub my knuckles. I'm proud of getting my idea this far, but I can't help the acute sense of relief that there's finally a grown-up involved.

'Everyone at the theatre's still up for it,' I go on as they all settle down again. 'Costumes, set, box office. Oz over there is in charge of publicity, and sorting out the cast party.'

Oz waves, then goes back to scrolling through his screen.

'What about the band?' asks Eunice.

My eyes widen. I have forgotten the band. 'Under control,' I lie, making a frantic mental note to track them down and beg them to stay in the show. 'We need to redo the posters though.'

'What's wrong with the old ones?' Henry asks.

This is the bit I haven't broken to them yet. I brace myself.

'We're renaming the show *What an Ado About Zombies!*,' I announce, before adding a little unnecessarily, 'because we're having zombies in it.'

Patricia spits out the large mouthful of wine she's just slugged.

'*Zombies?*' says Maria in horror.

'Genius!' blurts Tabby.

Everyone else is nodding or looking quietly stunned. I take this for encouragement.

'I've conducted some research and there's a definite market for shows with zombies in them.' My research has stretched to a few punts around Twitter, but no one needs to know that. 'Especially in this town, which as you know has got students everywhere.'

'Students never come near us,' Eunice says, a little sadly. 'Present company excepted.'

'Your usual audience won't like what we're doing, so we have to think wider,' I say. 'Hence the change of focus. Which brings me back to my point about the posters. Anyone handy with a spray can? I need someone to go around the town centre adding *About Zombies!* to all the posters that are already out there. It'll be fiddly, but it's cheaper than reprinting. It'll also look kind of street, which is important if we're trying to get a younger crowd through the theatre doors. Volunteers?'

Two of the older members of the chorus – I don't know their names – look at each other and raise their hands.

'I use a can of hairspray most days,' says one. She nods at her even more elderly companion. 'So does Dorcas.'

I scrutinize their solid grey helmets. 'Er, OK,' I say, overcome with a mad urge to laugh and bolt for the hills. 'Thank you, Dorcas and . . .?'

'Gladys.'

I'm curious. 'Do you like zombies, Gladys?'

'Mad for them,' Gladys says comfortably.

Maria pushes back her chair with an angry scraping sound.

'Babe,' Sam says, reaching out a hand to stop her. 'It could work.'

'It's the most stupid idea I've ever heard,' Maria spits, shoving his hand away. 'Not in a million years am I doing it. The agency scouts will *laugh* at us.'

'Director's vote still rankling?' says Warren.

For the first time, as Maria blasts him with a look of withering fire, I see a glimmer of likeability about Warren.

'Leave if you want to, Maria.' Patricia has come to stand beside me at the bar, wine glass in hand. 'We'll pop Tabitha in as Beatrice instead, find someone to sing Hero. Shouldn't be too tricky. God knows, you're flat half the time.'

227

I almost feel sorry for Maria, who sits down again.

Patricia has slid so naturally into the role of director that I wonder why she hasn't been directing things from the start. 'I think Delilah deserves a round of applause for getting us here,' she goes on, looking round the room. 'She's not even in the show, but she's stepped into the breach like General Gordon. Bravo.'

Everyone claps. I wonder who General Gordon is, but look around the room and try to enjoy the smiles being aimed in my direction.

Sam is looking at me oddly.

'What?' I say, feeling defensive.

'Why are you doing this?'

How long have you got? I think. 'Lots of reasons,' I say out loud. 'I don't want the Gaslight to lose business, I don't like anything being wasted, I like zombies. Anyway, it's not me that's going to be doing it. It's you.'

'But why zombies?' Maria says in a plaintive voice. 'They're so *ugly*.'

I hope my ultimate weapon will prove the last piece in this extremely exhausting puzzle.

'Will you excuse me a second?' I say.

I hurry to the toilets, remove my top and hoodie, press them firmly up against my chest, swallow my blushes and hurry out again. The cast boggles at me as I present my back. Warren makes a kind of mooing noise.

'The girl who did this has a team,' I say, peering back at them all over my shoulder. 'She rang me ten minutes before you got here, confirming that they'll do the make-up for the whole cast. You're all going to look unbelievable.'

'If it's on, why aren't we meeting at the theatre like normal?' asks Rich.

'I didn't want Val to think it was on again, in case you all decided not to go for the new approach,' I say. That is half true. 'It wouldn't have been fair, getting her hopes up that you'd all be back buying drinks at the Gaslight if, well – you weren't.'

'But we'll be there tomorrow,' says Patricia, taking charge again. I am so grateful I could kiss her. 'Usual time. *What an Ado About Zombies!* is our phoenix. Or to be more accurate, our Frankenstein. And Maria, if you go to that bar even once before the break tomorrow night I'll demote you to the back row of the chorus.'

Several people cheer.

'More wine!' shouts Niko.

Tab rushes over to me as everyone gets out of their chairs and aims for the bar. 'That was *amazeballs!*' she says, bouncing around me like Tigger. 'What made you think of all this?'

'Repentance,' I say. I clutch my clothes a bit closer. 'Don't ask me any more, OK? Just go and chat up Sam. I have to go home and zombify a load of lyrics.'

In the little bathroom I pull my top and hoodie slowly over my head, and examine my face in the mirror over the sink. Yup, still me. Still breathing. I've done this thing, and now it is up and running. My stupid idea has come to life.

A zombie theme has never felt so apt. I want to sleep, but I still have stuff to do. Calling the almost-forgotten band for starters.

My phone rings at eleven. I lurch upright from where I have been snoozing on my desk.

'We're coming over.'

Tabby sounds strange.

'Who's we?'

'Me and Sam.'

My eyelids fly open like shutters in a thunderstorm. 'You and—'

'We got talking at the bar tonight and I mentioned how you were going to re-write some lyrics tonight and he said he's good at lyrics and suggested we come over to help you!'

From the bright, loud way Tab is talking, I gather that Sam is within listening distance and I am not allowed to say anything stupid like: 'Have you kissed him?' which he might overhear.

'Awesome,' I say, and gratefully lay my pen down over a heavily hatched area of paper where I've written *heart / cart / fart?!* 'I'm discovering that rhymes aren't really my forte.'

'Hi Delilah. Don't worry about the rhyming thing. I did poetry at GCSE.'

Sam has a nice voice. Deep. I picture him snuggling his ear up against Tabby to hear the conversation, and am amazed I can't hear Tabby wheezing beside him with badly suppressed desire. Maybe they are on speaker.

'Sam?' I say. 'Can I talk to Tabby on her own for a minute?'

There is a bit of rustling at the other end.

'He's still listening even though I just walked ten feet away from him down the road,' Tabby says in a low, agitated voice. 'Maria left half an hour ago – she's still in a massive strop about the show-as-zombies thing – but Sam stayed. And we started talking. And he truly honestly suggested the lyric thing all by himself.' Her voice starts rising. 'Lilah, do you think—'

'Don't think,' I order. 'Just get here. We have eighteen songs to rewrite, zombie-style.'

On the other end my best friend laughs hysterically.

'You might want to tone that down,' I advise. Despite my own pathetic situation, it is impossible not to smile. 'Girls who cackle like Vincent Price may not float Sam's boat.'

'We'll be with you in half an hour.'

I tidy my little room as best as I can. Check Dad is securely in front of the TV and OK with the prospect of guests this late. Locate three packets of Skips from the back of the cupboard in the kitchen. I don't examine the sell-by dates too closely. I line up the kettle, teabags, three mugs, a pint of milk and a box of sugar cubes. I am contemplating running the vacuum up the stairs when I hear Tab's tentative knocking.

'How far have you got?' Sam says, edging himself sideways through our skinny door.

'One song,' I say. 'Not great for two hours' work, sorry.'

'*Kissing?*' I mouth at Tab behind Sam's back. She blushes and shakes her head. I make encouraging faces. The fact that Sam is here at all is worth at least ten before the evening is out, in my opinion.

'This zombie theme has given me lots of ideas.' Sam puts his jacket neatly on one of the hall pegs. I hope the peg doesn't fall off the wall. Dad's DIY is patchy. 'Where's your room?'

'He's suprisingly forceful without Maria,' I whisper as Tabby and I follow him up the stairs.

'I know,' Tabby sighs.

I've never fully appreciated how small my bedroom is. Sam lounges across my bed with his feet dangling off the end. I perch at my desk. Tabby curls up on the carpet by Sam's feet and stares at his toes with longing.

'The first song, "Sore about the War".' I start singing it, while doing my best to ignore the startled expression on

233

Sam's face. Tab has heard my voice before so she doesn't react, much. '*Pretty sore about the war, pretty sore—*'

'*All this fightin' ain't excitin' but a bore,*' Sam and Tabby both sing out loud, him low and her high. Then they say 'Sorry' and blush and look hard at me as if I'm the most interesting thing in the room.

'I thought,' I say, after an awkward pause, 'we could rhyme *gore* with war instead of sore. *Love the gore in the war, love the gore.* And we call the song "Gore in the War" instead.'

Sam and Tab look expectantly at me.

'That's it,' I say.

'Good thing we came,' says Tabby the diplomat. 'We can work on the rest of that song later. What's next?'

'"Bad Baby Bea",' says Sam.

He and Tab start tentatively working out zombie rhymes. They both seem jumpy. The way they edge around each other makes me think of unfurling flowers ready to pull back into their buds at the first sign of a frost.

'*Bad Baby Bea,*' Sam hums, '*became a zombi-ee?*'

Possibly the worst lyric ever. GCSE poetry is going to be no help at all.

'Comfort break,' I say, getting up. 'Dazzle me when I get back.'

I stay in the bathroom as long as I can without appearing constipated. Pushing open my bedroom door very gently, I consider – with some disappointment – that Sam and Tab are sitting in exactly the same positions as before, hot mugs of tea in their hands. They have switched back to 'Gore in the War'.

'. . . So far we've got, *Love the gore in the war, love the gore, All this bitin' is excitin', not a bore.* Next line: *We need wine, we need women, or a vat of beer to swim in,*' Sam is humming. 'What can we do with that? *We need blood, we need brain . . .*'

Tab steadfastly studies his socks. The steam from her tea is misting up her glasses. 'We are all a bit insane,' she says vaguely.

'Brilliant,' says Sam in admiration, writing it down in big loopy writing. 'You're really good at this, Tab.'

Tab's whole face turns puce. 'I am?'

I write some new lists to soothe myself as they work through the rest of the song. The band – they call themselves the Slaughterhouse Seven – are still on. Have I covered everything else? Will Jem agree to join Ella's make-up team? Will she tell him I'm the cause of this new direction, this opportunity to showcase his mad skills to a wider world? If I know anything about Ella, she likes causing trouble. I feel a bit sick.

We move on to 'Who Needs a Wife', Benedick's big number. It's a tick list of women he's known and why none of them are wife material. You can see why I get wound up by this musical.

It is instantly improved by Tabby's rhyming genius. She is coming up with some absolute stonkers, fuelled by tea and the encouraging presence of Sam, who can't take his eyes off her. Soon we're all loudly singing, '*Ah dearest Katie, from sunny Haiti, she ate my eyes to my surprise and grew quite weighty, and lovely Linda, we met on Tinder, left her rotten and forgotten when I binned her. Who needs a knife, not I! Who needs a knife, not I!*'

We wallop through an astonishing eight songs. 'A Weddin' and a Shreddin'' is perhaps my favourite. We hardly have to touch Tabby's 'Love Eternal', because it's all about loving someone till you die, and as all the characters are already dead it's full of unintentional gags from start to finish.

'Tod Slaughter wrote a show for zombies without even realizing,' I say in delight.

Sam trumpets with sudden laughter. 'Tod *Slaughter*!'

It turns out that Tod means 'dead' in German too.

It's two am when I kick them into the night. They both promise to deal with the remaining lyrics over the rest of the weekend.

'Get Tab home safe and unmolested, Sam,' I say at the door without thinking.

I get a heavily loaded look from Tabby.

'Of course,' I say hurriedly, '*you* can molest her as much as you like. I was thinking more along the lines of weirdos in the shadows. Though of course with you going out with Maria and everything, I'm sure you wouldn't dream of it!'

My best friend does a finger-across-the-throat thing.

'I'm going to stop talking now,' I say before I make

236

things worse. 'I can't make the rehearsal tomorrow – today, I mean. Studying to do. Hope everyone likes the new improved lyrics.'

'I look forward to killing you,' Tab says in my ear as she kisses me goodnight.

'Thanks for the tea and crisps,' says Sam, shepherding Tab down the path. Leaving her by the gate, he comes back towards me.

'I'm an honourable guy,' he says in a low voice. 'Tabby's safe with me.'

That's what I'm afraid of.

'Great,' I say out loud.

I offer a limp fist-bump which he returns with vigour, and wave as they walk off together down the dark street. What's with all these honourable guys? They're more trouble than they're worth.

Fatima arrives on Tuesday. Actually, 'arrives' doesn't really cover it. 'Blasts in' is closer, or 'teleports'.

She is draped on the doorstep like a dying opera singer as I come in through the gate after a long day at college. She can never do anything without turning it into performance art.

'*Cherie*,' she husks, propping her head up on one elbow. 'I arrived since three hours and your father is not here and you don't answer your phone innit. A lot of English people say this on YouTube.'

I've been so preoccupied with the show and my endless looping anguish about Jem that I forgot her plane would come in today around lunchtime.

'I wouldn't lie there,' I advise, grinning. 'Mr Djembe next door's dog likes to pee on our mat.'

Fatima leaps to her feet with speed. For someone of her

size, it's an amazing thing to watch. She kisses me on both cheeks and puts her finger under my chin.

'You have a lot to tell me,' she observes. 'You will keep nothing back. Why don't you answer your phone?'

'New phone,' I explain. 'New number. Sorry.'

Fatima gazes around Wyvern Court, the different coloured doors, the walkways strewn with bicycles and potted petunias that all look brown in the street lights. Probably are all brown, actually, it being October.

'England is a nice place,' she says.

I decide to overlook the tone of surprise. 'Want to dump your stuff and hit the town?'

'We must hit your town until it falls down,' she agrees.

As she puts her sleeping bag and rucksack on my bed and disappears to the bathroom, I track down the old camp-bed mattress to its place of hibernation under the stairs. My room isn't enough to contain Fatima Ammour. This whole *block* isn't enough to contain her. I wonder what on earth Dad is going to make of her.

'You will now go in the bathroom and make yourself sexy,' Fatima declares, billowing out forty minutes later in an eyewatering cloud of perfume. Her eyes are ringed with kohl like the Algerian gypsy that she is, cascades of black hair falling down her back and dark berry lips gleaming.

'I'll feel as sexy as a slug next to you,' I confess.

'Go to the shower and we will make war on your face together.'

239

Half an hour later, with my hair bullied into shining curls and my eyes smokier than a barbecue grill, we slide out of the door.

'We can walk or take the bus,' I say, glancing cautiously at the sky. In the streetlight, it resembles old brown leather. 'Either way, I think we're going to get wet.'

'I have a better idea,' Fatima says.

She knocks on Mr Djembe's door before I can stop her. Mr Djembe's dog starts barking like a mentalist.

'Allo,' she purrs when Mr Djembe opens up.

'Sorry, Mr Djembe,' I say, firmly taking Fatima's arm. 'My friend knocked on the wrong door.'

'I see that you have bicycles, *monsieur*,' Fatima says, undeterred, gesturing at the two bikes chained beside Mr Djembe's door. 'We can borrow them?'

'I . . . suppose so,' says Mr Djembe, bemused.

Fatima kisses him twice, one on each cheek. The man looks half-fossilized with shock.

'We will return them very soon or you can tell Delilah to the police,' she says generously. '*Allez*,' she says to me. 'We can ride now.'

'You're unbelievable,' I yell when we round the corner, Fatima gliding ahead and me peddling my little legs like a maddened hamster to keep up. 'I've spoken to Mr Djembe twice in my life. And you steal his bicycles?'

'I don't steal.' Fatima leans in towards the kerb, one knee almost grazing the tarmac. Her long ebony hair billows behind her like a black pirate sail, the chiffony bits on her tunic threatening to tangle themselves in the spokes. 'I ask very nice and I borrow. Hey, you ride in the front. I don't know where I am going for the hot spots.'

A couple of cars parp us for riding without lights. I haven't ridden a bike since Mum left. The wind drives cold fingers through my hair, raking my scalp deliciously. Somehow I don't care all that much that my skirt is short and – with every corner, every gust of wind – steadily getting shorter. I whoop and crash through a set of traffic lights on amber. Pedalling behind me, Fatima sails blithely through the red, nearly taking out a couple of pedestrians and blowing such generous kisses of apology over her shoulder that one of them blows a kiss back.

Ten minutes later I stick one hand out and veer towards Aphrodite's Moon as we approach the station. It isn't the best place to drink in town, but when you are underage there aren't many options. Niko will turn a blind eye as long as we pay our bill. Dismounting, I hoik my skirt back down to a respectable length.

Fatima swerves right across the path of an oncoming Range Rover to join me at the pub door, earning a horrified blast on a horn.

'These English drivers are very bad,' she says, lowering the finger she has proffered at the shocked blond lady behind the wheel.

'Have you got a death wish?' I yelp. In a head-on collision with a Range Rover, even Fatima's indestructability would be tested. 'Cars drive on the *left* in England.'

Fatima's face clears. *'Desolée!'* she shouts, waving in the direction of the disappearing 4x4. 'So,' she says to me, gazing at Aphrodite's boobs swinging in the breeze. 'This bar has men?'

I glance through the window. The view isn't promising. 'It has Niko, the bar owner,' I say. 'He'll love you. But there's a problem. We can't leave these here.' I indicate the bikes. 'Not if we want to return them to Mr Djembe later. There's a bike rack at the station we can use, maybe.'

'Pah.'

Which is how we end up wheeling Mr Djembe's bikes through the door of Aphrodite's Moon, avoiding punters' ankles as best we can and giving Niko our most winning smiles. After an initial frown, he catches sight of Fatima.

'What can I get you?' he says in excitement.

Fatima shoots him her most smouldering stare through outrageously sooty lashes. 'I think you can maybe get me to heaven,' she murmurs, upping her French accent to heroic proportions.

Three free drinks later, and we have exchanged most of our gossip. Mine pales in comparison to Fatima's, but it's hard to compete when you're talking to someone for whom conquests are as frequent as buses. Half the drinkers in here haven't taken their eyes off her since we arrived. At least four guys try to hit on her as we talk, offering drinks and phone numbers, but she swipes them away like flies. I've never felt so invisible.

When I have brought her up to speed on generalities,

we move on to my present situation. I leave out certain details, like my real reason for resurrecting the show *à la* zombie and the bit about the swipe machine. The memory still makes me flush with shame from my head to my toes. I also fail to mention the Gaslight by name, and leave out precisely how hot Jem is. I'm not about to give Fatima Ammour ideas.

'So you like him, and you kiss him, and now he don't like you?' she summarizes, twirling her bottle of cider.

'It's not that simple.'

She clicks her tongue. 'With men, it is always simple. With Laurent, it was simple. With Dave *le bâtard* it was simple.'

There is nothing *simple* about my feelings for Jem.

'I can't work at the bar any more,' I groan. 'I can barely walk around my own town without knowing that I'll see him somewhere.'

'All of this searching in the soul,' Fatima grumbles. 'All you do is to have sex in the wardrobe.'

'We *didn't* have sex,' I say. 'And you make it sound like we were crashing around among coat hangers and lavender-scented drawer liners.'

Niko is hovering. Fatima gives him a devastating smile, and dazzles him into handing over two more bottles of cider and a free bag of peanuts.

'Niko never gives away free stuff,' I marvel.

'I think he is in love with me,' she says with satisfaction. 'But he is very old. *Salut*, Delilah.' She raises her bottle at me. 'I will tell you about the man in the airport today. He was very beautiful but his nose was too small. They say the nose is very important when you judge a man.'

She looks meaningfully at me over the top of her drink, then checks out the rest of the bar. 'This is the best you can show me in this town?' she inquires, looking disappointed.

'It's only Tuesday,' I bleat.

'Tuesday is the best night in Argole-sur-Mer,' says Fatima, unimpressed.

I check my watch. Nine-thirty. Rock on. I feel panicky. Pubs aren't really my thing. Nightclubs in this bit of Surrey are thin on the ground, and non-existent on Tuesdays. Fatima will be on the next plane home if I don't rustle up something better than this faded joint.

'I'll text Oz,' I say, fumbling for my phone. 'If anywhere's rocking tonight, he'll know about it.'

HELP.
French friend arrived tonight.
What's going down?

> Gaslight's banging. Totally the
> venue for Halloween. Get ur butt
> over here.
> Zombie on. <O>

'What is Gaslight?' Fatima reads over my shoulder. 'Pub? Nightclub?'

'We're not going to the Gaslight,' I squeak in a state of panic.

'Pah,' says Fatima for the second time that night.

I've forgotten how single-minded Fatima can be when in search of entertainment. I stutter at her as we wheel the bikes out of Aphrodite's Moon, deeply regretting how I failed to mention the Gaslight by name when I had the chance. We roll down the High Street and swing past the river towards the mouth of Hell with me hissing like an enraged goose all the way.

'Don't make me go in there,' I implore as we come to a breathless halt at the foot of the Gaslight steps.

Music pumps into the street from the bar, enticing as a siren on a rock in the middle of a stormy sea. Fatima looks up at the pink-lit basking-shark windows approvingly and starts up the steps, where the glass doors swing shut behind her and Mr Djembe's best bicycle. I sigh and plod up the steps after her, heaving my wheels behind me.

The place is swamped. A younger crowd than normal

swarms the bar alongside the post-rehearsal cast of *What an Ado About Zombies!* and there is a buzz about the place that takes me back to the start-of-term party. I can't believe my eyes. College kids, here? Mid-week?

Fatima slings her bike behind the sofa by the double doors and absorbs the shoving throng, assessing, dismissing, noting the talent with lethal precision.

'I am glad we come,' she pronounces.

Towering over the top of stretching arms and heads at the bar I make out Jem's hair, glossy and gorgeous as ever. I stuff my bike behind the sofa alongside Fatima's and wonder if I'll fit back there as well.

'Delilah!' Val shouts, fighting her way towards us with glasses held high above her head. 'This place has turned into a lunatic asylum. Did you know the show's back on? They're rehearsing every night this week, and bringing the world with them. You want your job back? You can get behind the bar right now before Jem collapses under the strain!'

'This is the place with the man and the wardrobe?' Fatima says in surprise, turning to me.

'And it's too late to leave now,' I mutter. 'She just offered my job back.'

'That is good! You always say you are broken.'

She drives me *mad*. 'Didn't you listen to anything I told you? I can't work here because *he* works here!'

Fatima strafes the bar. Her gaze slows at the sight of Jem's long, muscular arms reaching up to the optics. 'Oof,' she says with a deep, sucking intake of breath.

Jealousy bites down hard with sharp green teeth. 'Don't,' I say.

Her gaze is now sliding along Jem's jawline and down into the neck of his black T-shirt until she is practically licking the shadowed dimple of his collarbone with her eyeballs. Fear grips me by the throat.

'Promise me,' I almost shout.

'OK, OK,' Fatima grumbles. 'I don't go near him except for a little drinking. And maybe sexy talk?'

'No sexy talk!'

'You want the job or not?' Val shouts at me over the hubbub.

'I will work tonight,' Fatima announces.

It's a solution, I realize, once I've got over the surprise. With any luck I'll have sorted the Jem situation by the time Fatima leaves, and my job will still be waiting for me on her departure. Theoretically.

'I will keep Jem warm for you, *cherie*,' says Fatima, fluffing her hair as Val nods and mows on through the crowd. 'Like a chicken with an egg.'

More like a lioness with a wildebeest, I think.

'Delilah!'

Oz stops dead at the sight of Fatima clearing a path towards the bar. Even from behind, she is magnificent.

'I thought you said your French friend was brainy,' he accuses, his eyes like saucers.

'Sexy and brainy aren't mutually exclusive, Oz.' If Fatima

248

gets off with Jem, I'll kill her. 'What's going on? The Gaslight's never full like this.'

Oz is still watching Fatima recede. 'I . . . what?'

'She affects everyone within a two-hundred-metre radius. Like plutonium,' I say kindly. 'The bar? The action?'

'It started with your posters,' says Oz when he gets his focus back. 'Those grannies you armed with spray cans have done a fantastic job. Apparently they got stopped by the police on the High Street, and had a time explaining themselves. Meanwhile I've been putting out the word that this is the place to be seen. I'm combining tickets for the fancy-dress party on Saturday with tickets for the show. Take-up's already looking good.' He looks in Fatima's direction again. 'Where's she going?'

'To serve a lot of beer,' I say.

'Mine not to question why, mine just to get the beverages. What are you drinking?' He looks me up and down. 'You're looking good tonight, by the way. Liking the boxer eyes.'

'Lilah!' says Tab joyfully, leaping to her feet as I make my way to where half the cast are sitting at a table. 'I thought you were never setting foot in this place again?'

'Never say never,' I mutter. 'Fatima rocked up on my doorstep a couple of hours ago and now she's behind the bar. Say what you like about that girl, she's a fast worker.'

Word on the new barmaid is out. Half the room – the male half, by and large – has surged towards the bar for sudden refills. Oz finds our table and plonks several bottles down, a far-away look in his eyes.

'I'm in love,' he says. 'She's bringing the rest of the order in a moment.'

'Her surname's not "Ammour" for nothing,' I say.

Tabby cranes her neck towards the bar, eager for a glimpse of the legend that is Fatima Ammour, but is foiled by a sea of boys' backs.

'Musical in a Month should officially be renamed Miracle in a Month,' Patricia enthuses to me. 'I can't believe this zombie business hasn't been tried before. The songs fit perfectly and Sam and Tabitha's new lyrics are terrific. I can honestly say that I haven't laughed this much since Alan died under that tree.'

'How's Desmond?' I ask.

'A little better I believe.' Eunice tugs her cashmere cardie around her body. 'Mortality is such a ghastly thing.'

'Mortality's a hard topic to avoid when you're playing a zombie,' Patricia says. 'I can't decide if telling Desmond about our new approach will push him through the Pearly Gates or shock him back to this life, so for Eunice's sake we're holding fire.'

'Patricia,' Eunice protests, blushing.

Sam and Maria are sitting together at a table across the room. I want to hurl my cider bottle at the girl, chase her off Tabby's property like an aggressive guppy.

'It's OK,' Tab says, doing her best to sound serene. 'He told me a few times on the way home on Saturday night how crazy he is about her.'

'Are you sure he wasn't just saying that to keep himself

on the straight and narrow with you?' I check.

A glimmer of hope wanders across her face, a lost duck in search of a pond. 'I wish.'

'Drinks, *mes biches*.'

Fatima leans in at Oz's eye-level, placing bottles and glasses in front of everyone. Our table is suddenly swamped by boys sticking out their chests and doing little chicken struts to get her attention. It's hard to introduce her amid the madness, but I do my best. She does the two-kiss thing to everyone around the table, even Warren.

'I have already twenty pounds in the tips,' she confides, patting her bosoms.

'How's Jem?' I ask casually.

'I don't talk so much with him yet. We have no time. We already change two beer barrels. I must go back. Laters, alligators.'

She runs a finger thoughtfully down Warren's nose and chucks him under the chin before the crowd swallows her up again. Warren touches his nose in wonder.

'I love her.' Oz props one elbow dreamily on the table and rests his chin in his hand. 'Did I already say that?'

'Even I fancy her,' says Rich.

Henry frowns. 'You don't.'

'I do. But I fancy you more.'

'She reminds me of myself at that age,' says Patricia as Rich and Henry beam at each other. 'Fatima Ammour. Are we sure that's not a stage name?'

'She's Algerian,' I say. 'Descended from bandits.'

'She can rob me anytime,' Warren mumbles.

'There's more chance of our little zombie hell freezing over, I fear,' Patricia says to me, in a low voice for once.

I consider Warren's nose. It's actually kind of enormous.

'I wouldn't be so sure,' I say doubtfully.

My stomach folds in half at the sound of Jem's voice calling last orders at eleven. I've been sitting with my back to the bar for maximum avoidance of eye contact, and have been relatively successful. The only time he looks at me is when I weave my way a little unsteadily to the bathroom, eye make-up probably running down my face like Usain Bolt in sooty shoes. His gaze is dark, his face set in a frown.

By midnight the bar has cleared. Tabby has left with stoic kisses, Rich and Henry with high-fives, Eunice with a delicate wave and Patricia a less delicate one. It's strange, watching the evening's action wind down from a punter's viewpoint instead of with my head dipping in and out of the dishwasher.

'You waiting for Fatima?'

I leap out of the sofa like I'm wearing a pair of jumping

stilts. He's approached as quietly as a ghost.

'I – what?' I say. Slick, I think.

'She's disappeared somewhere. Probably the bathroom.'

'Oh,' I say. 'Yes. Thanks.'

There is an awkward silence. What is a girl supposed to say to a guy who thinks she is a waste of space?

'Fatima's . . .' I watch him hunt down a suitable adjective. 'Something,' he concludes.

'Mmm.' Oh crusty carpet, swallow me now.

'Not really my type though.'

I decide to take refuge in attack. 'Why? You catch her with her fingers in the till?'

He doesn't answer that. 'How are you?' he asks instead.

Drunk, I realize. 'Me?' I say out loud. 'Oh, I'm brilliant. Fantastic. Like one of those swans.' He looks puzzled. I paddle with my hands. 'All elegance and refinement on top but swimming for my life below.'

'Right,' he says.

'What do you care anyway,' I say morosely.

He stares at me like he's trying to peel back the layers and get to the nerve endings beneath my skin. Trying to burn through to the truth. 'Just taking an interest.'

'Didn't think I was worth your interest.'

He fiddles with his ear. 'Delilah—'

'I'm not up to a repeat of our last conversation, if that's where you're going.'

'I'm not,' he says. 'Trust me.'

Why should I trust you when you don't trust me? I think.

More silence.

'What were you doing at the collective last week?' he asks at last.

'Ella asked me.'

'Oh,' he says. He pauses. 'I didn't think you knew her that well.'

Ella hasn't shopped me. Part of me is a little annoyed. I know I asked her to stay quiet, but having Jem know I am trying to put things right would be . . . comforting.

That isn't the point, of course.

'Guess I know her better than you think,' I say waspishly.

'Guess you do.'

This conversation is flowing as smoothly as molten fudge. It's Willy Wonka's chocolate river, warm and rich and fulfilling. I stare out of the double doors for a bit, at the dark brown night. Perhaps he'll go away.

'I keep seeing you in my head,' he says eventually. 'Laughing.'

'Oh, I'm a laugh a minute,' I agree. 'Though of course, criminal intent runs through me like Brighton rock. Which is a flaw.'

Where is Fatima? I am getting reckless with this strange grief I am feeling.

'I hated it.'

'What, Brighton rock?'

'You, laughing. With him.'

'You put me on trial,' I say, angry suddenly. 'You found me guilty. So what if I laugh with someone that isn't you?'

'What were you laughing about?'

'I was laughing about my impending villainy,' I say. 'Wasn't I?'

We both hear a strange noise. It seems to be coming from the box office. Jem glances at the closed ticket window, then looks back at me.

'All I know is that I hated it,' he says.

'What are you condemning me for here?' I demand. 'Having a laugh with the wrong person or planning my heist?'

We are both angry now.

'How can you *joke* about this?'

'Best thing to do in desperate circumstances. If you're so convinced that I'm a thief, why didn't you tell Val?'

'What makes you think I didn't?'

'She offered my job back.'

Lightning flickers across his eyes. 'So why didn't you take it? Not many thieves get a second opportunity. Busy bar tonight. Plenty of profit.'

'I thought I would find the working environment a little trying,' I say through gritted teeth.

The odd noise has started up again. It's definitely coming from the ticket office.

Jem swears loudly. 'Got one of your pals in to clean out the safe?' he inquires, striding towards the ticket office.

'If that's a thief,' I roar after him, 'they're the noisiest . . .'

I suddenly realize something with ghastly clarity. Jem does too.

'Is it just me,' he says, his footsteps slowing, 'or does that sound like—'

Warren's head pops up over the ticket office desk. A long hand with dark red fingernails slaps across his mouth and pulls him back down.

Fatima means 'abstinence' in Arabic. Talk about ironic.

'*Vive la France*,' Jem says in wonder.

'I wish I could say she isn't normally like this,' I squeak through my fingers in an agony of embarrassment, 'but we all know how you feel about lies.'

Jem indicates the kitchen diplomatically. 'Perhaps we should . . .'

'Right behind you,' I mumble.

By the time we reach the kitchen and shut the door behind us, Jem is nearly paralyzed with laughter. 'Know any good songs we could sing?' he chokes out, leaning against the lockers for support. 'You know – loudly?'

The only one I can think of is 'My Generation' and look where that got me. 'Nothing's coming to mind,' I say weakly. 'You?'

'*People try to put us down*,' he sings close to my ear.

My knees actually buckle. Fold sideways and lose anything approaching substance. His breath is warm.

'Not that one,' I say.

He stops laughing and visibly collects himself. 'Sorry.'

We concentrate on the sink, wiping and stacking. I have never been so aware of him in my life.

Val comes into the kitchen from the back yard. She stops when she sees us, back to rigid back, silently scrubbing the kitchen surfaces.

'Isn't Fatima supposed to be doing this?' she says.

The kitchen door opens. Fatima sweeps her fringe out of her eyes. ''Allo,' she says, sounding a little breathless. Over her shoulder I see Warren sliding out a little unsteadily through the double doors.

Val lobs Fatima her pay packet. 'Great work. Same time tomorrow?'

Tomorrow? I never work Wednesdays.

'I will be here,' Fatima says gaily.

Jem keeps scrubbing surfaces and doesn't look up as I tow Fatima towards Mr Djembe's bicycles, still stashed behind the sofa.

'You are a true piece of work,' I hiss. '*Warren?* Are you insane?'

We push the bikes through the doors and bump them down the steps. Warren has disappeared. I hope he's fallen down a drain.

'I think I will teach Warren many interesting things,' Fatima says in a contented voice.

The doors clatter open behind us.

'You'll want lights for those,' Jem says.

He tosses me a set, then a second lot for Fatima.

'*Chéri*,' Fatima gasps, examining the lights like they are

258

precious jewels. 'They are adorable. For us?'

'Someone left them here last week,' Jem says shortly. 'Try not to get run over between now and tomorrow.'

'He is so pretty,' Fatima sighs as he closes the doors. 'It is a shame about his nose.'

Ella's call takes me by surprise on Thursday.

'What, the whole cast?' I say, my canteen sandwich halfway to my mouth.

'No, just the ugly ones,' she says, dripping sarcasm like rain off an umbrella. 'Of *course* the whole cast. Everyone's got different faces. Different angles, different elements to work with. We've done our designs but we need to practise them. Can you get them here tonight?'

'Can't you do it at tomorrow's dress rehearsal?'

'Need to know what paints to bring to the theatre. You want this make-up to look good or not?'

Ella is jittery. It strikes me she is just as nervous about this as me.

'Maybe we can take a portable keyboard and rehearse there,' Tab says, listening in. 'Run through the songs while we're being painted.'

'Sort it, Delilah,' says Ella. 'As close to five as you can. There's a lot of you to get through.'

The buzzing tone informs me that she's rung off.

'Do you think Patricia really will agree to rehearse at Ella's flat tonight?' I ask Tab, lowering my phone uncertainly.

'I don't see why not.'

'But the show's in two days' time! You need to be on the actual stage, with your props and everything. Don't you?'

'Done the staging already,' Tab says. 'We've all gone up a gear since your brainwave. Call Patricia and give her details. I can't wait to try my zombie look,' she adds with enthusiasm. 'I hope I get flaking skin. Maybe bleeding eyes.'

She taps Ella's address into her phone, pulling up a map.

'Hi,' says Warren, appearing at the end of our table. 'Is Fatima around? I didn't get a chance to, er, talk to her last night.'

I left Fatima on her camp-bed mattress this morning, draped like a flamboyant starfish across half my carpet after another full evening behind the Gaslight bar. I haven't told Tab the full facts of Tuesday. They are too gruesome.

'Is she working at the theatre again tonight?' Warren says hopefully. 'I'd kind of like to see her again.'

'And I'm sorry to report that she'd kind of like to see you again too,' I say.

Warren adjusts his face with a transparent attempt at nonchalance. 'I'll er . . . do my best to fit her in.'

'We're getting painted tonight, Warren,' Tabby says. 'I'll text everyone directions to Ella's flat. We're meeting there from five. I guess we'll all head to the Gaslight afterwards.'

'Great,' says Warren. He shifts from foot to foot. 'Sorry I've been a bit of an idiot about the whole lesbian thing.'

'We're not lesbians,' says Tabby patiently.

Warren's phone beeps. He pulls it out and stares at Tab's message. 'Five tonight?' he says, walking away with his nose to his screen. 'Cool.'

Tabby gets busy with her list of cast members' mobile numbers and attaches the map. I picture the directions being fired in thirty different directions from a load of tiny cannons on the tabletop.

'You'll have to do it the old-fashioned way with the oldies,' I remind her. 'Phone them up. Post them printouts.'

'Gladys is on Facebook. Dorcas has a iPad. Everyone's covered.'

At four-thirty I stand shivering at the bottom of the High Street. Despite Tab's texted directions, a mass of calls from assorted cast members asking for someone to guide them through the scary maze of the poorly lit Watts Estate has resulted in an old-fashioned element after all: me, waiting to escort old ladies Gladys and Dorcas and students Sam, Maria, Warren and Tabby like a tour guide with an umbrella in Piccadilly Circus.

Fatima has come along for the ride. She flaps her arms. 'English weather,' she grumbles.

'Your coat's too thin,' I say. 'You could get one of those long downy ones you see in *Grazia* with your Gaslight earnings. I can't believe Val had you working last night. I only got Fridays and Saturdays.'

'Tonight too. I am popular,' Fatima says without apology.

'Everyone ready?' I ask as Gladys finally turns up.

'Thunderbirds are go,' says Dorcas.

'You will be my 'ot water bottle, *chéri*,' Fatima shivers, linking arms with Warren and making his cheeks light up.

'That girl's rather obvious, isn't she?' Maria says loudly, one gloved hand tucked into Sam's elbow. 'She shouldn't get Warren's hopes up like that. Anyone can see the poor boy's developing a crush.'

The road is steep. Dorcas rubs at the panes on a greenhouse and admires the tubs of growing things inside. Fatima sings French marching songs, stamping her booted feet and moving in synch with Warren, as I shepherd and cajole and warn of puddles like a teacher on a school trip.

'Why aren't there any posters along here?' says Dorcas as we climb.

Gladys pushes her sleeves up. 'Set to, Dorcas.'

Dorcas pulls spare posters from her handbag and sticks them on fences as we pass. Gladys gets industrial with a spray can of yellow paint she has tucked in her rucksack.

'I've got a stitch,' Tab says. 'Is it much further?'

We reach the double doors of Ella's building at around five-fifteen. The lift is too small for all of us, so we go up in two groups. Patricia answers the door in a fug of marijuana smoke and the wall-shaking sound of a boom box at full volume. Her face is red and fleshy and covered in unpleasant welts.

'You look rotten, Patricia,' says Dorcas and giggles.

'Bang on for a first attempt,' Patricia shouts over the music. 'Eunice and I got here half an hour ago.'

Eunice waves at us from a chair in the middle of the room, her face half-painted in the same style as Patricia's.

'Those with honest jobs are coming after work.' Patricia is holding something that looks suspiciously like a joint. 'Pick anyone you like, darlings.'

'She's stoned,' whispers Maria disapprovingly to Sam.

Patricia points the reefer at Maria. 'I can hold my smoke better than your boyfriend can hold his drink. Looking ugly's going to do you the world of good, girl.'

Sam is coaxed away with a lad whose head is half shaved and whose nose looks like it won't support much more in the way of metalwork.

'Can you make me a *pretty* zombie?' Maria asks plaintively as a willowy jet-haired boy – the one Ella was painting with angel wings the first time we met – leads her towards a stool.

'I'll go, shall I?' I say to no one in particular.

'Oh, don't!' says Tabby at once. 'Ella, can't you paint Delilah again?'

'I'd love to, but I have to make that chick look like a corpse.' Ella nods at Gladys.

264

'Shouldn't take long,' says Dorcas naughtily.

I keep meaning to leave, but somehow stay. Maria skulks over to the camera, looking as miserable as a green-faced zombie can, as Kev takes photos and chats her up. Sam is enjoying himself a lot more with Mr Metal, to judge from the gales of laughter sweeping through the room from their corner.

At six, Rich and Henry blow through the door with wine and a twelve-pack bag of crisps.

'You all look like hell,' says Henry admiringly as Rich uncorks the wine and sloshes it generously into polystyrene cups.

'Mission accomplished,' says Patricia, her second joint of the evening drooping between her lips. She has set up a small portable keyboard. 'Do you mind turning your music off, Ella love? From the top, you half-dead darlings.'

There is something both odd and awesome about hearing old-style musical tracks sung by zombies. A couple of Ella's team members wrinkle their noses. Sam's Mr Metal adds a few *Be-dooby-dooby-doo*'s during 'Gore in the War'.

'This music is like Marmite,' says Ella. She adds a layer of ripped skin to Gladys's neck. 'You spend the whole day trying to sponge it off your vest and by teatime the bastard's still there.'

'*Merde*,' says Fatima suddenly. 'I am late for my job.'

'Don't worry about it,' says Jem, coming through the door as she races past him in a billow of chiffon. 'Mum will only rip your head off.'

His T-shirt is dark red tonight, and fits his chest like someone has painted it on to his body. Not unlikely, in present company. Our eyes meet. Flick away. Meet again. Kind of like those magnetic dogs that sniff each other's rear ends but leap apart when you put them nose to nose. The air shrieks with awkwardness.

'*Hey*,' I picture myself saying brightly. '*You know this whole zombie make-up thing? I came up with it because I'm crazy about you and you like painting blood and bones. Yes, of course you can apologize for getting the wrong idea about the swipe machine and kiss me in your hot red T-shirt until I forget everything you accused me of. Go right ahead.*'

'I should probably . . .' I say instead, edging towards the door.

'If you say so,' he says. He set his paints down beside Dorcas, who is halfway through the soppy 'Love Eternal' with the rest of the chorus.

'*Say you love me*,' Dorcas warbles, '*for my flaws . . .*'

'Oh, I do,' Jem assures the old lady. Pulling a brush from his pocket, he twirls it between his fingers. 'Can I make you super-evil?' he asks her with the kind of smile to floor a girl.

'*Say you'll hold me*,' Dorcas sings dreamily. She looks a little pink. '*With your claws . . .*'

I open my mouth, shut it again and flee.

'Wait, Fatima. WAIT!'

I gallop through the double doors and wallop straight into Studs.

'Watch where you're going, bitch,' says Studs, startled, arms up in a defensive position as I bounce him against the bins. I am pleased to see he has a nasty split lip that is only just beginning to heal. Offering a hasty finger in non-apology, I keep running.

'For God's sake WAIT FOR ME!'

Fatima stands on the road ahead, arms folded. I fall into step with her, my little legs pumping a bit harder than her great long ones as we negotiate the cracks and tilts in the pavement. A car squeals by, driven by a couple of lads looking way younger than seventeen. I imagine Studs at the wheel with Jem beside him, the crump of metal on man and dog, and shiver.

'Shouldn't you call Val?' I ask as we trot. 'Remind her you're late because of the show that will make the Gaslight a fortune this weekend?'

'She need me,' Fatima says matter-of-factly. 'I bring in the customers.' She looks at me sideways. 'Why do you do this with the zombies and the show? You don't like these shows. There are things here that I don't understand.'

I decide to be honest. 'Because I'm up to my ears in love with Jem,' I admit. 'And I've realized it's no good telling someone you love who thinks you've lied that you haven't lied, because they think you're lying. *Doing* is different. I have *done* something here. Something he can be a part of. It's mental, but it appeals to my control freakery on pretty much every level.'

I'm hoping for Fatima's approval. I don't get it.

'Don't do this for him,' she says.

'What, like he's any worse than all the other guys I've organized zombie shows for?' I joke, feeling a prickle of unease.

'He has a girlfriend, *chérie*. I see her in the kitchen at the Gaslight.'

I trip over a bit of pavement, banging my shin on the kerb. 'W . . . what?' I stammer, shocked almost beyond speech. 'Who?'

'I don't see her face but she is tall, it is all that I know.'

Tall would be right, I think, feeling dazed. No cricked necks or bent knees required, unlike with little flea me. The pain is red-hot, and not just on my shin.

'Men are simple,' Fatima reminds me, and pats my hand.

Everything is blowing around me like dust. Smashed and irretrievable, a priceless vase in a food processor. I thought I had developed a girlfriend-o-meter after Dave, but the gauge has failed me just when I needed it most. Maybe Jem started dating this girl after we broke up, or maybe he's been dating her all along. However you look at it, I am the stupidest girl in the universe.

I walk beside Fatima in silent hell, torturing myself as far as the High Street.

'I won't come to the Gaslight tonight.' My voice sounds rusty when I finally use it again, the squeal of a key in a badly oiled lock. 'I have a load of college work that won't do itself.'

'If I see this tall girlfriend in the bar I will pour beer on to her,' Fatima promises. She kisses me on both cheeks and sways across the road towards the theatre. A lone car drifts sideways, a slack-jawed man at the wheel, then rights itself just before striking the traffic island in the middle.

It's amazing how soothing it can be, learning Newton's laws of motion by heart. And Lenz's law, and Kirchoff's. And every other law of physics ever proved. Their worlds are ordered and devoid of pain.

'Did you know,' I say, the minute Fatima comes through my bedroom door at ten past midnight, 'that at any junction in a circuit, the sum of currents arriving at the junction is *exactly* the same as the sum of currents leaving the junction?'

269

'She don't come in the bar tonight,' Fatima says.

I lift up a finger. 'In other words, *charge is conserved*. If this didn't happen, you'd either get a massive build-up of electrons at a junction in a circuit or you'd be creating charge from nowhere. *Nowhere*. Of course, it makes perfect sense. All science makes perfect sense.'

'I said—'

I shut my Physics book with a bang. 'I heard. Did the others reach the bar with their zombie faces on?'

Fatima kicks off her shoes. 'They look so terrible that some girls do screams. Then it was like rock stars, you know? Everyone love them, talk to them. The old ladies too. Your friend Oz can sell all the tickets, maybe two times if he want to cheat.'

The word 'cheat' makes me think of Dave. I toy with calling him up, to check whether the shadowy beings behind his pathetic fraud attempt have done terrible things to him. Then I remember I don't have his number any more.

'I already buy your ticket before they all sell,' Fatima adds. 'I will be working but my tips tonight buy you a very good seat.'

'Cheers,' I say, trying to smile. 'You're back early, did you hitch a ride?'

'With Val. They live not so far from here.'

'And Jem was . . .?'

'Somewhere else.'

Meeting the tall girl. Kissing the tall girl. Going

270

somewhere private with the tall girl. I haul myself back from the edge of paralysis. 'I hope Maria and Sam had a massive slanging match.'

'Slanging, no. But Maria spend a long time in the bathroom tonight. I don't think she like her green face so much.'

'And I hope Tab was chatting up Sam in Maria's absence?'

'If you are so interested to know everything, you must come next time,' says Fatima, wagging her finger at me. 'Sam and Tabitha, they are so *English*.' She unclips her back, wriggles a bit and pulls a huge black lacy bra out of her sleeve like a transparent rabbit. 'They skip around each other like lambs. I want to say to them, "Go and have the sex, little lambs." But no. Instead it is "Do you want . . ." "Is it OK if . . ." This look super strange when they are zombies. So polite. "Could possibly I drain your blood and eat your brains?" "By all means. Be my gusset."'

Fatima climbs out of the rest of her clothes and wanders in supremely unconcerned nakedness into the unlocked yet occupied bathroom.

'Bloody hell!' Dad yowls.

I speed to the bathroom with a blanket I've snatched off my bed. Dad is leaning against the wall behind the bog, shielding his eyes and hyperventilating as Fatima makes a vague attempt to cover herself with the blanket.

'Sorry, Dad,' I choke, tugging her back to my bedroom. 'Sorry . . .'

'*Desolée*,' Fatima adds helpfully.

I slam the bedroom door behind us and wipe the tears from my eyes. 'Fatima, you . . . Don't you have a dressing gown or PJs or something?'

'He look very surprised,' Fatima says.

Which sets me off again. God it's good to laugh, even in such heinous circumstances. For a while tonight, I wondered if I'd ever laugh again.

The *What an Ado About Zombies!* publicity campaign proves so successful that, come four o'clock on the Friday of the dress rehearsal, there is a queue up the Gaslight steps full of college kids celebrating the start of half-term, looking forward to the Gaslight's zeitgeist brand of zombie *craic* and hoping to sneak a preview of the show. Several are wearing masks, fangs and flashing horns.

Oz has been quick to capitalize.

'We're using raffle tickets,' he says, waving a fat book of blue ticket stubs as Tabby, Fatima and I mount the crowded steps for Tab's make-up call. 'A fiver for a sneak preview. Give the crowd what they want, I say. Checks out with the boss.'

He thumbs at the auditorium doors, where two hideous creatures in shredded security-guard uniforms are talking to an enthusiastic gaggle of early comers. I look more closely. The creatures are Patricia and Eunice, dressed as zombie Night Watchmen Dogberry and Verges. Patricia's double-breasted jacket magnifies the size of her stomach to epic proportions, and she adjusts her hat as we approach.

'We've got an audience already, isn't that tremendous?' she says with a ghastly, bloody grin. 'We'll be stopping and starting like old motorbikes as we and the band get used to each other, but no one seems to care. Ella's just doing Gladys, as it were. You're next on her list, Tabitha. I'm sorry, my darling,' she adds to a girl in devil deelyboppers sidling up to the auditorium doors, 'but no one's going in until seven-fifteen. And if anyone tries, I'll pull their throats out the way they taught me in zombie school.'

'The band's doing a warm-up in the auditorium,' Eunice tells us as we hear the strain of familiar tunes wafting through the doors. She looks ludicrously chic in her uniform and face paint. 'Go and have a listen. It's super.'

Fatima wanders off to the bar to see if she can blag an extra hour's work, trailing a few groupies behind her. Tab shoves me through the doors of the auditorium, talking at a hundred miles an hour.

'It was such a good night last night, Lilah, seriously, I totally wish you'd been there, Maria was a total cow to Sam, I think even Sam was quite shocked at the way she was acting, and he was incredibly sweet to me and bought me a Coke and we even managed to laugh about the summer music thing we did when we first, you know, and it was fine, it was actually OK . . .'

Go and have the sex, little lambs. I hear Fatima in my head, loud and clear.

'Jem has a girlfriend,' I say. 'A tall one.'

The sound of a violin from the Slaughterhouse Seven soars about the auditorium roof with perfect timing.

'No,' Tabby says, aghast.

'Fatima saw her in the kitchen on Wednesday night,' I say sadly. 'He's supposed to realize I did this to give him his first proper gig, and then he's supposed to apologize for being an arse, and THEN he's supposed to kiss me to death in blind gratitude and love. But I've done it for nothing.'

'Hardly that, babes,' Tab protests. 'Every single member of the cast owes you big time. Don't you realize?' She waves at the set, the green lighting scheme, the band percussionists in vampire masks. 'What you've done is immense. Musical theatre history. You are a proper legend, Delilah. Not a Greek one this time; a real one. A modern one.'

I feel quite teary at the warmth in her voice. 'But you aren't with Sam,' I say miserably. 'I'm not with Jem. Nothing's worked out like it's supposed to.'

'It's gone way beyond that, Delilah,' Tab tells me.

She pushes me past the Slaughterhouse Seven in their pit and through a rubber-sealed door marked 'backstage'. A sudden wall of chatter, laughter and music smashes into me.

The cast of *What an Ado About Zombies!* is getting ready for the dress rehearsal. We pass clothes rails of costumes, some of which I recognize for certain painful reasons. A skull-patterned rucksack spilling hairspray (Gladys, I suspect), old lady support shoes (Gladys again), Mr Metal loudly singing 'Love Eternal' as he applies a disfiguring latex scar to Sam's cheek, an abandoned iPod beside a library book on wild flowers on a greasy make-up counter. I do a double-take at Warren, halfway through his make-over. With his green-blue zombie face on, he looks almost fanciable.

'You've thrown me in a room with people born in the second world war,' says Tab, raising her voice above the riot. 'Looking hot, Gladys.'

Gladys waves from beneath Ella's paintbrush.

'You have made a death-metalhead embrace musical theatre,' Tab goes on as Mr Metal sings a bit louder on the 'Love Eternal' chorus. 'You have allowed a Monster Munch love story to unfold.'

'Pickled onion flavour,' says Henry, halfway into his outfit, and Rich smiles fondly.

'You've introduced me to a scary girl who isn't scary any more.'

'I'm still scary,' says Ella, offended. She looks wired and super-jumpy. 'You're done, Glad. Get your backside in my chair, Tabitha, or you'll go from Hero to zero in less time than it takes me to blink.'

'And that doesn't even *touch* on how I will shortly be singing a lead role in a proper theatre covered in peeling flesh before the professional gaze and extensive note-taking of agency scouts, thanks entirely to you,' Tab says, settling

276

obediently into the seat Gladys has vacated. She sweeps her hands around the room, bringing my attention to every single thing and person in the chaotic but purposeful space. 'Other things maybe didn't work out like we thought. But tell me again that *it's all been for nothing.*'

In a back corner of the room, Jem is finishing off the masterpiece that is Dorcas's fleshless, putrid jaw bone. His black hair hangs in his eyes and he has a smear of green paint on one cheek. He hasn't seen me come in. Or maybe he has, and is choosing to ignore me. I feel insanely jealous of Dorcas.

'Don't lose faith,' Tab says, catching my hopeless glance in his direction. 'You said that to me once, about Sam. Your words have got me this far. Try applying them to yourself.'

'And remember what they say in undead musical theatre,' Ella adds, wiping her brushes with trembling fingers. 'It's not over till the zombie lady's head drops off. I badly need a smoke.'

I realize what's missing back here: the heavy haze of hash. No wonder Ella is stressed.

'How are we getting on, darlings?' says Patricia, striding into the room. 'Some big bouncer chap just turned up. Friend of Oz, summoned on red alert. I've put him on the auditorium doors. If I were twenty years younger . . .'

'He'd be a foetus,' says Eunice.

'I wish I knew more about this girlfriend Jem's got,' I mutter as the rest of the room bellows with amusement.

277

'You know, whether she'd been around for ages or just . . . since me.'

'Jem hasn't got a girlfriend,' says Ella, applying bluish paint to Tabby's face in swift, sure strokes.

'Apparently he has,' Tab says. 'And she's tall. Fatima saw him with her.'

Ella looks slyly amused. Her eyes flicker up and down my petite frame. 'Got bored of doing it on a stepladder, did he?'

'Ella!' Tab protests.

'I'm just *saying*!' Ella grins. 'Stop moving. You're going to look like something from the meat counter in Sainsbury's, and not in a good way.'

Maybe Jem has taken the tall girl to our wardrobe. Perfect spot, perfect privacy. Comfy furs.

'Break a leg or whatever,' I say, getting up abruptly.

'Delilah—'

'Tabitha, I said *stay flipping still*!' Ella hisses.

I climb over Gladys's rucksack and through the rail of costumes that smell of memories, barge out of the stage door and back through the auditorium. The gentle waltzing sounds of the band working through 'Love Eternal' make me walk faster. Mum is on the stage, singing and dancing and waving two fingers at me. I have to get out of here before I break down like an old car on the sticky carpet.

'Everything all right, Delilah?'

I hold up one hand wordlessly at Kev on the auditorium doors and keep walking through the lobby, through the

278

glass doors and down the big steps outside. The cheerfully dressed queue has grown, and is almost winding back to the High Street itself. I want to tell them all that life is a goatskin of steaming camel urine and the sooner they take off their devil horns the happier everyone will be.

This is *all* Aphrodite's fault.

'You will come,' Fatima insists.

'Tabby will understand,' I say stubbornly.

Fatima glares through fantastic Hallowe'en eyes, spider-web falsies shimmering on her eyelids. '*Lâche.*'

'So I'm a coward,' I say, lifting my chin. 'I'll apply for membership to the Coward Society, get a little yellowbelly badge, bury my head in sand, whatever. I'm not coming. You go. Val'll want you there as early as possible tonight.'

Fatima doesn't move.

'Just go, will you?' I say weakly.

My phone rings. Tab. I don't answer, hating myself for it.

'If you don't come,' Fatima declares, 'I will tell to Jem that you love him and so you don't come because of this.'

I gape in horror. 'You wouldn't.'

She jabs at me with a fearsome blood-red fingernail.

'I will tell to him everything. The show. The so-sad tears.'

'Fatima, you—'

'You *English*,' she says impatiently. 'Why must I explain everything? How glad I am that I am French. You must put on your nice clothes and your pretty eyes and you must show him you are not scared. Love is the war. If you don't fight, you will lose.'

She is getting dangerously loud. Dad will start taking an interest in a minute.

'I've lost already,' I whisper. 'I—'

'I will put on *Facebook*,' Fatima threatens. 'Then everyone will know. The tall girlfriend will know.'

She whips out her phone and starts typing. I fly across the room at her, knocking the phone from her hand.

'You win, you total cow! I'll come for the show. But that is IT. I am leaving before the party. Is that clear?'

'*Bon*. Now dress.'

She goes through my wardrobe like a whirlwind. Dresses discarded, shoes ignored, scarves thrown across the bed.

'That?' I say, cautiously looking at the black lace thing she is thrusting at me. 'It's a vest.'

'It is super-sexy minidress.'

'I'll freeze my butt off!'

She shakes it at me, firmly. I put on the vest, adjusting it around an old black bra she located at the back of my sock drawer. I am relieved when she hands me black leggings next. For a nasty moment I thought she was going to send me to my doom half-naked.

'Hair.'

'Straight?' I say hopefully.

'Boring as a boring English person. Curls, *chérie*. They are your most sexy thing.'

She tugs my hair out of its scrunchy, making me yelp.

'So pretty,' she says with satisfaction as it cascades around my face. 'Big earrings, red lipstick, *boum*. You are a little goddess.'

A goddess is the last thing I want to be. Fatima opens her make-up bag and shoves me into the bathroom.

Fifteen minutes later and more frightened than ever, I insist on putting my trusty parka over the top of the strange, lace-clad, sooty-eyed, red-lipped creation that is post-makeover me. Fatima is appalled.

'It's *November* tomorrow,' I hiss as she tries to pull the parka from my shoulders for the third time in as many minutes. 'And I'm *not* wearing heels.'

I am close to running back to my room and locking the door behind me. Wisely, Fatima allows my Vans and parka to stand.

We walk, at my insistence. Fatima tries to urge me forward at more than a snail's pace. 'You think he will not be there if we are late?' she goads. 'He will be there. The person that you don't want to be there will be there, with this tall girl. They will be kissing. Picture this worst thing and prepare for the war.'

I picture the tall girlfriend dead. It's bad of me, but I do. It's surprisingly easy. My emotions feel like a ticking bomb, packed with venom for a girl I've never even met. The anger and upset I felt over Dave are nothing compared to this.

As if I have conjured him through the sheer power of thought, Dave walks around the corner, holding hands with a sulky-looking Louise. He leers excitedly at Fatima, then realizes she's with me. Guilt and caution are suddenly all over his face.

I am in no mood for small talk. 'I hardly recognize you on foot, Dave.'

'Where have you been, Dee?' he says, recovering. 'I've been calling you for *days*.'

Louise is holding tightly on to his fingers, preventing him from slipping his moorings. The news that he's been calling me isn't going down well.

'I got rid of my phone,' I say. 'Thought I'd got rid of you too.'

The urgent eyebrows Dave aims at me give him the look of a startled stoat. 'What happened to . . .'

'It got broken,' I say.

He deflates before my eyes, a sad individual in a naff leather coat.

Louise fixes Dave with a basilisk stare. 'What's she talking about? Why were you calling her?'

Propelled by the strange surge of empowerment Fatima has triggered, I address Louise. 'Does Dave still have his testicles?'

Looking surprised, Louise nods.

'Why do you still have your testicles, Dave?' I ask.

'I sold my car,' he mumbles.

'You sold your car,' I repeat.

'I sold my car.'

'*You sold your car?*'

Louise interrupts irritably. 'He sold his car, OK? God knows why I agreed to go out with him again.' She bends down and rubs at the back of her shoe. She is wearing extremely high heels.

Fatima says something long and venomous-sounding in French.

'What?' says Dave.

'Trust me,' I say, struggling to contain the volcano. *You ruined everything for me when you could have just sold your car.* 'You don't want to know.'

I leave him with Louise moaning on the pavement about her shoes. I'm so furious, I can feel myself turning green and expanding with every step I take.

'Dave *le bâtard*,' Fatima states, keeping pace with me. 'Yes?'

I tell Fatima everything in a tumble of fury. The ATM robberies, my lost money, my found money. Dave and the swipe machine. Dave and his flaming car. I don't know how much she follows. When I'm angry, I talk even faster than I walk.

'His contacts are probably the same guys who ripped off the ATMs. Who else would he get a fake swipe machine from? Jem goes ape at *me* while Dave simply sells his car, pays what he owes and gets his girlfriend back!'

Judging from Louise's face tonight, Dave won't last long without his car. The thought gives me a degree of savage satisfaction.

'How do you get your money back?' Fatima asks, doing her best to keep up.

'The bank refunded me. I think Jem knew about the scam somehow, he kept telling me to talk to the bank. He's got dodgy friends, he must've asked arou—'

Click, whirr. A sudden bright ray of understanding.

Fatima clicks her fingers under my nose. ''Allo? You nearly walk into the lamp post.'

I am like Buddha but skinnier with more hair, and infinitely more stupid. *I know it all.*

'Studs was part of the fraud,' I say in wonder. 'The skinny weasel I nearly bumped into at Ella's flat. You must have seen him. Diamonds in his nose. *Studs!*' My brain is at fever pitch. 'Jem would never give Studs up to the police because they are friends from way back. But Jem guessed Studs was involved when I mentioned my bank problem . . . He went to find him – talk to him – fight – black eye . . .'

I got this for you.

I clutch my head. Comprehension hurts when it comes at you as fast as this. 'Jem's the one that gave Studs the split lip,' I whisper.

'He must love you very much to do this,' says Fatima.

The strength of my shame, my longing and my total idiocy nearly knock me off my feet. 'I guess he did, once,'

I whisper. 'But now he's got a better deal with Miss Burj Khalifa.'

Half a moon peeps out from behind a frost-edged cloud overhead. Aphrodite, listening in.

'This is all a very big mess,' Fatima says after a long silence. 'But you must still fight, *chérie*. If he love you once, he can maybe love you again.'

I shake my head. All the fight has gone out of me. I am a sad, punctured balloon flapping in the wind. There is no way back. 'What did you say to Dave back there, by the way?' I ask, rubbing my nose and blinking back the tears that are about to turn my mascara into several shades of hell.

'I say he is like the corpse of a dog in my mouth with the maggots inside.'

'Story of my life,' I mutter.

It is nearly six o'clock as we force our way up the crowded steps, through the double doors and into the throbbing pumpkin-decorated lobby. For an instant, half an instant even, I think I see Studs slipping through the depths like a piranha. This many punters in one place spells showtime in more ways than one.

'Fatima!' Val roars over the mass of heads already crowding the bar. 'You're LATE!'

'You will be OK?' Fatima asks me. She looks genuinely worried.

I know without checking in a mirror that I look more undead than all the zombies, ghosts, vampires and slasher-murderers pushing and shoving around me put together. But then she is swept into the crowd and is gone.

I fight my way through to the auditorium doors. Kev looks spectacular, a great gaunt skeleton in a headset.

'Looking hot tonight, Delilah the vixen,' he grins and lets me through.

The velvet thump of the doors behind me cuts off the chaos. Members of the theatre's lighting crew are scaling the rigs at the back of the stage, adjusting spotlights and attaching filters. Someone has their head inside the piano, filling the air with the monotonous *bom-bom-bom* of strings being hit and tightened and hit again, while a broken piece of scenery is nailed together and cables firmly gaffer-taped to the floor. The air is thick with expectancy. You can almost open your mouth and take a bite.

Beep.

PLZ PLZ CALL I NEED YOU
xxxx

'Delilah!' Appearing at the stage door, Rich looks anxious and dishevelled. 'Thank God. Tabitha's going nuts trying to reach you. Apparently you haven't been answering your phone. Can you go and see her, talk to her?'

On top of the emotional exhaustion, I suddenly feel scared. 'What's happened?'

Backstage, Mr Metal is staring at his empty make-up chair, mindlessly twirling the metal in his nose. Somewhere in the background, in the toilets maybe, someone is screaming with fury. Despite the apparent focus, the swish of brushes from the make-up team, it is clear that the whole room is trying to hear what's going on.

A half-painted Tab almost knocks me down, ignoring the multi-coloured swearing from Ella with her brush held in mid-air.

'You came,' she sobs. 'I thought you weren't going to come, I've been messaging you and calling you—'

'I wouldn't miss your big night, would I?' I lie, feeling bewildered by the drama that has descended from nowhere. I have almost forgotten what it feels like to have Tab needing me like this. 'Of course I came. What's up?'

She shoves her phone at me with trembling fingers.

Leave my boyfriend alone bitch

'Charming,' I say, extremely relieved that it isn't anything more serious than a fresh Sam situation. 'Maria?'

'I didn't *do* anything,' Tab wails. '*He* sent the text to *me*.'

'If you don't sit down, I am going to redefine ape.' Ella looks mad-eyed with nerves. 'I'll walk out of that door and you will get on that stage looking like a camel's rectum.'

I steer Tab back into Ella's make-up chair and pat Ella on the arm.

'And I will *bite* the next person who tries to calm me down,' Ella snarls, fixing my patting hand with the stony glare of Medusa. Her pupils are like pinheads.

'I got a text,' Tabby sniffs. 'From Sam. He wants me back.'

It is remarkable to discover that I can feel like death yet

289

also winded with delight *at the same time*. 'Wow!' I gasp. 'Just like that? Can I see the text?'

I've messed up. I love you.
Go figure.
S x

Short, sweet, despondent. *Totally* what is needed. I am seized with a passionate longing for the message to be for me, from Jem.

'But that's fantastic!' I say, pressing the phone back into her hands.

Tab shakes her head. 'Maria saw the text on his phone and went ballistic. Sam hadn't said anything to her about breaking up. Not a word. We're on stage in just over an hour, Lilah. About to tell a love story that, right now, isn't going to happen.'

'Of course it's going to happen!' I say, aghast. The show can't go belly-up now. Not *now*. Not after everything I have done.

'Beatrice is meant to be in love with Benedick,' Tabby wails. 'But now all she wants to do is kill him. She's insane with rage and refusing to get her face done and threatening not to do the show at all. This is all my fault!'

I try to keep a grip. 'It's all Sam's fault, surely?'

'Lilah, you don't—'

'STOP TALKING,' Ella howls.

'Everyone needs to calm down,' says Patricia. Beneath

her demonic make-up, she is grey with anxiety. 'Maria wouldn't be so unprofessional as to let us down now. There will be agents out there, and press, and—'

Maria's shrieking pierces the toilet walls. 'YOU SPINELESS SKUNK! YOU FAT COKE-DRINKING FLATFISH!'

'She's a charmer, that Maria, isn't she?' says Jem.

I have been so absorbed in Tabby's drama that I have totally failed to clock Jem making up Dorcas two chairs further down the room. It is a miracle that I don't wet myself then and there. He is looking right at me.

Sam crashes out of the toilets, breathing hard. A bog roll comes flying out and clonks him in the back of the head.

'BASTARD!' Maria screeches from the toilets.

'I can't do this,' Sam says. 'Sorry, Patricia. Sorry everyone.' The look he gives Tabby is one of hopeless longing. 'Sorry Tab.'

He hurries out of the fire escape at the back of the room. Ella leans her hand hard on Tabitha's shoulder to stop her leaping out of her chair and running after him, muttering warnings of death by hideous means.

'Oh dear,' says Eunice helplessly. 'No leading man now either.'

'Come on,' Jem says to me as a shrill, desperate chatter breaks out.

'Where are we going?' I say in surprise.

'I've finished Dorcas. I don't have anything to do. You don't have anything to do. Everyone else is busy, terrified

291

or both. We have about an hour until curtain-up. We're going to talk to Sam.'

He holds out his hand to me. I stare at it in disbelief.

'You will bring him back, won't you?' Tab implores.

'Do our best,' I mumble, sliding my hand into Jem's. My whole body is boiling hot from the pressure of his fingers. 'Can't promise anything. Someone else will have to get Maria to put her toys back in the pram.'

Jem threads me through the room and out of the same fire escape Sam has just used. A relieved wave of applause follows us out, cut off abruptly by the slamming of the fire door. The cold air wallops into me.

'Should have grabbed my jacket,' Jem says, shivering. 'Can't really go back in now, can I? Not cool.'

'Like leaving a party,' I blurt, for want of anything better to say. 'When you say goodbye to everyone really loudly and shut the front door and then realize your phone is upstairs.'

'In the bog,' Jem says.

'In the bog,' I agree. His tall girlfriend wouldn't approve of this hand-holding, I think.

Sam is standing by the rushing river, his big back in silhouette under the dirty brown lights. He turns slightly as we approach.

'You probably think I'm the biggest idiot in town,' he says.

'I can think of a bigger one,' I say, with complete honesty. 'Your timing's a bit off, though. Couldn't you have held it in until after the show?'

His eyes are pained. 'I've been thinking about it for ages. Since . . . well, basically on and off since I ended it. It's just . . . my pride took a kicking at that party. And then there was Maria. I was still holding a candle for Tab at the start of our relationship, but suddenly Maria was right under my skin.' He looks puzzled. 'She was incredibly sexy, somehow. Do you know what I mean?'

'Don't look at me,' I say.

Jem has finally let go of my hand.

'I was in a mess,' Sam groans. 'Did I like Maria, or Tab? Tab or Maria? And today I finally realized I had it all wrong. I was thinking with my—'

He stops apologetically.

'I get the gist,' I say.

'Anyway,' he goes on, 'I started thinking with my heart and my head instead. The minute I did that, everything became clear. I had to act before I lost sight of what mattered all over again. And so . . .'

'You sent the text to Tabby,' I say.

'As soon as I'd sent it, I felt like a total bastard.' Sam looks appalled at himself. 'I never thought I'd be the kind of guy who'd do that. And then Maria borrowed my phone without me realizing and . . . She's right to be angry with me.'

'You can't let everyone down just because you feel bad,' I object. 'There's a whole cast in there, dangling on a thread. Hundreds of ticket holders all looking like they've been through some kind of body shredder. The band, the set . . . Everything is ready to go. Are you really going to dump everyone in it?'

Sam groans again. I turn the last serious screw I have in my arsenal.

'This is Tabby's big night, Sam. She's worked really hard on this. If you really love her—'

'I do,' Sam says.

Lucky, lucky Tab.

'If you really love her,' I repeat, 'you'll do the show. Because if you don't, she'll never forgive you. And then you won't have anyone.'

I have a feeling Tab would forgive Sam most things, even this – eventually. But I say it with as much conviction as I can.

'Maria loathes the sight of me,' Sam says desperately. 'How am I supposed to make her act like she loves me?'

'She's meant to hate you, isn't she?'

Sam looks doubtful. 'Yes, but she's meant to love me too.'

I glance discreetly at my watch. Not long to curtain-up. 'But not to begin with, right?' I prompt.

'True,' he concedes.

'Tell her something to get her on that stage. There are agents in the audience, Patricia said. Tab says she really wants an agent.'

Sam nods.

'Tell her an agent has come specifically to see her,' I say, struck with sudden inspiration.

'But they haven't,' Sam says, startled.

'Lie,' I order him.

I wait for Jem to protest but he is staring at the ground. Sam squares his shoulders and goes back inside. The fire door swings gently shut behind him.

'Well you were a fat lot of use,' I tell Jem, a little crossly.

'I'd only have said the wrong thing,' he says. 'I've done a lot of that lately.'

There is a long, weird moment, full of rushing river and freezing wind. He takes my hand again. His lips are so close and his eyes are so dark.

The fire escape bangs open. We leap apart.

Val is ashen. 'There's been an incident,' she says. 'An ambulance is on its way. I need your help.'

I stare at the spattering of vomit on Val's shirt. Picture a pair of wired Medusa eyes with pupils like pinheads. I see Studs the piranha in my mind's eye as a ghastly dread creeps through me. Has Ella done something stupid?

'One of you, either of you, both of you, I don't care. Oz is with her now. I can't leave the bar for much longer. Everyone else is needed for curtain-up and *someone* has to go to hospital with her. Move, will you?'

I know Fatima is mad, but I never thought she'd be idiotic enough to buy whatever Studs was selling.

The ambulance speeds through the town, sirens going. I am thrown back and forth, sometimes crashing into Jem and sometimes into the oxygen canister taped to the metal wall behind us. I look at Fatima's dark hair spread on the ambulance pillow and the mask strapped to her face. She is taped to the gurney, her spider-web lashes closed and her chest moving erratically. Monitors bleep.

'What did she take?' I ask the paramedic fiddling with the drip feed in Fatima's arm.

'We won't know until she wakes up and tells us.'

This is every kind of nightmare rolled into one.

'Studs was at the Gaslight,' I spit at Jem.

He runs his hands through his hair. 'He wouldn't deal anything dangerous.'

'You think?' I rest my head against the oxygen canister. 'It must be nice to have so much faith in your friends.'

'Delilah,' he begins. 'I—'

I hold up my hand. '*So* not the time.'

We listen to the keening wail of the siren over our heads. There is a little telescopic window set in the back doors of the ambulance, and I gaze out at a shrunken world of headlamps and streetlights and reflective cats' eyes.

Five minutes later and we are squealing into the special parking bay outside the Royal Surrey's Accident and Emergency department. The paramedics leap out and yank Fatima on to the tarmac.

Jem and I are allowed to follow her inside, but then we lose her. We are ordered to sit like dogs and wait. People slump in the red plastic chairs around us, with bandaged fingers, or bloody heads, or cradling wailing children. The smell of disinfectant is eyewatering.

'*New Scientist*?' Jem suggests, dangling a tattered magazine at me.

'Not really in the mood for reading,' I say. 'Funnily enough.'

He puts the magazine back, reclines on the chair next to me and crosses his long legs. It is comforting having him there. I wish it wasn't, but you take what you can get.

'I worked it out about Studs and my money,' I say. I don't care any more. 'And your bruise.' I flap my fingers around my face to illustrate.

He looks wary. 'You worked out what, exactly?'

'You fought about it. Cut Studs' lip. I don't know how it all connects – something to do with the cashpoint I used at the Gaslight maybe.' Studs was there, the first time I saw Jem. The night everything began. 'It was a lot of money that I couldn't afford to lose, and I never said thanks. So . . . thanks.'

'I didn't put your money back,' he says. 'The bank did.'

'It's still what you fought about. Isn't it?'

'Studs has always worked the shallows,' Jem says after a short pause. 'But he met some guys recently who pushed him out too deep. He needed me to reel him in again.'

'And the fishing rod gave you the bruise.'

He gives me a look.

'You started the whole fishing metaphor thing,' I say, blushing slightly. 'Why is it up to you to babysit him?'

I am getting echoes of another conversation he and I once had, about a mother duck and her duckling. How times have changed.

'You know why,' he says, closing me down.

We stare for a bit at a poster about handwashing hygiene taped to the opposite wall.

'I know what you did too,' he says eventually. 'Saving the show, changing the theme. Ella told me. You saved my mother's neck. The bar, the business. That makes us even, I think.'

'I told Ella not to say anything,' I say, embarrassed suddenly now my plan has been revealed in all its pathetic glory.

'She told me on Thursday. She was bored of waiting for me to figure it out for myself.'

Does he know I did it for him? Do I want him to know? He's looking at me so intently that I have to stand up and walk to the desk.

'Talk to me,' I say to the receptionist on the counter. 'I'm being bothered by the guy in the red T-shirt.'

The receptionist has a head of tight curls and a face like a dormouse. She stares at me in wary surprise, making me wonder how often people talk to her about things not related to critical injuries. Her badge tells me to call her Shelagh, should I feel the need for first-name terms.

'I was jealous, OK?' Jem says, following me. 'Of that idiot in the car making you laugh. It clouded my judgment. I know you were never going to rob the bar.'

'Oh, but I was.' I fiddle with the RSPCA charity box chained to the reception desk. It seems you can't even trust people with life-threatening injuries not to nick stuff. 'The one-way ticket to Rio was booked and everything.'

'Why are you still fighting me, Delilah? Can't we—'

His phone starts ringing.

The receptionist comes to life. 'All phones should be switched off in the hospital,' she barks, her tight curls vibrating even more than Jem's phone.

'I'll take it outside.' He fixes me with burning eyes. 'Don't go away. We are going to talk about this.'

He heads through the hospital doors and stands in a streetlight with the receiver to his ear. It's probably Val.

299

Or Miss Long Legs UK.

I don't want to talk! I mentally scream after his back.

More sirens, another ambulance. A kid on a trolley, lots of blood, a woman whose skin looks as clammy as a toad's. I stand to one side with my arms tightly folded into my sides, wishing I could block out the horrible noise the woman is making as the boy is checked in. Finding a few coins in my pocket, I drop them in the charity box because it has a cute dog on the front and I am in need of distraction.

The receptionist looks up at the sound, her dormouse face suddenly animated. 'I'm an animal lover too,' she says. 'Dogs, cats, budgies.'

'I've got a fish,' I say, feeling the need to somehow prove my animal-loving worth.

Apparently Marie Curie gets me into the club. All of a sudden, the receptionist grows chatty.

'Hit and run,' she says, nodding at the boy's trolley being rushed down the hospital corridor. 'Always nasty.'

I glance out of the doors. I wish Jem would come back. Then again, he probably doesn't need reminding of what happens in hit and runs.

The receptionist is still talking. 'A lovely Staffie was knocked down with his owner five, six years ago. Couple of joyriders up the Watts. Scarpered, of course. Police never got them, the little criminals.'

Jem and Studs hit a man with a dog.

'Barney survived,' she adds, registering my expression. 'I

can see that you're wondering.'

I'm suddenly wondering a lot of things. I am also looking very hard at the receptionist with the kind of pinpoint focus normally reserved for microscopes. Now, I feel, might be the moment for first-name terms.

'Was Barney the dog or the owner, Shelagh?'

Shelagh looks slightly amazed by the question. 'The dog,' she says.

It's a coincidence, of course. Joyriders must hit dogs all the time. I have visions of the Watts Estate filled with flying four-legged bodies. But still, I have to ask the question.

'Do a lot of dogs get caught up in hit and runs around here?'

'No, thank goodness! It's the only case I've known in fifteen years on this desk.'

I need to keep this conversation going because suddenly I have to know how it ends. 'Dogs have better senses than humans,' I say.

'They do,' Shelagh agrees warmly.

'Shame about the guy,' I prompt.

'What guy?'

I really hope I get a receptionist like this the day I get knocked over by speeding teenagers. So interested in the human element of a tragedy. 'The guy with the DOG,' I say.

'Oh, a broken leg won't kill you,' Shelagh says. She frowns again. 'Unless you're a racehorse.'

She returns to her paperwork, completely unaware that she's just made a seismic shift in my world. The only case in fifteen years? Both man and dog survived? This is *colossal*. This . . .

I sit down to stare at the handwashing poster again. More sirens. Another ambulance. Moaning, crying, puking.

'Apparently it's all kicking off back at the Gaslight,' says Jem, returning. 'They clawed the show back from the brink, but it's touch and go they'll make it to the end. Val has Oz and Kev on the bar as back-up, but she really needs one of us back for the interval or the whole place will implode.' He looks at me properly. 'You look like someone just hit you round the head with a mallet. Are you OK? Has Fatima—'

A bemused-looking doctor with a wispy beard approaches us. 'You came in with Fatima Ammour? She's awake and chatting up my gastroenterologist. You can see her if you like.'

It's like resurrection day around here, I think a little hysterically. Now Fatima isn't dead I can kill her myself, at my leisure. As we follow the doctor up the corridor, my hand creeps up Jem's arm and grips him tightly at the elbow.

'Are you sure he died?' I blurt.

His face tightens. 'What?'

'The guy Studs hit.'

'Of course I'm sure.'

'You saw him lying there? Him and his dog?'

'Why are we talking about this now?'

'Did you see him?' I insist.

'We left,' he says shortly. 'I got the details from Studs later. What—'

'The receptionist remembered the dog,' I say. 'They didn't die, Jem. Neither of them died. You didn't kill anyone.'

Fatima is sitting up.

'My stomach feel like an elephant is jumping on me,' she croaks crossly, trying to smooth the hospital gown over her belly. Her voice sounds rough.

'They pumped you out,' I say. 'Does it hurt?'

Fatima flops her head back on the pillow. 'I cannot even fart, it hurt so much. Imagine this. English drugs don't agree so much with me as French drugs. When I see that skinny weasel man again I will kill him.'

Jem is standing by the window, staring out into the night. He hasn't said much since the man-and-dog bombshell. Nothing at all, in fact.

'When did you meet Studs anyway?' I ask, squeezing Fatima's hand to reassure myself that she really is talking to me.

'He offer me something outside Ella's place but I don't want it. Then he is at the Gaslight tonight. I want to relax, enjoy the party, you know?'

'But you were *working*,' I say.

Fatima looks surprised. 'Why does this matter?' She nods at Jem a little woozily. 'You see his tall girlfriend yet? Do I miss the fight?'

I shush her, alarmed.

'Whose girlfriend?' Jem says, turning round.

'Tall. With the curves like a violin.'

Fatima motions with her hands. She is still pretty out of it. Jem looks at me like *I'm* the one who owes *him* an explanation.

'Cats never stay in bags, Jem,' I say, deciding to have it out right here and now. 'I mean, why would they? They're cats. You can't even keep potatoes in bags. They go green and sprout. Imagine the state of a blinking *cat*.'

'What are you talking about?'

'You tell me,' I challenge.

'I can't tell you what day of the week it is right now. My head is spinning like a wheel. I can't take any more surprises.'

'Fatima saw her in the kitchen at the Gaslight,' I say. I wish I could sound more triumphant about this. 'Talk your way out of *that*.'

Jem raises his hands. 'I've said sorry for not believing you about the swipe machine. You just dropped the nuclear news that I have never killed anyone and now you're talking about potatoes and cats. Have we slid into another dimension? Fatima, I'm really glad you're OK, but right now I have to leave before my imminent alien abduction. I'm going back to help Val at the bar.'

He leaves, hands in pockets, head down and shoulders up.

As the door closes I burst into tears. Emotional

intelligence is so *exhausting*. I long to be fourteen again, getting with Ali Frampton while simultaneously eyeing James Collins at the fruities.

'You have him very bad,' Fatima observes as I weep all over the hospital blanket.

'I've only been in love twice,' I choke. Bogies are going everywhere. 'And both times they've had girlfriends and lied about it. What are the chances?'

Fatima strokes my hair.

'It's because I annoyed Aphrodite,' I gulp. 'I tried to interfere in her plan for the universe. And now it's all pinged back and walloped me in the face. I don't think the gods like it when you interfere.'

She makes a tutting noise. 'This is Laurent, yes?'

'What's Laurent?' I wail.

'Aphrodite.' Fatima looks at me indulgently. 'I have the kiss of Aphrodite, mwah mwah. You kiss him in Argole and you catch fire in your pants and you think this is the power of Aphrodite because he tell it to you. He tell it to all the girls. He tell it to me one time, even. But the truth is more simple. French boys kiss like movie stars.' She looks a little smug.

Oh. Right.

Yes.

What?

'I never really believed him,' I mumble. My face feels scarlet. 'Not really. Not a hundred per cent. I'm a *scientist*. I mean, it's a great line and everything, but . . . Tab believed

305

it but I didn't. Kind of didn't. I'm a total pillock.'

'It is because you are human and stupid,' says Fatima. 'You want to believe that someone in the universe know what they are doing because for sure you don't. Maybe Aphrodite, maybe God. This explain a *lot* of religion.'

I rub at my tears. I am a truly ridiculous example of an idiotic human.

'You need to rest,' I say, and wave at the door. 'I should go.'

'Don't go home and cry on your pillow.' Fatima's head sinks back. 'Go and see Tabby's show, if there is still some show to see. She will want you to be there. Love will come when it is ready, *chérie*. Not when Aphrodite is horny.'

The lobby and bar are half full, but the main action is coming from the auditorium where I can hear whoops and whistles and the jolly thrum of band music. No Jem. Nowhere I can see, at least.

'I hear Fatima's going to be OK,' says Kev on the auditorium doors. He clasps my arm in comradeship. 'There's some bad gear about at the moment. She was lucky. How about you?'

'I'm not the one who's had a load of fertilizer rinsed out of my guts,' I say, touched by his concern. 'I'll live. How long until the interval?'

'Ten minutes. Five, maybe. Wanna go in?'

The auditorium is packed. Plastic glasses of beer line the steps, and devil horns flash, and the crinkle of crisp packets cheerfully battles with the band as the chorus thumps through that old Shakespeare hit, 'Sigh No More, Ladies', with Tabby's signature twist.

'*Die no more, ladies, die no more,*' carols Gladys.

'*Zombies deceive us ever,*' Dorcas carols back.

'Whoever savaged that granny did a sweet job,' says a transfixed Grim Reaper perched near the doors.

The cast are dancing around Warren, Rich and Henry on stage. Sam and Maria are nowhere to be seen. Lurking in the background, Patricia and Eunice seem to be on red alert.

I check my ticket. Someone is sitting in my seat. As I dither over what to do next, Oz grabs me and pulls me on to the armrest at the end of the nearest row.

'What have I missed?' I whisper. 'Any assassination attempts?'

There is a sudden commotion in the wings. The audience sits up with interest as Studs ploughs through a gaggle of green-tinged chorus members and pegs it across the stage, ducking the scenery, his skinny legs and white trainers a blur.

'It was insurance!' he squeals over his shoulder. 'You'd have done the same . . . You know how it is . . . We're still mates, yeah? We're still . . .'

Jem powers after him, hurdling over a bench and a tub of paper flowers. 'I'll wring your bloody neck! I would've stuck by you *whatever*. And don't get me started on what you sold Fatima . . .'

The rest is lost in the wings on the far side of the stage. The audience erupts, whooping and drumming their feet on the ground, and the curtain comes crashing down on Act One.

'Delilah, thank God.' Val is pulling my arm, heaving me through the auditorium doors on the crest of the flood. 'Despite promising to help on the bar, Oz has vanished and Kev's on crowd control and Jem's somewhere else and I am on my knees and the serious drinking hasn't even started yet and I'll pay you six quid an hour— no, seven, plus tips, just *do it.*'

The bar is already fat with people waving tenners in the air. What else can I do but serve, and serve, and serve again, picking my way through the queue bargers and the big spenders and the banter merchants like I haven't already had the most frantic evening of my life?

'It's a miracle the show's made it this far,' says Oz, unaware of the death glares from Val as he squeezes in between two girls at the bar to order beer. 'The tension on the stage has been sensational. It could have been scripted.'

I wipe my forehead with one hand and siphon soda with the other. 'You seen Jem anywhere?'

'Strangling that skinny guy, I imagine. Enjoying the show, ladies?'

'It's amazing,' gushes a girl with Morticia Addams hair on his left.

'AMAZING,' agrees the smaller witchy one on Oz's right.

'And you lovelies are pretty amazing too,' Oz beams, putting his arms round them both.

We sell an unbelievable amount of alcohol in twenty

minutes flat. And then the bell goes and most of the hellish Hallowe'en army returns to their evening's unpredictable entertainment.

'These kids will be the death of me,' Val wheezes, banging her chest with a fist as the auditorium doors swing shut. 'Shortly after they have funded my retirement. Get this lot in the dishwasher, will you?'

I carry armfuls of dead glasses into the kitchen, stack them in the machine and wonder what on earth I'm doing. The money will be handy and everything, but I am *supposed* to be watching Tab. And yet here I am, in the heart of Jem's lair. I sneak a glance at his locker. It hangs slightly ajar, his jacket on view. He is still around then, somewhere.

At about ten-fifteen, I wipe a table beneath the elbows of a pair of singing werewolves and throw my cloth on the counter.

'Going somewhere?' Val says beadily.

'I thought I'd catch the end of the show,' I say, edging towards the auditorium doors. 'We're quieter now, and I thought—'

Val points at a small crowd hanging around the bar who have decided to quit the show in favour of getting extremely drunk. 'They need serving.'

She dives into the cellar. I serve a few more rounds of drinks, wondering if I'll get to see any of the show at all.

The door which leads straight to the wings on the right-hand side of the stage suddenly opens into the lobby.

'I need a drink,' Maria announces, marching towards the bar.

The singing werewolves point at her, study their crumpled programmes and break into a cheery rendition of 'How Do You Solve a Problem Like Maria?'.

'Is it over?' I ask. I haven't heard any final-sounding applause.

'It's Patricia and Eunice's big "comedy" number,' says Maria with a sniff. '*Big* being the word, where Patricia is concerned. Hasn't she heard of the Dukan diet? I deserve a nice cold drink for everything I've been through tonight. It turns out Sam has been lying to me about agents too. I heard Rich talking to Henry in the wings. The agent Sam said was here is at the show in *Woking*.'

I can hear Patricia and Eunice's duet through the open door. They are getting plenty of laughs. But if the leading lady is at the bar on her next cue, the laughing is going to stop pretty fast.

I come out from behind the counter. 'I'll bring something backstage if you want,' I say, flapping my cleaning cloth at her like I'm trying to usher a chicken back into its pen. 'But I really think you should go back—'

'Give me something now.' Maria pulls off her long dark wig and ruffles her blond hair. 'That lot can wait.' She gave her make-up guy so much grief that her zombie look is more pale and interesting than outright dead.

'Aren't you on next?' I say helplessly.

'I don't know if I can be bothered,' Maria says with

supreme indifference. 'Anyway, this song takes ages. They'll probably do an encore too. Fanta, with ice.'

'Maria, what are you doing?' hisses Sam in terror, putting his head round the stage door. 'We've got the finale in five minutes.'

'Don't you start with me,' Maria spits.

'I'm sorry about the agent thing – I'm sorry about a lot of things – but you can't let us down now!'

Tabby peeps round nervously next to Sam. Maria curls her lip.

'And as for *you*,' she begins malevolently.

The main double doors clang open, bringing with them a gust of cold evening air. Jem's hair is sticking straight up and his cheeks have a glow that brings me out in a rash of purest longing.

'Is it over?' he asks breathlessly, resting his hands on his knees.

'No,' say Sam, Tab and me together. Well, I make an odd snorting noise.

Jem looks at Maria. 'Then what—'

'I'm having a DRINK,' Maria says.

'Where's Studs?' I manage to ask.

'Halfway to Dorking, if he knows what's good for him,' Jem says darkly.

A burst of applause rocks the lobby. Patricia shoots through the stage door to join the fun at the bar, along with Rich, Henry, Gladys – pretty much everyone, really.

'Get back on stage,' Patricia shouts at Maria. 'It's the

finale! Hero and Claudio, Beatrice and Benedick – the *wedding*!'

'Encore!' roars the crowd. 'Bring back the dead coppers!'

Eunice grabs Patricia's uniformed arm. 'We need to go again, Patricia. They'll have to sort this out themselves.'

'Thank God for encores,' says Sam as the orchestra starts Patricia and Eunice's song again. He looks ill with nerves. 'Maria, you have to come back.'

'You have no right to tell me what to do,' Maria says mulishly. 'Not after the way you've treated me.'

'Sam,' says Jem, 'there's something I should tell you round about now.'

Maria goes very still as Sam scrubs at his eyes like a tired child.

'Hit me,' he says.

Jem looks abashed. 'Maria and I kind of . . . hooked up a few weeks ago.'

There is an astonished silence, not least from me. The assembled cast goggle at each other.

'Don't believe him, Sammy,' Maria says, in a voice that instantly tells me that every word is true. Not that I need Maria to tell me that, of course. Jem being Jem.

'You're kidding me,' Sam says to Jem.

'I wish I was, mate. Kissing *one* of your girlfriends is bad enough, I know. Kissing two is—'

Sam's fist flashes out – WHAM – and Jem hits the ground, holding his jaw.

'Punchable,' he agrees, through a mouthful of blood.

'It was only once,' Maria says quickly. 'And he kissed *me*, Sammy. I swear.'

I'm trying to keep up, but I'm struggling. So's the cast. In the background, Patricia and Eunice are on their second verse again.

'When did you kiss her?' Sam demands, standing over Jem's sprawled body on the floor.

'Night of your first rehearsal,' Jem confesses. 'And for the record, she's lying about who kissed who.'

Sam shakes his fist out and glares down at Jem. Laughs, suddenly. 'Guess *I* hit *you*,' he says. And laughs again.

The singing werewolves and assorted other drinkers watch, enthralled, as Sam extends a hand to help Jem back on to his feet. They exchange manly nods.

'Don't ever bloody kiss Tab again,' says Sam.

He takes Tabby's hand and squeezes it. Tabby goes bright pink with excitement.

'What about me?' Maria bleats. 'Don't you care that he kissed me?'

'Nope,' says Sam.

Taking Tabby's face in both hands, he kisses her gently. The kiss becomes extremely ungentle, extremely fast. Over their heads, the theatre lights sputter and fizz and glow again in a flash of pure comic timing.

Ella rockets through the stage door next, armed with a murderous glare and a fistful of brushes and powder puffs. 'STOP SNOGGING. You're wrecking those masterpieces on your faces BEFORE THE SHOW'S

314

EVEN FLAMING FINISHED!'

Maria storms for the glass doors and the outside world. Abandoned on the bar, her wig looks like a deboned Persian cat.

There is a fresh explosion of applause. Patricia and Eunice's second encore is over, and the leading lady has left the building.

'We'll have to go on without her,' says Sam, his arm tightly wrapped around Tab's shoulders.

There is a look on Tabby's face that I've never seen before. I know that if Sam takes his arm away, she will keel on to the carpet face-first without even putting her hands out to save herself.

'I'll think of something,' Sam says heroically. 'I will.'

There's no point having a run of genius ideas if, when the chips are down, you don't have the final genius idea that brings everything together.

'Tab, put Maria's wig on,' I say. I grab the Persian cat-a-like and thrust it into her hands. 'Warren, you're marrying Rich.'

'Goodee,' says Rich. 'Don't worry Tabby poppet, I know your words. If I keep the veil on, no one will know the difference. Everyone always watches Beatrice and Benedick

316

in this scene anyway. Give us your wig, there's a darling.'

'Tab, do you know the words to Maria's last song?' I say.

Tabby tears her eyes from Sam's face and manages a nod. She starts slowly putting Maria's wig on while Ella attempts to repair the kiss damage to her face, stabbing in and out of range like a furious hornet.

Patricia flies through the stage door with Eunice as the audience roars its appreciation. She hunts wildly through the assembled cast. 'Where's that bloody girl? Rich, why are you wearing Hero's wig?'

I feel Jem slide his hand into mine. I will allow it just for now. Just until we get through this crisis.

'Delilah has everything under control,' Jem tells Patricia, rubbing his jaw with his free hand. 'Tab's taking Maria's part. The rest of you are fudging it.'

'We can do that,' says Gladys.

'You always do that,' Dorcas observes.

Judging from the sound of chatter and throat-clearing in the auditorium, the audience is starting to get bored. The band plays on brightly, à la Titanic.

Patricia squares her suited shoulders. 'Time to kill this, zombie style. On we go, my little chickens. Quick quick.'

The lobby feels strangely empty without the cast. The werewolves aren't singing any more, and the barflies are having a silent moment of contemplation over their beers.

'Guess we're the only ones left in need of a happy ending,' Jem says.

317

'Two Magners and some pork scratchings please,' pipes up one of the werewolves.

I prise my eyes from Jem's molten gaze and my hand from his hand and I walk to the bar. 'There's no happy ending,' I tell him as I find the Magners and the scratchings. 'You've got a girlfriend.'

'Funnily enough,' he says, following me to the bar, 'all I can think of right now is you.'

I push the ciders and scratchings at the werewolves and face him.

'You kissed Maria?' I demand. 'You kissed Maria AND you kissed Tabby?'

'Sam's women apparently find me irresistible,' Jem says. 'Tabby kissed *me*. Maria kissed me too, as you may have gathered. She was pretty insistent. Caught me in the kitchen, out of the way. It would have been rude to refuse. Oh, and my jaw hurts like hell, thanks for asking.'

'When did you kiss Maria?'

'First rehearsal. I just told Sam that.' He frowns at me. 'What? This was before you – after you – OK, I guess in the middle of you. You're not thinking of hitting me too, are you?'

I am thinking about the fizzing lights above Sam and Tabby's kiss. The scent of pine woods and oregano seems to waft through my nostrils, and I try and fail to put it down to Val's brand of toilet cleaner.

Jem attempts to catch me around the waist. 'Now, all that kissing has got me in the mood and you are looking gloriously gorgeous tonight. Kiss me.'

I strike at him with my fists. 'Tell me about your girlfriend first.'

'I don't have a girlfriend,' he says patiently. 'Read my lips. Scratch that, kiss my lips.'

I wriggle away from him and rush into the sanctum of the kitchen. My mind is a wreck.

'Fatima *saw* her,' I insist as he follows me in like a really, *really* annoying dog. 'Right here in this kitchen.' I'm not being the other woman again. I'm NOT.

'What does my girlfriend look like?'

'She's *tall*,' I shout.

I am up against the lockers now, my back flat to the metal doors like I am somehow hoping to melt my way through and escape. Jem leans his arms on the lockers either side of my head and does his stripping look at me.

'I don't go for tall women,' he says. 'I prefer them dinky.'

'Dinky?' I say, offended.

A locker door creaks open just beside my ear and Jem's jacket flops out on to the floor. Stuck to the inside of the locker door is a long, naked back, painted with a silver zipper on a black ribbon. An unfeasibly long neck with just a few dark blond curls on show. The body curves in and out again like a violin.

'Why have you got that picture in your locker?' I say, shocked.

'Because it's the most beautiful thing I own. Kev gave me a copy, but only after I begged. Did I cause the chip in

319

your heart or was it the guy in the car?'

There is a long, long pause.

'Bit of both,' I whisper.

'I have been having sleepless nights about you for weeks,' he says, running a finger down my cheek. 'I haven't felt this strongly about anyone since I crushed on a *Blue Peter* presenter.'

I gaze at the picture. My picture. Me.

'Fatima said she'd seen a tall girl in the kitchen,' I mumble.

'Did she now.'

'I thought—'

His lips come down on mine, sweet and soft, cutting me off. My whole body goes whoosh like a firework and I finally – properly – kiss him back.

He pulls away after five minutes, ten minutes, forever. 'I'm going to the police about the hit and run in the morning. You've given me back my life, Delilah Jones, and I love you for it. I hope you won't mind having a boyfriend with a criminal record.'

'I'm looking for an accomplice for my next heist anyway,' I say, utterly breathless. 'You, me, the Bank of England and a trusty getaway Ford Fiesta.'

'I'm in,' he says and kisses me again so passionately that I think I might burst into flames on the spot.

'I'd better call Studs,' he says, coming up for air once more. 'Just to check the idiot's OK. And also to let him know he's coming to the cops too.'

A roar of thirsty party-seekers floods into the bar on a wave of tumultuous applause from the auditorium. The show is over. All I need to complete the moment is a fly-by. Maybe a couple of cannons.

'Tomorrow,' I say as I curl my fingers wonderingly through his thick dark hair. 'Do it tomorrow. Now shut up and kiss me again.'

There's no moon filling me this time.

Just the most blazing of sunbeams.

CREDITS

Lots of people to thank for a book I had way too much fun writing.

Special thanks to Jasper Mann, handsome and dashing former General Manager for Caper & Berry at the Yvonne Arnaud Theatre, Guildford. Carolyn and Sheila at getmadeup.com who revealed a tiny part of the amazing world of body art to me. My come-as-a-pair experts Jenny and Paul Brocklehurst: Jenny on banking and Paul on policing. Pamela Belle, from whose beautiful poem 'The Moon in the Water' I stole Oz's philosophy about the importance of having dreams in your life. Thank you all, and apologies wherever I have taken liberties with information supplied.

Sorry, Sir Patrick Moore, for messing around with the full-moon calendar to fit my fiendish needs. Richard Burton and Elizabeth Taylor, you were the perfect celebrity couple to represent the power of Aphrodite's Kiss, and I apologize for putting words into your mouths.

Thanks also to Naomi Greenwood and the Hodder team for believing in *The Kiss* from the start. Thanks to my husband Will because he's lovely and I couldn't write half what I write without him. And finally, I should perhaps thank the French boy who once kissed a teenage me among moonlit Mediterranean sand dunes. It's only polite.

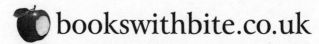
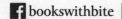